TRUE BORN

L. E. STERLING

TRUE

TRUE BORN TRILOGY

BORN

Entangled Publishing, LLC
2614 South Timberline Road
Suite 109
Fort Collins, CO 80525

Entangled TEEN is an imprint of Entangled Publishing, LLC.

Visit our website at www.entangledpublishing.com.

Edited by Liz Pelletier
Cover design by Louisa Maggio
Interior design by Toni Kerr

HC ISBN: 9781633753198
PB ISBN: 9781633756045
Ebook ISBN: 9781633753259

Manufactured in the United States of America

First Edition March 2017

10 9 8 7 6 5 4 3 2 1

For my own little Storm

1

When we came into the world, silent and cowled, my sister and I were attached by our big toes. They waited a whole day to separate us, and for that one perfect day, Margot and I were one. After the separation, they tell us, we cried for days, would not be pacified except when we were laid side by side, touching. Our toes show the scars from our being ripped apart. Mine is brown in the shape of a blotchy lock. Margot's is long and thin with little teeth that make it look like a key. We decided this as young girls, as we stared at the freckled flesh that has long since become a part of the story of us. I pull my foot free from my leather boot and wiggle my toes, staring at the inky blot that marks me one of two. Beside me at the courtyard table of our exclusive private school, my sister throws back her hair and looks around for teachers or guards who might be able to convince her to come inside—since I clearly can't.

"I'm not skipping the whole day, Lu. Just this period. I'll

be back after lunch. Promise," Margot reasons, staring back at me with a look one inch shy of mischief.

We are supposedly identical, but despite carrying the same long chin, we don't look precisely alike. Our mother tells us I'm built like a bird: thin and small, with a cap of deep shadow-brown curls and dark gray eyes. Margot is a smidge taller, fuller, her hair a shade lighter and three shades straighter. Her eyes are a mystery: green and gray and a glint of gold. And when Margot walks into a room, she commands all eyes while I, the sparrow, sit unnoticed and observe. Margot is fire: bright and ready to burn out of control. I am the less exciting twin, the responsible twin.

Despite Margot being older by one and a half minutes, it has always fallen to me to watch over her. I'd not call her wild—our parents wouldn't stand for a wild child—but she does know how to skate the boundaries. Still, though I've not given our parents a moment's worry, Margot is the family favorite: the one our mother most enjoys and our father coddles. And me? I'm the one who keeps her out of scrapes so she can enjoy her favored status. It may seem like I'm doing a lot of work, but I get something out of it, too. As long as I keep Margot in the limelight, I'm not the one our parents expect to entertain visiting businessmen and politicians. Which is the reason I'm currently outside in the cold arguing with my sister instead of sitting in my favorite class.

"You can't skip, Margot. I mean it. Besides, what do you think you're going to do? Half the city is on lockdown today."

This is Dominion, after all. The Plague has escalated the last few years, sweeping over the world on its dark horse and gobbling everyone with its diamond teeth. Whole sections of the city are kept under constant martial law to prevent the lawlessness that comes with rising body counts.

I stare up at the gray, moody sky before turning back to my twin, who busily packs up her things. A fat raindrop falls with a *plop* onto my inky blot of a birthmark. I sigh. She'll not listen. This I know for sure.

"What are you even doing, Margot?"

She's been skipping a lot lately. Meeting someone in private. I suspect she's going around with Robbie Deakins, the boy she's had a crush on since seventh grade, although I can't see it when they're together. We live in a very small world. It's nearly impossible to keep secrets in our set. But between us, my sister and me, it's even harder.

"Just heading out for a walk with some friends. Don't worry so much," she scolds.

"It's not like you to keep secrets from me." I shove my toes back into my boot and regard my beautiful twin shrewdly. "And I know you're doing more than going for a walk."

We are not like other people, despite how normal Margot likes to imagine we are. Our mother tells us we are like pieces of the same puzzle, and she's right. When we're apart, I can feel us stretching to fit the pieces together, no matter the distance.

We should have died at birth. They thought about killing us: two babies dressed in our bloody cowls and so supernaturally quiet that the doctors and midwives were looking for hammers. But we lived, and as we grew, we slowly came to know that we were unique, though two. At times I think I can read her thoughts, like bells in my mind. And what Margot feels, I feel—sometimes more sharply than even she does. Her pain, her joy. Her excitement…

It's our secret, and one we guard closely. *Lock and key.*

There's one secret more. We never speak about it, but

I'm different still. Sometimes I can say with certainty who's going to catch sick next. I know when the street preachers and their rabble will erupt into violence. Today's death and violence is nothing compared to the ugliness of tomorrow. She has her own special gifts, my sister, but this one, this secret, is mine alone.

I also know when I'm wasting my breath. I stand up, pulling my coat closer around me as the sky opens in earnest. "Fine," I tell her sternly. "But I won't cover for you. You get in trouble, you dig yourself out."

"Fine," she says, then leans over to kiss me on the cheek before rushing off in a blur of color, cheeks bright, eyes shining. "Love you," she tosses back over her shoulder.

But as I make my way to the doors on the other side of the large courtyard, jumping over gray-black puddles and getting drenched, a traitorous thought—all too familiar of late—flashes through my mind: *why does Margot get to have all the fun?*

I yank on the heavy oak door and barrel through, fuming over Margot's latest caper. Grayguard Academy is as old as the hills and we've been attending it practically since birth. I know every nook and cranny, every dip in its polished marble halls, every loose joint in its four-hundred-year-old wooden stairway. So I'm flapping my wet coat free of rain rather than looking where I'm going as I fly from the hallway up the flight of stairs, a route that will take me to my class more quickly.

And smack right into something as hard as bricks.

I bounce and careen backward, losing my footing. My arms flail, but I can't catch anything but a whiff of real danger and the fact that the object is a man. He reaches out to grab my hand, but my arms have already started sailing over my head. Images of splattered brains all over the highly polished marble floor flash through my mind as I fall back, back, and snap still in mid-air. Adrenaline spikes through me as my head-over-heels tumble is suddenly halted. I'm not dead.

And the man in front of me, a gorgeous wallop of a man, holds me from certain death by the hem of my skirt. I'm lucky, I muse as, teetering on my heels, I'm suddenly cast back to the time when a much younger Robbie Deakins held Margot suspended in the same position and bartered a kiss for her freedom. Back then I kicked him in the shins and Margot told me I knew nothing about boys. As I take in the one before me, I reckon that statement still holds true.

"You should watch where you're going," the stranger says, but the words are delivered without a sting. For a moment I'm struck dumb—not by my escape from a near-death experience, since I continue to dangle over the stairs at an odd angle—but by the man before me. At first I'm caught by his lips, just the right kind of full, the lips of an angel. Then I take in his cheekbones, high and carved in a face more long than square, with a nose to match that flares slightly wider at the nostrils. Though it's all the rage in Dominion, he has no facial hair, making him seem younger than he likely is. I see a sinfully long, dark sweep of eyelash, a dark arc of eyebrow topped with a mop of messy blond locks that fall over one eye. The other eye is an intense, moody blue that rakes me from head to toe.

He carries himself with all the menace of a trained killer.

"You…you shouldn't be here," I splutter haughtily, feeling heat rise to my cheeks, though whether I'm more embarrassed or concerned I can't tell.

"But I am here," he says in dark, rich tones. He peers

scandalously down at my legs, "and you're welcome."

I gasp in outrage. I try to bat at the hand that holds my skirt, but I can't reach, and somehow this makes me feel even more helpless.

"Let me go," I fume imperiously.

"If I do that, you'll fall," he tells me reasonably enough. But there's nothing reasonable about the way he looks me over: frank, assessing. The gaze of a true predator. Nor how each scrap of my skin seems to tingle under his heated gaze. His lips curl into a smile. But the worst part: I don't like what it does to me. "What will you do for me if I let you go?" And there, in that singular second, the stranger crosses the line between potential friend or foe. He is not one of us, this vulgar, magnetic stranger. Every instinct in my body warns that this man is not safe. No one outside the Upper Circle is safe.

I narrow my eyes at the intruder. For intruder he surely is. They don't allow non-students in this wing, not even the mercs who watch over us after school. And he surely can't be a merc. Mercs wear House uniforms, while my self-proclaimed savior is in a black shirt faded almost to gray. On the front is a stick figure skeleton painted in a flaking white. Even from here I can see a frayed hole in the knee of his pants, the strange nakedness of his toes. He's wearing sandals. No one wears sandals. He seems too beautiful, too self-assured to be rabble, but one never knows.

I lick my lips. "Tell you what, Laster. I'll give you a head start before I call security."

His eyes sharpen. They must be catching the light, I muse, as for a moment a flash of emerald sweeps across his cornea before turning back to a dark indigo.

"Well aren't you a ray of sunshine?" He leans back. "What

are you, anyway, some sort of nun?" he asks, taking in my high-necked white blouse and dark-blue wool skirt that falls below the knee.

"What are you," I throw right back, "some kind of blind hermit? You've not seen a single school uniform while you've been traipsing through our halls? If you know what's good for you, you'll get out of here."

"No, I haven't. Not one like this," he says, suddenly quite serious, all but ignoring my warning. At his words I stop trying to break free. Something passes between us, quick as lightning. It's so unexpected, I can't catch my breath.

I'm so distracted I almost don't notice the sound of fabric ripping.

"Uh oh," says the stranger, lips curling into a sinful smile.

"My skirt is ripping."

"Yes it is."

"Let me go!" I yell in my most imperious tone.

But the stranger just shakes his head and clucks at me as though I'm a small and naughty child. "Terrible manners."

It takes me a beat to understand he's serious. He'd as soon see my skirt rip off than let me go. "Fine," I fume. "*Please* help me out of this ridiculous position so I neither lose my skirt nor scramble my brains, *kind* sir."

The stranger cocks his head at me. That one lock of hair falls back away from his eye, revealing a face of stark perfection. He cups a hand over one ear, holding me effortlessly in place with the other. "What was that you said, Princess?"

Reeling in mortification, I mumble, "I said 'please.'"

I hate his arrogance, his certainty as he reels me in, one fistful of skirt at a time as though I'm a fish hooked on his line. Worse still, I think as I watch the play of bulging muscles under the thin and fraying layer of his shirt, it costs him no effort.

When I'm two fistfuls from upright, I lunge for his arms. He's slender but broad of shoulder. Beneath my grip his arms are rocks that I grasp on to for dear life.

And then we are far, far too close for comfort.

The beautiful stranger's eyes glitter as he stares down at me. He looks as though he'll say something when a fleet of feet sound in the hallway below, accompanied by the cultivated voices of my schoolmates, drawing away his attention.

With a pang, and utterly against my better judgment, I realize I want it back.

He sweeps an arm behind my back and sets me squarely on the step below but makes no other motion to leave. His other arm sweeps around me, locking me against his body. We're so close I can smell cinnamon on his breath, can feel the rise and fall of his chest as he breathes. It occurs to me that I still have his biceps locked in a death grip. I swallow past my embarrassment and loosen my fingers one by one.

The stranger's eyes marble into vibrant green again. His eyes narrow, and for a moment I feel like I'm staring into the face of a wild beast. On the heels of that thought crashes another. *Maybe he's True Born.*

I dismiss the errant thought as quickly as it comes. There are no True Borns at Grayguard.

"You'd better go before they arrest you, Laster," I tell the stranger, taking a trembling step down the stairs. When had my legs started shaking?

The stranger's arms remain around my back, though they loosen somewhat. He glances down at me with something like regret stamped on his features.

"Some day someone is going to have to teach you how to behave," he tells me cockily.

"And I suppose you'll be the one to do it?" I throw back, shrewish. I am not flirting, wouldn't even know how. But the man before me is surely not accustomed to being rejected by any woman, let alone a school girl, and most Lasters don't know their place. He throws me a lopsided grin.

My heart lurches again at the appearance of a sharp dimple. I stare at his white teeth, the curl of his lips. Concentration melting away, I remove my hands from his arms. Having nowhere to go but his flesh—which, my fevered brain reminds me, I must avoid at all costs—they dangle uselessly in midair.

"Maybe I will be," he finally drawls. His hands trace from my back up to my shoulders. He gently holds me in place while he steps around me, then bounds gracefully down the stairs. I turn and watch the lithe muscles in his back shift under his shirt. He has the spare and supple movements of a cat, I think, as he hits the landing and turns back to me.

The stranger flicks a glance at me through a lock of his hair. "Be seeing you, Princess," he salutes before waltzing down the hall as though he owns the place.

Once he's gone I give myself permission to sink down on the step, knowing my shaking legs won't support me a moment longer. My heart races, though for the life of me I can't figure out why. I'm not the sister who chases after boys—no matter how gorgeous they are. And I certainly wouldn't chase after one like that, so rude, so messy. We Fox sisters are Upper Circle. Our parents would make sure I'd never see the light of day. Worse, they'd marry me off to the nearest middle-aged senator in ten seconds flat.

Still, as I sit there and shake—a delayed reaction from a near-death experience, I keep reminding myself—I can't help but relive, over and over again, the way he looked at me. His eyes had raked every square inch of me as though he knew me better than my own sister did. Better than I know myself.

Hand to my chest, I close my eyes and pray to all the gods in Dominion that I never see his face again. Because for some absurd reason I can't shake the uncanny feeling that maybe I will.

2

By your eighteenth birthday you're supposed to know. They're supposed to tell you.

Splicer. True Born. Laster.

Margot and I, though, all we seem to be getting for our eighteenth birthday, still over a month away, is another round of Protocols at the Splicer Clinic.

The rain comes down in stripes as we're bundled into our father's shiny black Oldworld car and stall at the sooty iron gates surrounding our home. Two sentries ride shotgun on the electric gate. They hold machine guns with one hand and iron pegs with the other as the gate slowly glides open. Fritz, the one with the steel-colored flattop, is our newer merc, ex-army. Shane, the one with the Celtic knot work bulging over his biceps and the crazed glint in his eyes, has been with our father since we were girls. He's one of only a handful of people in the world Margot and I trust.

I spy the first sign as the car crosses through the gate and

wades into a sea of people. *Evolve or Die.* I don't understand
these signs. Father says they indicate that a lot of rabble have
gone mad.

The boy holding it up can't be more than twelve, but
you can never tell these days. He's got the startlingly gaunt
frame of the starving or sick, his face smeared with dirt and
desperation. Chances are he's either a goner himself or his
family has been wiped off the map and he's providing for
himself.

Sometimes they get religious, the orphans. Sometimes
the zealots get them. He aims a look right at us, at *me*, as we
drive by. I want to sink down in my seat and never be seen
again. But of course, that's impossible even if our father would
allow it.

Is he out there? I search the crowds for a particular face,
a face I haven't been able to get out of my mind for the
past few days. It's been a constant knot within me. At night
I've unraveled those moments on the stairs again and again,
wondering for the billionth time who the stranger could be. A
preacher's man? A merc? Though if the stranger protects one
of my classmates, I'd likely have seen him after school when
all the mercs come to pick up their charges. More importantly,
what is he? I know most of the Splicers in the city, so he'd
likely not be one of us. A Laster? Surely he's too vital, far
too arrogant....

As I pick over the moments feverishly, I wonder if I
should tell Margot about what happened. No, I remind myself.
That would give the man more importance than he deserves.
I'll likely never cross his path again. Somehow the thought
doesn't lend me comfort.

A creeping sensation pokes at me. Margot hasn't moved,

but I catch the flick of her eye in the opposite direction. There, on top of a burned-out car the color of storm clouds, a man wearing a long, dirty white robe smiles gently down at the crowds—weird enough for these times. A shiver crawls up my spine as he watches us, his eyes piercing black under thick, bushy eyebrows. His smile grows thicker, kinder.

"Who is that?" I say under my breath. Only Margot can hear me. We're quiet-quiet. It's a game we've practiced our whole lives.

"Preacher man," she murmurs. You don't usually see the preachers. More often than not they stay hidden in the basements they call churches. The government frowns on the preacher men, calls them "seditious." This one, though, seems bold as daylight. It's a thought that jolts another shiver down my spine.

Our father shifts on his seat, a grim expression stamped across his stern, handsome features. As always, he's impeccably dressed in his gray pinstriped suit and black overcoat. He holds his gloves absently across his lap. He's never apart from these shiny black leather gloves, so soft they feel like butterfly wings. Margot thinks he needs them like he needs the car, his suit, the towering gates around our house: totems to keep him safe from the rabble. Even sitting across from us he doesn't notice our eyes drifting to the lone figure atop the carcass of a car. All around the preacher man, milling and standing and sitting, are people. Dozens of people, some missing limbs, most with a look in their eyes I'd as soon call frantic. Lasters.

In Dominion they have a saying about the Lasters. Those who can, Splice. Everyone else comes in Last. There's another one, too, not much used in polite company, as our mother likes to remind us.

What's a Laster? A dead man.

They say the Plague started when people did—it just took its sweet time warming up and getting good and ready to strike us all dead. There was another name for it at some point, before the scales tipped and nearly everyone was dropping from the wasting disease: bodies turning traitor and gobbling up people from the inside out. That's all forgotten now, as useless as the crumbling towers without enough people to light them up. As useless as the hospitals that can't keep people alive, not anymore. People used to survive the Plague, we've been told. It would come on more slowly, folding people up slowly, one day at a time. Now when it strikes, you'd better kiss your babies goodbye. Most people don't last the week once the symptoms start.

If you're lucky, like us, you can become a Splicer. If you're born in the Upper Circle, you can hop in your private car and drive to a private clinic with enough guns and gates thick enough to be called safe. Nice doctors and nurses in white gowns and dripping with gold jewelry wheel you into a room where they use long needles to sew medicine into your DNA. New DNA to take over where your own falls apart and starts to go rogue.

Our mother has gone in three times already. When she thinks we're not listening, she likes to tell her friends that there's more new DNA hardwired into her than old. Practically a test-tuber. Our father hasn't been struck yet, but we all know it's just a matter of time. If you're born, you're living on borrowed time.

But there are others they don't even whisper about.

One day you walk into a store and everyone is either a Splicer or a Laster. Next thing you know, in walks a pale woman with a shark fin sticking out from a slash in her blouse. Can't be a Splicer. Splicers can't grow the extra hardware.

True Borns are born with it.

They don't want us to know. In the Upper Circle they talk openly of the Splicers and Lasters. But no one wants us to hear about the True Borns. No one from our Circle will hire one. Oh, maybe our Circles across the sea will. From what Robbie Deakins tells us, the True Borns make great security detail, special ops, merc, army. People to ride the gates and shotgun our cars. Our Circle encourages others to pretend they don't exist.

What we know we've gathered from listening in at their late-night cocktail parties. When the laughter gets more desperate and dies down. When the voices go low and the women start to cry.

Sometimes the Splicing doesn't work, you see. Sometimes they come out and say there's nothing they could have done. They never mention the "L" word.

But in the Upper Circle, the week you turn eighteen, they throw you a party tó Reveal your fate, good or bad. After that, they're supposed to give you the test results. By the time you're eighteen they can pretty much pinpoint when your genes will blow. The earlier they Splice and dice, they say, the better your chances are.

We reckon you can pretty much predict what the results are from when you're told. Carrie Olsen's parents sat her down after throwing her a magnificent party and gave her a round trip ticket around the world. Two days later she came to school blotchy and wild-eyed. We all knew her first Splice would be her last. Just like her mother, who'd already lost both her legs despite multiple trips to the Clinic. And then she disappeared.

Robbie Deakins, on the other hand, was given his results the day before his party. We'd never seen him so relaxed. He smiled and danced with us both, even though he only likes Margot.

The slogan is scribbled everywhere in Dominion, a constant reminder. EVOLVE OR DIE. It is spray-painted on the sides of buildings, most gap-eyed and crumbling. On looted and abandoned storefronts, on cars without windows, on homes half torched for heat. It's painted on the sidewalk, the long, dripping letters red as blood as we roll into the private testing and treatment compound known as the Clinic. Just before the steel gates squeeze shut behind us I cast another long glance at the rabble, hoping to catch a glimpse of my strange savior. I swallow my disappointment when he doesn't appear. Then a moment later we're escorted into the building by men with yet more guns, and I don't have time to ponder it any longer.

A smiling, slender blonde in a short snow-white dress greets us at the door. Her legs are long and thin and delicate, the limbs of a colt. Huge blue eyes sit in a flawless face. She ushers us down the long halls while our father goes with one of the genetic doctors into a private room, and she seats us in identical white leather reclining chairs.

The nurse gets chatty with us. "So not long now until your Reveal, yeah? You gals must be so excited. You going to have a big bash with rock stars and celebs or what?"

I share a look with Margot. Our nurse obviously doesn't have clearance to access our background file. If she did, she'd know we would never be allowed in the same room with rock stars. Our father is one of the most important people on the continent, let alone Dominion. Father is Chief Diplomat of the continent-state of Nor-Am, a position second only to the Prime Minister and surely ranking above the Senators. Father's job is to wield influence. It's because of him, he's fond of telling us, that the cities and villages still counting survivors haven't gone completely lawless. He's the reason that other continent-states not yet hit so hard by the Plague haven't invaded. Father tells us his job is to look out for the interests of every outpost of humanity still remaining in the once-great continent-state of Nor-Am—it's just that Dominion, the most populous and influential city remaining, is the most important. It's common knowledge that most of those outposts are even worse off than we are.

And as we're constantly reminded, in Father's line of work, appearances are everything, so we Fox sisters need to set an example. Our Reveal party will be small and sedate. On the guest list will be the Mayor of Dominion, the Prime Minister of Nor-Am and his family, and a handful of the most important Senators and foreign dignitaries. One or two people our age will be shipped in to dance with us, sons of dignitaries twice as boring as their fathers. We will be expected to mingle and serve our guests as befitting our family station— regardless of our results.

Margot reaches her hand across the small space between us. I take it automatically, a hand I know as well as my own. She doesn't turn her head. Nor do I.

"Isn't it a little weird that we have to do our tests again? Was there some kind of mistake with the first one?" Margot says it innocently enough, a slight twang to her voice to match the nurse's rabble-like twang.

"Well, hon, sometimes they get mixed signals, you know? Like when you think a boy likes you but then he goes all hot and cold?" She winks. Margot's fingers tighten on mine.

"Uh huh." Margot nods. "So there's a problem with your machines? Or with the staff?"

The nurse frowns. "Not this staff. They're five-star amazing. Must have just been a bad sample or something. Try not to worry about it, sweetie." She pats Margot's arm just before she shoves the needle in my sister's vein.

I squirm on my seat. The skin on my arm crawls from the sharp pain originating in my sister's arm. Relaxed beside me, Margot doesn't move a muscle. She knows what I'm feeling even if she can't do anything about it. This is just how it is with us.

"How much are you going to take this time?" My voice shakes as our coltish nurse comes around to me and drives a needle into my arm. It doesn't hurt nearly as bad as Margot's did. Our hands stay folded together. There's a note in our file about letting us. One of the perks of being born us.

"Oh." For the first time she looks a little dismayed. "I'm sorry, hon. Didn't they tell you? We gotta go through the whole Protocol again. The whole shebang."

My twin and I did know. We'd been told. Still, it bothers us. A full day's worth of giving blood, going through tests, having your organs measured and documented. Urine samples, more blood samples, hair samples. We'd already been through this two times in the last two months. We no longer believe they'd gotten "bad" samples—not that we're going to let on to the nurse.

And funny thing is, each time we come, the Protocols Nurse is new. This is the third we've had, each as clueless as the last.

We know better than to ask our parents. The deepening silence and constant rounds of testing and lies must mean the news is the worst. Late at night we lie together, holding hands and whispering under the deep canopy of one or other of our beds. We've thought about what it will mean if one of us turns out to be a Laster. We've talked until dawn about what we'd want, what we'd do. I tell Margot I'd want to go with her, but she's against the idea.

"One of us needs to survive," she said to me, her gray-green eyes as serious as I've ever seen them.

"What if it's not that?" I asked her.

"What do you mean?"

"What if we're, you know," the words mere whispers, "True Born?"

Margot laughed. "Us? I know we're different but really, Lucy."

"No, I'm serious," I told her as I pulled a strand of tawny brown hair away from her face. "Do you really think they'd keep testing us if it came out we were Lasters? Does that sound like them?"

"No," Margot admitted.

And that got us to thinking. And listening through the walls like mice.

True Borns don't worry about needing enough money and luck to successfully Splice. True Borns don't catch the Plague.

They say True Borns are genetic throwbacks. Something in their DNA has woken up and jumped back in time, back to the OldenTimes when we were animals, mutating and evolving into humans. Some of those genes hold the code for becoming dogs, or apes, or sharks and other fish, reptiles. Some True Borns look a lot like the origins of their DNA:

long limbs that hang to their knees, or tongues that loll out of misshapen mouths. A few, we hear, actually sprout fur or grow gills. True Borns can be extraordinarily strong, gifted at hunting and catching prey.

None of them, not a one, ever catch sick.

Evolve or die. That's what the True Borns have done, ever since the Plague began. The preacher and his people have a point.

"Can't be," Margot told me, shaking her head.

"Why not?" I asked, but I knew why. Margot and I, we look perfectly normal. We haven't sprouted fur or feathers. Our eyesight isn't 40/40. We are as human as our mother and father, bone and blood.

Lying back on the white Protocols chair, trying to forget the uncomfortable pricks of the needles, I can't help but think about the stranger again. The sheen of bright emerald rolling over his eyes. As I've done a hundred times since yesterday, I dismiss the possibility that he's one of them. You can tell True Borns just by looking at them, right?

And yet…

Nurse finishes with a big old Miss Dominion smile as she straps the blood into a tester case and tells us to hang tight while Clive comes for us. Then disappears with a clack of her heels.

This is not Protocol. This is not how it's supposed to go. Unlike the poor rabble, we of the Upper Circle are tested every year. Not for longevity, but for traces of the disease. Some of the more superstitious are under the impression the Plague might be catchy, like a virus. We know Clive, have known him for years. He's not supposed to come get us. The nurse is supposed to bring us to him. The blood can wait. The rest of the tests can't.

She leaves anyhow. I eye Margot uneasily until a few seconds later there's a knock at the door. A dark, swarthy man with a huge dimpled grin peeks in. Margot lights up.

"Clive!"

"There are my special ladies," he says. From behind his back he pulls two roses, one blue, one white, and hands one each to us.

"Thank you," Margot mumbles over her white rose. A suspicious stain spreads across her pale cheek.

"You're welcome," Clive says. "You ladies ready for your tour in the spotlight?" He hands out a line like this every time. We climb down and follow him through the long, antiseptic halls of the Clinic, Clive and Margot chatting away like old pals. As he guides Margot into a room with metal walls, metal ceiling, metal floor — all the better to keep things sterile, he's told us — I stop at the door.

"Clive, did Protocols change?"

His eyes shift restlessly. "Naw, we're just a bit short staffed this month. You know how it is," he says, grim-faced.

I nod. It's the one answer we can't argue with. We all know Lasters are becoming extinct. In the past two decades alone the population of the planet has dwindled by half.

And when I lie down and stare into Margot's eyes as we're wired in and put through the paces, I'm more scared than I ever have been.

Something deeply weird is going on.

3

The air feels charged as we glide down the stairs a little after three and wait outside our father's study. Margot beckons me into the alcove just off the heavy wooden sliding doors that lead to his sanctuary. Her voice hitches as she pulls on my pinky, a promise pledge. "No matter what's in there."

My smile is crooked and weak. "No matter what," I say.

No one needs a special gift or a crystal ball to tell us that something is going on. We hear a cough from inside. The door draws slowly open, revealing Shane. A man sits across from our father on the couch, the obligatory polite coffee untouched before him on the long glass coffee table. Another man and a woman stand behind him, giving off the alert and frighteningly efficient air of good mercenaries. Their eyes are peeled on us as we walk into the room, like lancets on our skin as they study, dissect, memorize our descriptions and stats.

But the roaring in my ears, loud as a drone, and the sudden

crazy lurch and tilt of my stomach, is not due to our father having hired new bodyguards without speaking to us. The man standing behind the couch is *him*.

No one should be so handsome, I think as I drink him in. A shag of sunlight blond frames a pair of cat's eyes, too blue, the color of indigo, twinkling now with something like amusement. My gaze drops to those chiseled cheekbones I've been daydreaming about, ending with a strong chin. I take in the faded blue jeans, the black shirt open at the collar. I clench my stomach against the sudden butterflies, nod to him and the woman, who at this point is just a bundle of details: long dark hair, pale skin, green eyes that laugh at me.

The seated man stands and the remainder of my breath tumbles out of me. It's not just that he's immense. He is well over six feet, although slender in that athletic way. It's not even that he's gorgeous, although he's that, too. As his gaze sweeps Margot's face, then my own, with eyes the color of a storm sky, I realize what it is. It's not often I see an aura of power shimmering around someone. Stepping back, I collide with Shane's chest. He grasps my arms and holds me there.

The tall man doesn't move. Just tilts his head like he's waiting to see what I'll do. I catch Margot's frantic gaze. She tries not to be conspicuous, but I've panicked her. I can feel her heart beating too fast. I take a deep breath and smile.

"Hello." I bob a small curtsy. Beside me, inside me, Margot's heartbeat slows.

Even though he says it softly, the man's voice rumbles from his chest like thunder when he speaks. "Hello, Lucy."

So, he knows which sister is which. That's a neat trick.

"Sir." I nod again. My eyes slide to the man standing behind him. He isn't acting like an ordinary merc. Mercs keep their eyes peeled to the world around their charges. This man studies me, bold as daylight, without even trying to hide the fact.

I'm so distracted it takes a moment for me to realize our father is speaking. "Sit down, girls. I want to introduce you to Mr. Nolan Storm."

No mention of the two others. Just Mr. Storm. I perch like a nervous cat on the settee. Margot, outwardly more serene, tucks in beside me. If they have been in negotiations, I'd have to say it didn't go as our father planned. He is in a rare foul mood. His cheeks bloom red while his eyes glitter like diamonds, ready to cut us. We sit like ice princesses, stone faced, hands in laps.

"Girls," our father's words are clipped and efficient, "Mr. Storm is a security expert. He and his team will be providing the family remote security in the coming days. It was important that you meet today so that you aren't alarmed should one of them appear to escort you home."

I take turns with Margot glancing at Shane from beneath our eyelashes. His jaw bulges and twitches as he tries to control himself. He won't like this, interference from outside.

"Lucy, Margot." In his pressed linen suit, oozing money, Nolan Storm could be one of our Circle. He'd be the most popular man in town, I think to myself as I watch him move. He can't be much older than thirty, but when Mr. Storm talks, he takes up all the space in the room. The air shimmers around him, as though it's waiting to split. I blink, trying to see beneath the strange illusion. Our father glares. He likes the help to be docile and speak only when spoken to. "You must be wondering why your father has hired a remote security team, since you already have a crack team here at home."

Shane puffs up. Crisis averted. "There have been no specific threats as yet, but we feel certain there might be one day soon. We'd rather be prepared than sorry."

Margot grabs for my hand. "Is something happening?"

Storm nods. "You may have noticed the number of zealots camped out around your gate has grown quite large of late. We have reason to believe their ranks are organizing, though for what purpose, we can't say. Your father just wanted to be prepared, and rightfully so." He tips his head toward our father. Score another point for Nolan Storm. "For whatever agenda they might want to advance."

Margot blinks. "Do you think they want to hurt us?"

"Do you really want to wait to find out? The Plague isn't flaming out. Times are uncertain."

True enough. We've given it more thought than our classmates, but even we haven't fully considered what will happen when the only people left are a handful of rich, spoiled Splicers, some True Borns, and a spoon's worth of very desperate Lasters. I know we're already seeing it, only in smaller scale. But is anyone paying attention? Just the other week our mother tried to keep the NewsFeed away from us. There'd been a hostage taking in Bremen, one of the rich suburbs north of us. An entire family, including a six-month-old baby, had been slaughtered by a Laster crew looking for a big payday for a Splice and dice. It was so stupid. All those unnecessary deaths. I thought everyone knew: for the past few years all money has been barcoded and tracked. By our people, the Splicers of the Upper Circle, the people who run everything. Had the Lasters escaped—the NewsFeed only said the fugitives were apprehended at the scene, but we know that means fried—they would have been turned down at every clinic except Black Market. And who knows what dirty genes would be sewn into your body there?

Margot and I are aware of the strange divide between us and the rest of humanity. We are the lucky ones who sit in our gated mansion. We stare from our windows and listen to the peppery sound of gun wars as we watch the world burn. Fires break out all over Dominion like they're on rotation: for the last three years the power grid has been shut down for all but the very rich, so people have been pulling down whatever they can to heat their homes. There aren't enough people to put out the fires. Homes like ours—high fenced, set far back and away from our neighbors—are life preservers on an endless, burning ocean.

Still, we aren't completely sheltered. It's not unusual for us to run across bodies in the street even though Dominion has gangs of people who go around collecting and burying as many as they can. Most of the corpses are dead of Plague, but a good number bear marks of violence. Jagged valleys ripped into chests; faces blown apart. In their blue HAZMAT suits, white handkerchiefs covering their faces, the cleanup crews look like soul-stealing bandits as they rove the streets looking for pickups. The city pays them by the body, and plenty say this has turned good men into murderers. But mostly the Rovers take the job for the pocket treasures they score from the Lasters. Even so, there aren't enough of them, we've heard— not enough Rovers, and not enough dead richies to feed them. We are paying attention. But there's nothing we can do to stop any of this. An image of the boy holding up his *Evolve or Die* message flashes through my mind. He was so rebellious and hateful as he made his stand on top of a car and held his sign. But then, why wouldn't they hate us?

"What do you think they want?" I'm curious to hear what Mr. Storm will say.

His eyes flatten me with a look. "Power." It's so simple it feels inescapable. "Whoever doesn't have it wants to take it away from those who do." Storm's eyes shift to our father, then back to me. I nod slightly. Mr. Storm knows exactly what's going on out there. And we're sitting ducks.

I glance at our father, who frowns at Storm as though he's said too much. My eyelashes quake with effort as I try not to look too long at the magnetic young man standing behind Storm. And fail. Which reminds me…. Not taking my eyes away from the blond merc I ask, "Mr. Storm, may I ask what 'remote security' means? Are you going to tail us?"

Storm shakes his head, his mouth a firm line. "No, I'm going to give you these." He fishes two flat objects out of his pocket, handing one to Margot and one to me with long, calloused fingers. I touch the screen and the display flutters to life. It's a pre-prog, but I see no apps and only one number. "Memorize the number in case you lose the phone. If you ever think you're being followed, call the number and don't ditch the phone."

I stare at Storm over the blinking display. "There's no name. Whose number is it?"

He doesn't answer. "Someone will pick up, day or night. Tell whoever answers what's happening, if you can. We'll extract you."

"Who are you really?" I ask, not sure which of the strange men I'm asking, and surely not quietly enough. My father's quick intake of breath is enough to know I've crossed the line.

He graces me with a crooked smile anyhow. "Right now, sweetheart, all you've got to know is that I'm your friend."

We're dismissed a few moments later. I stop in the hallway, pressing myself against the wall.

"You all right, Lu?" Margot asks.

I nod, not trusting myself to speak. Hot streaks of… *something*…jitter through my veins, and for the first time I recognize what until now I've only ever known secondhand from my sister. It feels as though my safe and perfect life is crumbling down around my ears, and I'm deaf to all but the roar, blind to all but a pair of indigo eyes. Eyes belonging to a *merc*, I remind myself, whose name I don't even know.

It's the waiting that gets to us—the endless waiting for explanations and answers that never come, days that feel a lot like holding out for some mythical Plague cure. Days after our meeting with Nolan Storm, Margot and I pack our school bags, go to school, come home again. Sunrise, sunset. Silence in between.

And not a single glimpse of my blond stranger.

It wouldn't be so bad, or maybe I'd call it typical, except that I can't shake the feeling that the secrets are mounting. Our father is more distracted than usual. We notice this because he forgets to be harsh with us on the long morning drives as Shane drops us off at school before taking Father to his office at the Capitol building.

Absently I run my fingers in my little purse until they clasp hard, cold plastic. The phone with its one number rides to school with me every day. At night it sits under my pillow, never too far from reach—much like my memory of meeting the merc with the sunlight hair, stamped indelibly in my brain.

"Girls." Our father suddenly stares at us with an odd expression.

"Yes, Father," we reply automatically.

"Something to keep in mind for your Reveal." *Our Reveal?* Father doesn't bother with the details of things like our coming-of-age party. And it's still a good six weeks away. *Unless there is something he needs to tell us.* My stomach churns with horror. I grip my sister's hand tightly between us, all thoughts of happiness fled.

Our father's gaze wanders out the window moodily, whatever he wanted to tell us forgotten. It must be bad. I can't stand the suspense. "What is it, Father?" I prompt.

He frowns back at us, the spot above his nose crinkling in displeasure. "We'll soon be hosting a very important business associate from Russia. I have to tell you"—our father leans over his knees, his black leather gloves snapping against the fabric of his pants as he stares intently at us—"this guest is the most important guest we have ever entertained." Beside me, Margot taps a slim finger against her wrist in exclamation. Our father has never sounded like this before. He pins us to our seats with eyes of fire and ice. "He will be present at your Reveal. In fact, he may escort one of you. I will expect you to play your part to keep him happy."

"Yes, Father," we say again. Waves of disappointment and relief wash through us. Not the worst news, then: not the "L" word. *But what of this?*

"Is there something we can do to help you, Father?" I say quietly.

A small smirk folds up the corners of his mouth. "Yes," he drawls, leaning back in his seat. "You can be the perfect daughters I raised. Stay out of trouble"—his eyes laser into

ours—"and when the time is right, do your duty to the family."
His words send shivers down my spine.

I sit in shocked silence beside my sister as our father goes
back to staring out the window. Outside, Dominion rolls by
in all its wrecked decadence.

"Father," Margot chirps beside me.

"Hmm?" Our father chokes the life out of his gloves as
he watches the streets. There is a strange moodiness in the air
today, like a storm is about to burst. We pass the checkpoint
fashioned of chicken wire manned by one of Grayguard's
blue-clad mercs.

"Deirdre Phalon told us that the Feeds were wrong. She
said there's an insurrection going on. Something to do with
the preachers and the rabble."

Our father shakes off his vagueness in an instant and
trains cold eyes on Margot. "Where did you hear that?"

"Deirdre Phalon," she says again.

"And where, pray tell, did Deirdre Phalon, that insipid
airhead, hear that?" His jaw clenches with anger. I wish
Margot would stop, but she's always been the braver one.
The one who asks what she shouldn't.

"Her parents, I reckon," her voice trails off.

"You shouldn't listen to idle gossip, Margot."

"But you'd know, wouldn't you, Father?" I chime in. My
hand finds Margot's on the seat between us. I cover her fingers.
Our signal that I'm coming in for a rescue. "They'd tell you
the truth."

"Yes." His clipped tones still spell disapproval, but his
mood lightens.

"I bet you heard the rumors, too, and that's why you hired
Mr. Storm. Just in case there is some kind of uprising."

His eyes crinkle in amusement. Our father slaps his gloves against his leg. "I suppose that's the case. Of course, Lucinda, if anything happens, you girls will be safe." Our father pats my knee.

But as Shane drives off with him a few minutes later, we know something else to be true. A lot of kids have extra mercs. Burly men who stand around the gates of the school, hands twitchy on gun triggers, smoking and pacing. The school has put out far more sentries, too. Blue-armed uniforms patrol the grounds and scan the nearby buildings for signs of trouble.

On the tall old brownstone just opposite the school someone has spray painted a pair of bright red eyes. They're trick eyes that seem to follow you no matter which way you turn.

A burst of gunfire wrecks the silence of our third period test. In seconds we are all at the window. A lone gunman stands on top of the brownstone and sweeps the school with bullets. Ms. Hojin makes us duck just as we hear the glass breaking in the windows all down the front of the school. As it shatters and falls, the glass sounds like an earthquake. Suddenly it's like a war has broken out, as any sentries and bodyguards still standing fire back. Ms. Hojin is on her feet in an instant and at the emergency phone. The alarm bleeps, and the steel security barriers collapse over the doors and windows, trapping us in the classroom. Soon the announcements blare distorted over the intercom. We're told to stay quiet, stay in our rooms until officials let us out. Not that we have a choice.

The gunfire disappears as we hear bigger booms to the east where the downtown core is. A while later, like in a dream, we're evacuated. Robbie Deakins finds Margot just as we get to the hall near the main door. His eyes are bright, almost feverish with excitement as he pushes a crumpled note into her hand.

"You guys okay? I heard Old Man Hicks was hit in the ass." His overly long front teeth gleam as he laughs.

"What's going on?" Margot asks. "Rabble again?"

"Yup, but my dad says there's something to it this time. Some new preacher is in town getting them all stirred up."

Robbie's father works at the Ministry of Defense. Our families know each other. Robbie is one of the boys on our "safe" list, invited to every party. Which just goes to show how much our parents collectively don't know.

"Gotta dash. Give me a call, gorgeous." Robbie flips his hands near his face like he's holding a phone. He pushes a lock of his dark hair out of his eyes and flashes his dimples at Margot.

"Wait." I grab his arm just as he's about to flee. "Robbie, who are they after?"

For a moment he looks confused. He backs up, shaking my hand off. "You're kidding, right?" Robbie asks. His Personal stalks up behind him. Robbie glances over his shoulder and says something to the impressive man wearing a bulletproof vest. He hands another one to Robbie, who slips it on over his collared shirt like it's a dinner jacket. "What, did you grow up in a tower or something, Lucy? Where have you been?"

"Don't you talk that way to my sister," Margot yells as he turns and flees. We're left standing in the hallway while all around us our classmates and their security swarm. I see a tall man with bluish, shiny skin standing silently near a classroom door waiting for his charge. I catch his eye, and he nods back at me politely before turning his attention to a pimply-faced freshman. A True Born.

Margot crumples up the note Robbie has given her and tosses it on the floor. Her bangs float off her face as she harrumphs in exasperation. "What a dozer." Margot sneers.

"What does he want?"

"To get into my pants."

"Are you going to let him?"

"I'm not interested in little boys," Margot says with a worldly sigh. She plucks at my arm and motions. Shane waits, grim-faced, beside the door. As he ushers us out he tries hard to shield us from the dead bodies littering the sidewalks, but it's impossible. Glass shards lay thick on the ground, like a blanket of broken snow. Windows are blown out everywhere. But the worst part is the pungent scent of iron and fire.

"Where are they, Shane?"

Shane holds up. "Where are who, Miss Lucy?"

I nearly choke on the words. "Mr. Storm's people. The True Borns."

Shane doesn't seem to notice my embarrassment. He just nods at the buildings beside the rooftop where the gunman had stood, then at the school. "Out there," he tells us, his jaw locking. "Kicking the hell out of them."

But if he's still out there—of course I'd been thinking of the blond stranger—I see no trace of him now. On the other hand, the evidence of our father's lies is everywhere. Grayguard Academy is in shambles. Shane slips us into the back of the bulletproof car and climbs into the driver's seat, Fritz, silent and watchful beside him. We know we won't be back at school tomorrow.

...

Margot primps as the night blooms fresh darkness.

"Don't go," I plead with my sister as I watch from her bed. "It's too dangerous. Besides, he'll know."

It's been three days since the "Downtown Siege," as the NewsFeeds are calling it. We haven't been back to school. Then again, no one has.

Our father laughed off the attack, calling it the work of amateurs out looking for a Splice job. Our mother said nothing, just fingered her pearls and ordered the servants to bring in dinner.

"Not to worry," our father told us, "that's why I've hired Mr. Storm and his team. Just in case we need a little backup. And already they're proving their weight in gold." He'd turned to our mother. "Now I don't know why I didn't hire these kind of people before, Antonia."

We know our father met with Nolan Storm the day after the attack, but he said nothing about it. There have been only three days of quiet while our parents and their friends kept up appearances. Still, everyone is buzzing about how our father's remote security firm kept the attack from becoming a slaughter. And every time I hear about it, I recall the stranger, his cinnamon breath, the feel of his muscles beneath my fingers.

"Who?" Margot halts midway while pulling on a stocking, looking back at me through the mirror. Her excitement zings through my veins like soda pop. I inhale sharply, hoping my distraction over the stranger doesn't show.

"You know."

"Father? He won't even notice I'm gone."

"Not Father." I exhale in relief, promptly changing the subject. "Though Shane is going to tattle on you if you keep this up, and you heard what Father said. I reckon we'll have to suck up to his mysterious business partner. I mean *him*."

Margot laughs and the sound—deep, pealing bells— is almost enough for me to shake off my feeling of dread. She hooks a tag of her hair behind a perfect, shell-like ear, showing off the diamond stud earrings she's wearing. A very Big Deal Date, then. Margot's mouth flattens into a hard line as disapproval drips from her voice. "We don't even know this Nolan Storm guy. I think he's just taking Father's money and isn't going to do a thing."

"You didn't feel it?"

Margot shrugs and shimmies into a tight black dress that ends mid-thigh. "Feel what?"

Lately it's as though Margot has built a wall between herself and all the things that make us special: our extra sense, how we touch each other's minds with ease. It's still there, but now Margot wants to fill it with boy intrigue, late-night getaways. Secrets she keeps from me, her other half, while I go about playing the dutiful diplomat's daughter.

She finishes strapping on her shoes and comes over to me. In her heels she towers over me, so her arms are too high when she hugs me. We don't fit anymore.

"Margot, please."

"It's okay, little sister," she whispers. Little sister. The name she calls me only when she's going to get us both in a world of trouble.

"No, it's not." I tug on her arm and force her to look at me. "Didn't you feel it? Storm's not… He's not a Splicer, Margot."

It's as though I'm wrestling with the bundle of impressions that have been haunting me for days, ever since I met the blond merc on the stairs. It's the only thing that makes sense. How is it they were able to route an entire scale attack on Grayguard and survive? How is it that we never catch glimpses of them?

Margot shrugs again. "So he's a True Born. So?"

"Margot, why would Father hire True Borns to protect us?"

This gives Margot pause, but only long enough to grab a wrap and make a face. "Because he's our father. He's got to make an impression. I'd bet you my allowance he wrote the rule against True Borns and made everyone follow just so he could be the first to break it."

She has a point. Sometimes people like to gossip with us about our father's exploits. The Ambassador of France once told us that in Europe they call our father "the Hunter," because his instincts for getting what he wants are—*how do you say?*—uncanny.

But as Margot heads down to the kitchen where she will slip out into the night with its zealots and crazies and Lasters bent on insurrection, I can't help but think that our father would never accept help from a True Born, not even the paid kind. Lukas Fox hates True Borns with a passion he reserves for those who have more power and money than him. Secretly I think True Borns are the only thing our father is actually afraid of, something too far outside his control.

That is, unless there is something to be very, very concerned about.

And as Margot disappears with a silent whoosh of the door, I have this crazy feeling I can't shake: that somehow my sister and I are at the root of a vast secret that blooms and blooms under the cover of night.

4

The grandfather clock in the hall chimes ten o'clock. It's a lousy day, gray and raining on and off. The house is silent. I sit at the large wooden table by myself and eat half a grapefruit, a delicacy of the rich. Mother and Father are gone without any word, and without any word on when they'll be back. "On business," Shane tells me, twisting his hands anxiously. I mentally translate: something bad is happening, and we're not supposed to know.

Margot is also not at home. Shane has the sneaking suspicion that she wasn't at home all last night. He'd be right. Every few minutes I hug myself and stare at my plate, and wonder what has happened to my sister.

The night had been one long erotic dream, images and sensations tugging at me as I tangled with my sheets. I felt sick over them, wanted to shut my body down against the treacherous feelings, so it wasn't until almost morning that I finally dropped off into a deep, dark sleep.

And when I awoke, my sister had vanished from me.

It was like going suddenly deaf and dumb. My hands shook as I quickly showered and dressed, then had to dress myself again as I discovered I'd put most of my clothes on backward or inside out. I kept poking at our bond, hoping to bring Margot's awareness back. It remained tied to me like a lifeless tree branch, but nothing moved. As deserted as the house I found myself in.

By the time I feel the first stirrings of life creep back to me it's a little after three in the afternoon. Margot is woozy, disoriented. Bright flashes erupt behind my eyes. I feel her throat burn as she throws up again and again, her stomach sick and empty. Another hour passes before she's somewhere back to normal, though a powerful sense of *wrong* still overwhelms me.

A little before five the phone rings. I dive for it on the first ring, certain who's on the other end.

"Lucy?"

"Margot, where are you?"

"Hey, little sis. Are Mom and Dad mad?"

I pause. "Are you all right?" Her voice doesn't even tremble. Then again, she was always the better actress than I.

"Hey, I've just been out partying with some friends. But listen, little sister. I forgot to tell you before I went out yesterday. Dad wanted us to go to the Clinic for another round of Protocols. Something about the last ones being duds. I'll meet you there, okay?"

"Margot, are you there now? Who's with you? Where are you?"

"Gotta dash, little sis. Gonna catch a few hours of sleep now. See you in a couple hours."

"Margot!" I yell. But it's too late. The line is dead.

I run up to my bedroom. The ultra slim phone is where I hid it, under the pillow. The number dials as I speed down the stairs. It picks up with a click. I know someone is there, but all they do is listen.

"Hello?" I grab a coat and pull open the front door. For a moment I simply stand there on the threshold and wonder what has happened to the day. The air is a blinding gold white, turning the streets hazy and strange. These days, when it isn't raining and cloudy, it's like this, as though someone has pulled a veil over the sky.

"Hello?" I say again. "You know who this is, don't you?"

"Yes," a voice on the other end confirms. It's a woman's voice, deep and clear. Maybe the same woman who accompanied Storm? I don't know as I never heard her speak.

"My sister is in trouble. Did she call? I think someone's holding her and been doing things to her. I need…I need…" I stumble over the words and bite my lip to hold back tears.

The voice on the phone remains coolly professional. "Where are you?"

"I'm leaving my house now. I've got to get to her."

"Stay where you are. We're on our way."

"It will be too late," I nearly yell into the phone as I slip through the locked door beside the wrought iron gate. "They're expecting me at the Clinic."

"Lucy," the voice is insistent, but by then I've pocketed the phone and am making my way through the eerie white streets.

As I thread my way on foot to the Splicer Clinic a good twenty blocks away, I have time to gather fleeting impressions of a city gone to ruin. I reckon the rabble has been busy. On quieter side streets, cars are parked one on top of another like tin can apartment blocks. I can't tell what holds them together, or what prevents them from collapsing from the weight, but at some corners they're stacked four high. Occasionally I see a head peep out from one of the car windows. Dirty hair, streaked faces. Most just kids. I wonder to myself why so many people are sleeping in cars when there are hundreds of apartments and houses unoccupied. But then I recall the gaunt, hungry look of the boy I saw the other day. And I think about our father. Would he let people squat in one of his buildings? No, he'd blow it up before he'd let that happen.

The light begins to fade as I walk. Bleached of its gold, the sky turns the color of bones. Old Victorian row houses sit chock a block on streets lined with tree trunks. "This used to be a good neighborhood when I was a girl," our mother told us with a derisive sigh. Most of the trees have been torn down for fires. It's only the people who can afford to guard their trees who still have any shade. Every few buildings the windows are blown out, making the stores look curiously blind. Sometimes there is a string of hollowed-out husks, where the buildings burned and burned and there was no one to stop the fire.

The farther I go the more people turn their hungry eyes on me. I shouldn't have left the way I did. I should have at least left Shane a note. But as I hurry on, Margot's fear bounces around inside of me, thickening until there's no room for anything else.

I'm so lost in thought that at first I don't notice the heavy pair of boots treading behind me. *Thud-clack. Thud-clack.* I pick up the pace and turn onto a busier street, one where the buildings are more intact. Even here I see signs of the rabble. *Evolve or Die.* It's written everywhere: sidewalks, bus stops, shelters. Abandoned windows. Store fronts that still have businesses — and people to run them. Heart in my throat, I turn again.

A figure appears from behind a corner. I recognize the skinny boy, the preacher's boy. Bones jut from his collar and face like all the fat has been sucked out from under his skin.

He glares at me as I pass, then falls in behind me, his steps light as a bird's and mixing in with the heavier tread. Panicking, I dart across the street and head for a store that I think is open. I don't notice until it's too late that just past the slightly ajar door shelves and boxes have been thrown all over the place. I turn another corner and end up in a small alley. I can't see anyone behind me and am about to hide when both of my followers appear. The boy says something to the heavyset man beside him. I get my first real glimpse of the other: a short man but thick as a house. His neck bulges from under a torn and dirty orange vest. They see I'm alone and advance on me. I scream and run as fast as I can toward the end of the alley as the two rush me. I'm nearly at the end, and nearly in their grasp, when a black van pulls up in front of me.

A side door opens and out slides a tall, thin woman with a black Mohawk. She's in a sort of skintight suit, something that looks like the texture of skin under a microscope, patterned in white, black, beige, and gray. Her face is all angles, eyes tilted strangely in her striking brown face. I skid to a halt. As do the men behind me.

"Hey, there you are," she chirrups in a friendly voice. She spares only the slightest glance for me before turning hard eyes toward the men in the alley. "Why don't you pick on someone your own size?" she says mildly.

The boy stays where he is, but the man with the bulging

neck pushes on, sucking at a crooked row of discolored teeth. "I like 'em small enough to use for toothpicks."

"That's fortunate." She bares her teeth at the bruiser, perfect rows of fangs, and a minute later I see a tail, long and ending in wisps of hair, swish angrily from her backside. Her eyes are dark pits of rage as she stalks forward and pushes me behind her.

A hand clamps over my shoulder. I scream and a second hand comes over my mouth, stifling it. The hands hook me back until I'm looking up into a pair of perfect indigo blue eyes.

My heart stutters and skips. He looks leaner in this light, as though he's hungry. A predatory light fills his eyes. He doesn't say anything, just looks me over as though thoroughly assessing me. Removing his hand from my shoulder, where it burns like a brand, he puts a finger to his lips. I nod, and he lowers his hand, only to drag me into the back seat of the vehicle.

"She's not happy unless she's showing off." He nods toward the woman before closing the sliding door and locking it.

I peel my eyes away from Storm's man to watch through the tinted windows as the woman's lithe form stalks the bruiser. I'm glad when I see the boy slink off into the emptying dark of the alleyway. At least one of them is smart enough to know when the game is over.

Mohawk kicks, her roundhouse so fast it's a blur of color as it connects with Bruiser's face and staggers him back. Just one punch, then she lunges at his neck. Bruiser screams, a high-pitched whine that fades as his jugular rips.

The woman leaps away as the big man crumples. Blood

splatters across her face and drips from her chin. She cracks her neck and walks back to the vehicle like she hasn't a care in the world, although I think I catch her studying every shadow in the alleyway.

Somehow they found me. Found me, rescued me. Even killed for me.

"That's twice now I've saved you."

I stare at the blond smiling smugly in the darkness of the back seat. Anger buzzes through me. "Seems to me that she saved me." I nod to the woman who climbs into the driver's seat and flicks the ignition. "And the first time we met you nearly killed me," I toss back breezily, telegraphing to the blond man that I am not pleased about his behavior at Grayguard. He could have identified himself. Why did he let me embarrass myself, going on as if he was common rabble, when he was in essence *spying* on us?

Mohawk twists in her seat and utters a strange, braying laugh. "Can't help but like this one," she says. "Hold on, chickies, it's going to be a bumpy ride."

The beautiful blond man's eyes narrow at me. He leans over and scoops the seat belt over my chest as I try to fend off his hands. He's too close, too close. My brain misfires as his hair brushes my face.

"I can do it myself," I argue.

But the man just raises his face, inches away, so close I can see a tiny scar by his mouth. Smiles wickedly. "I'm sure you can. But like you say, your safety is of the utmost importance, your Highness."

Mohawk puts the vehicle in gear and roars the engine, then peels out of the alleyway as though it's on fire. The van lurches sickeningly as we roll over the thick body of the man who'd chased me, and my stomach lurches along with it.

But it seems I'm not the only one who takes issue. "Did you have to do that?" argues the merc beside me.

Mohawk barely spares us a glance as she cheerfully replies, "Yep."

5

"We need to get my sister!" I argue with the rumpled blond slouching against the wall. If I weren't two seconds from hysterical, I'd probably still be drooling over him. Half bathed in shadow, his face looks like a sculpture. Besides the worn pants that fit his slim body like a second skin, he's got on an old moss-green shirt with "Girls are fun" scribbled on the front in neon pink.

Jared. On the drive over the Mohawk woman had called him Jared. Now I have a name. For a second I can't help but stare. He stares back. "You need to calm down. You know where she is, right?" I nod. "Then no problem, right?" The cold of the room, decorated with metal benches and equipment, doesn't seem to bother my captor in the least. "Hey now. It's Lucy, right?" A blond curl flips over one eye, and he tosses it back. Storm's man saunters over to me, thumbs hooked into the loops of his pants. If I weren't spitting mad and sulking, I might be swooning, although his personality has all the charm of the rabble. Which is to say, none at all. "Storm's on it. You really do need to get a grip."

I turn on him. "It's Jared, *right*?" His small smile tells me he doesn't get the sarcasm. "Well, Jared, why don't I let you in on a secret. I'm not some little girl you can park in your…science lab or whatever this is." I wave my arms at the gleaming benches. "And my sister is in real trouble. So if you aren't going to produce Mr. Storm *right now*, I'm going to walk out that door. Right after I throw you through it."

His head tips back as he laughs, knees bending like he can't stand up. I'm still glaring at his esophagus and wishing I had a knife when Mr. Storm himself breezes through the steel door.

"Lucy, sorry to have kept you waiting." He moves stealthily, every step measured and sure. I try to size him up but find I can't. It's as though he cast a net around himself and ties up all the air so you can't really see him. But then he smiles, a genuine smile, warm and gentle at the same time. "Come with me," he tells me, nodding only slightly at Jared as he pivots and marches out of the room. I follow, Jared's presence behind me poking me into a hot ball of nerves.

Storm leads me through winding hallways, some lit by lights I can't see, others long and broad and filled with hazy light coming in through floor-to-ceiling glass windows. I'm lost after the first turn, and by the time we enter an office with a living room set, I'm ready to sit down. My way in was much easier: Jared had simply slipped a knotted handkerchief over my eyes, right before he picked me up and carried me out of the car, whispering in my ear, "No peeking." I can still feel the hot band of his hands beneath my knees and back as he carried me into the cold metal room and dumped me on my feet.

Storm gestures for me to sit on the long, cream leather sofa, the soft kind that aren't made anymore. A woman with thick-framed black glasses in an olive green business suit brings in a tray with a pitcher of water and a coffee urn. Her hair is caught up in a tight, smooth bun, but I recognize the glimmer in her eyes. She's only pretending to be a secretary, I think to myself. She doesn't look at me, not even once, and I wonder what she's doing for Storm.

"Thank you, Alma," he dismisses her and sits. Even on the extra-large couch he's too big. He seems to gobble up all the air. And yet, I can't help but be electrifyingly aware of the blond slouching against the wall.

Storm pours me some water, himself some coffee, before launching in.

"Did you see her being taken?"

Storm shakes his head. "No, but some of my people were keeping an eye out." He raises one arched eyebrow at Jared.

"I don't understand. I thought you were hired to be remote security."

"This is a very particular job we've been hired for, Lucy. Your father doesn't want us to interfere with your lives unless you are in serious danger from…external parties."

Jared makes a scoffing noise behind me. I pretend to ignore him. "So we were safe the other day at my school? Those people with the guns—they're not a threat? I've heard it's a serious uprising."

"I didn't say that."

"Who is Father afraid of?"

There's a long pause before he answers. "I'm not certain."

"He didn't tell you?"

Over the rim of his coffee cup, Storm studies me. "As I'm

sure you're aware, Lucy, your father is not the easiest man in the world to work for."

Jared snorts. Annoyed, I turn around to glare at him, but I can't say I disagree with the sentiment. "Do you mind?" I turn back to Storm. "So why did you take the job? It doesn't look like you're hurting here."

"I took this job for my own reasons."

"And those would be?" I know as the question comes out of my mouth that he won't answer. Still, I'm disappointed when he sits there in stony silence. "Fine. Are we going soon?"

When he nods in agreement, I sag with relief. "But first we have a few things to discuss, you and I. Don't we?" It's clear this isn't a question. He won't be ignored. I can't help curling my hands in my lap, though, and sneaking a look at Jared, who lounges against the wall like a pin-up celebrity. "He's safe, Lucy."

It isn't so much the gentle way Storm tells me so much as the look in his eye that makes me believe him. Besides, despite what I've said, the man has repeatedly pulled me from danger. He may be a horse's behind but he's a good merc. And in the end, what choice do I have? Margot is lost somewhere, confused and in pain. To leave her out there, alone for a second longer...

And I know what Nolan Storm wants to hear.

"You're going to have to keep an open mind," I tell him, unsure of how to begin.

He laughs and leans in. "You already know I'm not like other people, Lucy," he says. "And we both know you and Margot aren't, either. Consider us even."

...

By the time I finish our story, Margot's and mine, it seems late and I'm antsy. Jared has hovered like a shadow at the door the entire time. Storm has been mostly quiet, too. He listened like he was recording everything with his mind. Every so often he'd stop me and ask me to explain something. The questions had always been good ones. "How does it feel when Margot is in pain?" he'd asked. "Do you feel it in your head or your body? Do you think the nurse suspected there was something going on with the Protocols?" He seemed to respect my read of a situation, too, like I mattered. That made me even more talkative, and I couldn't seem to help myself. I'd never had the chance to discuss the strange phenomenon between my twin and me with anyone other than Margot. It felt like a dam bursting: once I'd started there was no stopping it. The moment I'm through I'm swamped with guilt. How could I indulge in this storytelling while Margot is in danger?

Now as he sits back and stares at me I feel naked and alone. I have nothing else to barter with. I can't count on his help, and I don't know what he'll do with everything I've told him. It could cost us everything. Storm surprises me with his next question. "You know she's at the Splicer Clinic. Do you think you know who has her?"

I shake my head. "No. But it's someone she trusts."

He sits up straighter, eyes cold and calculating. "What makes you think so?"

I blush. "She was having fun at first. A lot of fun." I hear a chuckle behind me that I studiously ignore. "Then everything changed. They drugged her. On the phone she told me she was staying at a friend's house."

Storm cocks his head. "You think she was being fed a script?"

I'd considered this. But Margot had chosen every word very carefully. She'd called me "little sis," our parents "Mom and Dad." The tip-offs were obvious to me, but wouldn't be to anyone else. "No," I finally tell him.

Storm nods. "Okay then. Jared, fetch the others."

A heartbeat later I'm alone with Nolan Storm. And before I lose my nerve I need to blurt it out. I've figured out his people are all True Borns, even if I don't know what kind. But *what is he*?

"You're different from them"—I toss my head at the general direction of the door—"but I can't figure out how."

It's more than the concentrated way he sits, hands clasped together and an elegant elbow resting on a crossed knee. He's completely relaxed, but I know with every instinct in my body that he could spring in an instant. And though he's been nothing but gentle with me, I am confident he could rip a man to shreds with his bare hands. But it's something more, something that hovers just underneath the surface. Violent and dark and throbbing with undisguised power.

"I am," he replies after a thoughtful pause. "Suffice it to say, I don't think now is quite the time for explanations. One day I'll tell you a story, Lucy." He stands, offering me his hand. It swallows mine as he lifts me gently off the couch. "And for the record"—he winks—"I suspect you're as different as they come, too."

The "others" Storm alluded to appear. The woman with the Mohawk flings herself onto the couch with an offhand, "Hello, Dolly." Another man, a boy really, files in, followed by Jared, who grins cockily at me and resumes his guard duty as he shuts the door behind him. I stare him down with the haughtiest look I can muster. He looks away, eyes crinkling with laughter.

Storm doesn't waste time. "Routine extraction," he tells Mohawk and the boy. "Except the cargo here is extremely valuable."

"How valuable?" Mohawk arranges her lithe limbs over one arm of the couch.

"Think of the most precious commodity in Dominion, then up that." I blink at Storm's words. Our father is paying him well, and we're rich, yes. We're young and well-connected. But *precious*? The same thought must occur to Mohawk, because she sizes me up and down like she's measuring me for a plate.

She runs the tip of her tongue along razor-sharp teeth. "Delicious."

Storm shoots her a look that could freeze blood. She squirms and sits up a little straighter. "Torch," he barks.

The boy who's been standing behind the couch stands up straighter. "Sir." I'd barely noticed him in all the excitement. He has a way of fading into the background, like I usually do. Mouse brown hair. Dark, round brown eyes in a pale face but with the longest, thickest eyelashes I've ever seen on a boy. I peg him as a year or two younger than me. He's tall and rangy, with an awkward look to his limbs, like a tree whose branches have been growing at different speeds.

"Best way in?"

"North gate. Light artillery," he answers.

A thought dawns on me. "All this time you knew exactly where she was. Why didn't you go and get her?"

The room gets tense in a hurry. Jared peels himself off the wall. "Now hold on there, Princess."

I ignore him. "You used the situation to get me talking. Are you going to blackmail our father? You're just like all the rest." The air around Storm shimmers expectantly, as though something is about to happen.

"No." Storm's voice rumbles deep in his chest, deeper than it had been. Waves of heat or something else roll off him as he ambles over to me. I take an instinctive step back. The hairs on my arms stand up. "I know you're probably not ready to hear this right now, Lucy, but we're on your side. You're in our charge. It would be irresponsible to go into a potentially dangerous kidnapping situation without knowing as much as possible."

I take a moment to appreciate what he's telling me. "What about me? I'm going too, right?"

The room is as quiet as a grave. I try to ignore Mohawk's smirk and Jared's soft cough until Storm says, "Yes, you are," just as Jared hollers over top, "Not on your life!"

I feel a tug inside myself. A pinch. Margot pinches herself right there, right on the fleshy part of the thigh, when she's trying to get my attention. I lean over my toes, breathing deep, and clench my fingers. Sometimes it seems so unfair that the sensations only go one way.

"You can't be serious," Jared argues with Storm. "She's like, what—twelve?"

A twinge of disappointment rings through me. Do I really seem like a baby to him? I'm about to put Jared in his place when Storm beats me to it. "Nearly eighteen. And age has nothing to do with it. As you well know." He eyes Jared meaningfully. The blond merc stalks back to the wall and hitches one leg up as Storm reasons, "I'm not happy about bringing a client into an extraction, either. Frankly, we don't know what we're dealing with, and we don't know who's working for whom. She was nearly grabbed today. I doubt that was a coincidence."

I'd put it out of my mind as just another attack by hungry street thugs. Somehow hearing about what happened on the street from Storm's point of view makes my blood run cold. What if it hadn't been random? What if we are in more danger than we'd thought?

Mohawk picks at her hair. "Precious cargo is a liability."

"Yes," Storm returns coolly, "but she'll also be a valuable asset. Lucy's ability to sense her sister could determine the outcome." I blush as I feel three sets of eyes assess me with interest. No one has ever known about Margot and me.

Storm wheels on me as though he's reading my thoughts. "I know this was not my secret to tell, Lucy. I'm sorry about that. But in the current situation I need to place your safety as well as the safety of my crew above all other concerns. Suffice it to say"—the room grows downright chilly as he surveys his people—"if any of my people so much as hint at what they have learned here today, I'll put them to death myself."

I shiver and realize I believe him. Every word. As three covert glares come my way, I reckon his crew does, too.

6

The damp, moldy scent of the concrete is overlaid with notes of motor oil and a whiff of garbage. There's so much dust in the air I want to sneeze. As Jared shoves me up hard against the wall, I finally do, right in his face. Serves him right, I think, trying to ignore the shiver of heat that curls along my spine.

I'd thought I'd known what I was in for. The second we arrived at the Clinic the team went to work like a well-tuned machine. Mohawk slipped into the shadows to disable the cameras and cut the alarm. Jared got busy tapping on a small keyboard—disrupting phone signals, I was told—while Storm swiped between figures and a glowing floor plan of the place on his intel screen.

He nodded at Torch. "Now."

Every so often the peppery sound of gunshot broke the silence. Fighting in the quarters. I froze each time a gun popped. Storm's people kept their heads down.

The gangly boy, Torch, exited the vehicle and walked up to the fence. From my perch I could see current flowing through the wires, the faint sheen of electricity humming through it like the glow of a firefly. In the blink of an eye the current was gone. Torch glanced over his shoulder at Storm as though he liked what he saw. He raised his right hand to the fence, curling his palm around something. Moments later a glow erupted from his palm. Heat shimmered through the dark as the boy blew through the fence with a flame so hot it melted the metal links into puddles in minutes. A gaping archway just shy of my shoulders appeared. Torch peeled it back with a grin. He wasn't even sweating.

Then we'd run for cover, and at a nod from Storm, Jared hauled me into the darkness of the delivery bay…where I now linger in purgatory waiting for the extraction to be over so I don't have the mortal sin of murder on my hands.

As Jared snarls, "I said stay back," I wonder if he can tell that I'm dreaming up all the ways I'd like to kill him.

He's too close, too hot. I barely form the words, "I heard you," before he cuts me off with a loud, "Shhh. No talking." I glare daggers again, wishing he could see me, and try to pry his hand from my chest.

"I *said*, shut up," he says in a loud whisper.

"I wasn't talking," I whisper back, plucking madly at his hand. It might as well be a steel trap for all I'm able to move it. But even though I hate him, I can't seem to stop my traitorous body from tingling all over at his proximity. His entire length presses up against me, and I can tell from the way his eyes take on a faint sheen, a green I've never seen before, that he's noticing how close he is, too. I say nothing as he blinks and backs an inch away.

On this side of the Clinic the shadows are thick and impenetrable. Security is tight all around the Clinic but here in the delivery bay, where Storm has parked me and my demon babysitter, no one could hear me even if I scream. Between us and the fence is at least fifty yards of empty parking lot. Past the fence where Storm's van waits for us is a park whose greenery extends all the way up through the center of the city. We are cocooned in an island of darkness.

"It wasn't my idea to be saddled with you, either, you know," I mumble under my breath. Not that anything I say will matter. It's clear as glass that Jared feels stuck with me and resents the hell out of it. The thought sends a traitorous pang through me, and I remind myself that a merc doesn't need to like his clients to protect them.

Still, despite my babysitter's issues, it's quiet, almost peaceful. A soft rain ended not long ago, turning the streets of the city into shiny strips of dark wood. It always smells better in Dominion after a big rain washes away the stench of death. From where I stand I can pull a teasing whiff of clean, cool air mixed with Jared, something dark and mysterious and weirdly comforting, despite the fact that he wants to wring my neck. Every so often he tilts his head and whispers something. He's communicating with someone—Storm I guess, though I can't see where he's hidden his device.

He turns glittering eyes on me. "Uh huh," he says to thin air before speaking to me. "They've swept the first level and there's no sign. There are doors they can't get access to, though. Where do they usually take you when they do the tests?"

My fingernails bite into the flesh of my hands. "Protocols are done in C wing."

"Mid-section?"

"Yes."

He pushes a lock of blond hair from his face with an impatient hand. "Can you maybe use your spooky twin thing to hone in on her, Princess?"

I ignore the taunt and reach for my sister. Like slipping into her flesh, sinking into her body. Only this time—

A scream rips from me as my body jerks. Pain pulses through my lower belly, rippling up from the secret part of me to the tips of my fingers. I double up, try to protect myself. In an instant Jared is beside me, holding me up.

"What's happening, Lucy?" he asks with dead calm. "What's happening to Margot?"

But I can't breathe, can't think past the pain and horror. Can't stop, can't make it stop. "They're—don't know. So awful," I tell him. "Hurts." Tears leak down my face and cover his shirt. I look down and pull my fingers away, expecting to see blood. There's nothing there.

Jared pulls my head back and makes me look in his face. "Tell me where it hurts. Where are they hurting her?"

He doesn't look down to where I'm holding myself, to where my lower belly is being ripped to shreds by invisible knives. He keeps looking into my eyes, a witness to me living through my sister's torture. But he knows.

"Okay." His voice is gentler than I could have imagined. "Turn it off now, Lucy. Just turn it off."

My teeth are clenched so tight my jaw is wired shut. "Can't."

I barely feel his hands cradling my cheeks, pulling damp locks from my eyes. Then there's only Jared. Jared's eyes, feral and light. Looking straight into me again. "Come on. Do it."

I flick a switch I didn't even know existed. Margot's pain

shuts down, and I am alone, drowning in need for my sister. He catches me as I slip toward the ground. The only thing pinning me to the here and now is Jared as he grabs hold of my upper arms. The warm rise of his chest as he holds me close to him.

When I'm able, I lean in close to his ear. "I think she's in Protocols," I whisper.

"What makes you think so?"

I shrug, unable to put into words the complicated network of signals I share with Margot. He studies me for a moment. Without another word he hoists an arm around my back and hauls me up. I try to shake off my sense of disorientation as we move toward the big ugly cargo bay doors, gray and dented in a dozen places. Jared stops and props me up with a steadying hand and a military look in his eye. Pulling out a smart device he taps in a series of numbers, then holds the phone up to a small black box nestled into the wall next to the door, at the level of my head. A tiny red dot turns green and a *snick* sounds loudly in the quiet bay. He pulls the door back slowly, positioning me behind his body. Nothing and nobody comes out. So he grabs my hand and we slip inside.

The hallways are deserted, filled with tinny music. It's cranked so loud I want to cover my ears. Jared's hand tightens on mine as he hauls me into a doorway and presses me back.

"You don't move until I say so," he breathes into my ear. "You do what I say, when I say it, or I'm hauling you out of here by your hair."

I stare at him. Jared's face is raw: all bones, pinched nose, and a flat, thin line where his very sensual lips have been pressed together. I expect panic to swamp me, but it isn't there. Just the thought that, even though I don't know this man, I trust he won't do what he's threatening. At least, he won't drag me out by my shoulder-length hair. He'll choose another part of my anatomy. His face tightens as we consider each other.

"Lucy?" His voice is barely audible. I nod. He nods. Apparently we've struck a bargain.

I point down the hall. Built in the shape of a giant "H," the Clinic's half dozen testing rooms are tucked away in the hallway that stretches through the middle section. Jared holds me roughly by one arm, as though I can't walk on my own. Every few paces he stops, his head swiveling around. Looking, listening. His movements are so quiet it's as though I'm with a ghost. I hold my belly with one hand as tiny, razor-like licks nip into my skin and tiptoe awkwardly beside him, trying my best not to stumble. The rest of the team is nowhere to be seen.

He slows when we reach the corner. Over Jared's shoulder I catch a glimpse of a big man in a crisp white uniform, a goofy grin on his face as he whistles down the hall. Jared hauls me back with a look so dark it's painful. Then he slips out as the attendant puts his finger to the identi-pad outside a door. I hear the sickening *crick* of the man's neck as it snaps. He falls in a heavy pile on the thinly carpeted floor. Jared holds open the door and motions me over. I try not to gag as he lifts me over the body and into the room. I tell myself I should be better at this. I see dead bodies all the time. Dominion is riddled with them—although rarely this fresh. I can't even blame Jared. I would do anything to save Margot, and I'm grateful to him. Still, I'm struck by how unmoved he is, how routine this seems for him. As he ushers me into a small control room where the Clinic processes paperwork for the samples they take, it's as though the death means nothing to him. He moves around the room with the stealth of a professional soldier, eyes glowing with bloodlust. I shiver and wonder not for the first time who it is I've gotten tangled up with.

Jared cocks his head like he hears something. His nostrils flare as he sniffs the air. All I can hear is quiet-quiet, the pounding of my heartbeat, the faint tinkling of piano music outside the room. He mouths at me, *what's in there?* and points to a nondescript door leading from the anteroom. I mime a needle sinking into an arm. *Protocols*, I mouth back. He nods and pulls me back to the side of the door.

His breath tickles my ear. "Stay here." He bends into a half-crouch.

A second later he explodes into motion, so fast I can't see his limbs move. The door splits, partially tears from its hinges. Through the splintered pieces I can see into the samples' room. A tall man in white turns in surprise from an examination bed, holding a slightly bloodied syringe on a pan. A second man with a slack-jawed expression, also in the crisp white linen uniforms of the Clinic, gawps at us from behind a third. I can only see the top of his head, a scrap of his white uniform. A syringe with extra long tubing. And two slack, lily-white legs.

"Just one more," coaxes the man before my sister. He draws the words out, long and thin. "One more."

The cramping in my belly intensifies, as does the dreamy sense of floating outside my body as I stare at the pale face of my sister. She's on an operating bed, both hands stretched out and loose above her head as she cries out in pain. It takes me a second to process the thick bands holding her in place, the bright, cheery pink hue of her hospital gown in sharp contrast to the black leather of the bed. A purple bruise kisses the skin on her jaw. With her eyes closed, I can't tell if she's passed out as the man pulls the long tube of the syringe, glistening with fluid, from my sister's body. My belly feels so heavy with cramps it feels like death.

It takes me a second longer to place the blank and hungry look of my sister's captor to the plain face of the man we've known for years. The man who's brought us flowers every year since we were ten and the testing started. The jocular, chivalrous Protocols nurse. Clive.

A growl fills the small room, a low bass rumble that sets my teeth and hair on edge. Jared lunges at the men. I see only pieces of him: teeth extruding in long, sharp points as he tears into the necks of the two uniformed men. The ripping of sinuous throats into long pink ribbons left to dangle from thick holes. He moves so quickly that, as Jared turns his feral attention on Clive, the big man is still busy disentangling the syringe from my sister's hospital gown-clad body.

Jared's hands have sprouted into wicked-looking claws. He swipes, ripping a jagged line into Clive's chest before reaching in and pulling out the heart in one swift motion, then throwing it against the opposite wall with a thick *splat*. Clive's body keeps moving, the light in his eyes dying slowly before he crumples on top of the other two.

Jared roars, a sound so filled with primal rage that I cringe and step back, knocking loudly into the doorframe behind me. It's not the annoyed, grubby Jared that turns to glare at me. This is a demon. Even the shape of his face has changed: the chin elongated, his eyes gone a luminescent green, bright with blood lust, and four-inch claws drawn like daggers. *Panther?* my mind whispers. Sleek and beautiful and deadly. I cling to the wall, unable to move, certain that if I do he'll maim me.

"Jared," I whisper. His lips pull back with a snarl. I watch his features melt, the claws retracting an inch in the blink of an eye, the face reshaping itself into the striking features of the tousle-haired young man. "Jared," I croak again. We stare at each other across the space of the room, now liberally decorated with sprays of blood from the arterial wounds of the men. Thick red puddles ooze from beneath the bodies on the floor.

An alarm begins to shriek. I try to cover my ears, but it's too loud, the wailing of an air raid siren. The outer room door leading into the hallway slams shut and locks.

Jared turns his attention to Margot like there's nothing wrong. "Let's get her out of here. The others are on their way." The words come out slightly slurred, as though his tongue is too thick and no longer fits in his mouth. His eyes flash sinister as he rips at her restraints.

I try to collect my wits. Margot's clothes are piled neatly on a counter. I bring them over to her, slipping them on her unconscious form as quickly as I can with Jared's help, making sure to tuck the hospital gown against the seeping wounds on my sister's lower belly. I'm careful not to touch him, and I notice he's just as careful not to touch me. Every so often I see him shudder and draw in long breaths, as though he's taking in a bundle of scents. My sister is still unconscious when he scoops her up and starts heading for the door. It has sealed behind us. I'd forgotten it does that.

"We're locked in," I say unhelpfully. He doesn't even look at me, just stops at the three-inch thick steel reinforced door. His nose twitches, and he sneezes. He places Margot carefully on the floor beside the door, then motions for me to stay in the shadows with her. He has his ear to the door when the first bang comes, strong enough to knock Jared back and make him shake his head. Seconds later the outer door buckles and collapses.

In its place stands a monster. Jared springs for its face, ripping into it with freshly cut claws. It wasn't the prettiest face to begin with. The monster has got to be close to seven feet tall, draped in the baggy white uniform of the Protocols attendants. But that's where normalcy ends. The thing Jared attacks is a nightmare come to life: misshapen lips curled into a snarl, black piggy eyes set far back in a face covered by thickly ridged eyebrows. The arms are too long, forearms absurdly muscled. I watch the tendons in its neck stand out like ropes as it raises a ham-size fist and swats at Jared as though a six-foot panther man is no more bother than a fly.

Jared snarls as he rakes the thing's face, going for the eyes, and jumps away. The monster is strong, but even I can see how much slower he is than Storm's man. Jared is mid-leap at the monster's jugular when a slim figure appears from behind it and zaps Jared in the back with an electric gun. Jared lets out a high-pitched cat scream that makes my guts hurt before crumpling at the monster's feet.

I'm so shocked I don't realize I'm just standing there, dumb and staring, until the monster has grabbed hold of me with a hammy hand. "Don't struggle," the other man orders. He's skinny to the point of Plague-struck, his bones jutting into knots at the joints. The slim fit of the white Protocols suit makes his thinness even more pronounced.

"Who the hell are you?" I ask rudely, trying to put together what's wrong with his face. No eyebrows, no eyelashes to cover his red-rimmed eyes, the whites pink against pale blue irises. He has hair, but it's almost as pale as his skin. Albino, I reckon.

"Be quiet, Lucinda. My orders are to make sure you

and your sister are safe. But accidents can always happen." His voice is high pitched, with a strange lilt that reminds me of some of the foreign dignitaries who have dined with my parents.

"What do you think you're doing?" I back up, mentally screaming at Jared to wake up.

Behind me and tucked against the wall, Margot stirs and twitches, but it's not until the albino asks, "Where is your sister?" that I realize he hasn't spotted her yet.

"I was going to ask you the same question," I reply. It's a brazen lie, but I'd do anything for a few seconds to think. The albino steps over Jared like he's a suit of clothes. "Do you work for the Clinic?"

The albino's thin lips curl in an amused half-smile. "Something like that."

"May I inquire what your plans are for us?"

He laughs, sounding like a little girl. "Don't you just have such good manners," he drawls.

My attention is diverted by the monster, who holds up Jared's unconscious form and shakes him like a rag doll. Something protective rears up inside me. "Don't hurt him," I warn. Jared may be a stranger, a merc, but every cell in my body goes crazy when I think of him being hurt—protecting us, no less. I'll not leave him to be harmed. The albino's eyes turn sharp. "You want to rescue your friend here, do you? I'll tell you what. We'll make a deal. You get your sister and come with us without a fuss, and we'll consider letting your friend live."

No one is looking when Jared cracks open an eye with a bright green glow. "But I don't know where she is. We came in here looking for her," I whine.

"I think you do." The albino advances a step, something so incredibly off about him that I step back, realizing a second too late that it will expose Margot.

But in that second all hell breaks loose. The albino's back is turned when Jared sinks four-inch claws into the monster's chest. The big guy bellows and tries to shake off the attack as Jared leaps again. With a snarl and roar, Jared plunges his teeth into the monster's thick neck, the blood spraying across the whites of their uniforms and coating the albino's hair.

"Siggy," the albino barks. But it's too late. The monster crashes around in a blind, dull rage, knocking the albino off his feet as the blood pumps from his wound. They both land with a thud in a growing pool of red. I throw myself back. Still in the corner, Margot twitches and moans softly. I shake her, willing her to open her eyes, but they remain shut.

"Margot, please," I whisper, kissing her cheek and telling her everything is all right but that we've got to move. Nothing.

I turn my attention back to the spectacle before me. The monster's eyes are dull, lifeless, as he slumps over the albino. Jared straddles a beefy leg and brings his fist down on the albino's head again and again, until I hear a crack and the soft sighs coming from the albino cease.

Jared's head snaps up like he can feel me watching him. His arm halts mid-blow, and he pushes the albino's messy face down and leaps up, blood soaking his shirt so now the letters read, "*Girls -re f--*."

He doesn't so much as glance at me as he rips the rest of the reinforced door off its hinges and slings Margot up into his arms. She looks like a fragile doll as he hurries down the hall, like she's no weight at all. The minute we're out of the small room I'm no longer swamped with the iron-tinged scent of blood. I take a deeper breath, feeling slightly less nauseous.

Mohawk and Storm approach as we turn the corner.

"What the hell happened to you?" Mohawk flashes a quick grin. A hint of gray floats over her eyes as she takes a deep whiff of the three of us. "Never mind," she says darkly.

Beside her, air shimmers around Storm's uncannily still body. His fists clench as he tersely orders, "Get her into the van. Lucy, are you all right?"

I nod automatically, but I consider revising my answer. My legs are shaking badly. I sag against the nearest wall. Jared sighs and hands Margot to Storm before plucking me up into his arms. He glances down at me only briefly. It's not an expression I understand: annoyance and a dollop of confusion mixed with something territorial and just a bit smug, like I've been indelibly stamped as his property but he can't figure out how it happened. If it helps, I can't either.

We head back toward the loading bay doors. I don't say a word, even though he's got me pressed against his gory shirt, and neither does he. My arm curls around his neck instinctively. I want to close my eyes and disappear, but I'm too jacked up, my heart hammering away inside my chest, so I stare at the spot in his neck that pulses frantically and listen to the slow, steady beat of his heart. The deserted hallways echo with the tinny, generic sound of horns and strings as we walk.

I expect Jared to dump me outside the van and get as far away from me as he can. So I'm surprised when he opens the back door one-handed and settles me in the middle of the seat so gently I want to weep. He crawls in after me, his body hot and pulsing as he presses himself up along my side. A second later Storm buckles Margot in place beside me and hops into the driver's seat while Mohawk slides into the front passenger seat. Margot's head lolls back. I put an arm around her. The car jumps to life, and I start whispering in her ear, telling her she's safe, that we've got her. But despite the furnace of Jared's heat beside me, a coldness spreads inside my body. I am frozen to the core, and it starts in Margot.

"We've got to hurry," I say to no one in particular.

Storm glances at us through the rearview. "Fifteen seconds," he says enigmatically. As if on cue, Torch opens the back and rolls himself in before pulling the hatch down over him.

"Go." There's an urgent note to his voice. Storm steps on the gas, and we race down the long road that winds back into the heart of the city. Margot shivers fiercely. I hug her close to me and shiver myself. Jared stretches an arm around us both and with his other hand produces a blanket. He unfurls it one-handed and settles it over my sister, then me. I can't look at him as I murmur, "Thank you."

Jared says nothing. My body is such a confused mixture of heady awareness, shock, and terror that I keep my gaze, wide-eyed, locked on my sister. I will her to come back to me. *I need you, Margot,* I whisper into the space between us, the now silent and empty room of our bond.

7

It never occurs to me to ask where Storm is taking us. Still, I reckon I'm not surprised when his van pulls into the underground parking garage under the immense cobalt skyscraper in downtown Dominion. Storm takes my sister again, and we all climb into a private elevator. Mohawk opens a small black keypad, punches some numbers into the identi-pad, then puts her thumb to the scanner. The doors close silently. As we zoom toward the 60th floor, I try to stop my knees from knocking together. Jared holds my upper arm like he's certain I'm going to fall down. I don't pull away.

My throat is raw as I croak, "Do you think they'll come after us?"

Storm cocks an eyebrow at Torch. For the first time I notice the small box he carries in his hands, like a miniature banker's box. He sends me a lopsided grin and shrugs.

"Recording devices and security are kind of my thing," he tells me with sheepish pride, picking up what looks like a mini disc.

"For crying out loud, Malcolm, don't burn it." Mohawk slaps his hand so the disc falls back into the box. "We need that." His fingers smoke and leave tarry blue afterburns on the disc.

"It's *Torch*." He glares at Mohawk, who flips him a dimpled smile.

"Whatever, Einstein."

As the elevator beeps I catch her glancing at me, undisguised curiosity stamped on her exotic features. Her sharp eyes linger on Jared's firm grip on my arm, his body closer than it needs to be. Jared ignores her. I decide to do the same, repressing the blush creeping its way onto my face.

We're alive. Right this minute, that's all I can handle.

It seems like days later, rather than hours, that Margot is finally settled and Storm calls me into his office. I haven't slept, and at the moment I wonder if I ever will again. Every few seconds terrible scenes flash behind my eyes, each more incredible than the last. I sleepwalk over to the couch and stumble to a sitting position to stare at walls a color our mother would describe as "buff." My face is numb, covered in grit. I rub at it, hoping to stir myself enough to get what I need. Answers.

"It will get easier," a gentle voice tells me. "You need some sleep." Cracking open my eyes I see a pair of ultra-expensive brown leather men's dress shoes poking out from under black tailored slacks. I crane my head up to see Storm peering down at me. Around his head floats a ball of energy, crackling lines of lightning that dart out from his brain. I blink. The faint luminescent glow fades. Storm frowns and sits across from me.

"You must have a lot of questions," he says.

"Do you know where my parents are? Have you called them?"

I don't like the way he studies me. "Do you want me to?"

"I don't think… Margot…" I bite my lip.

He nods like he understands. Maybe he does. "They're in Europe. An emergency business trip," he lies smoothly.

We both know the real story goes so much deeper. "This is the first time they've both gone away without telling us," I reply like a true politician's daughter. And hanging in the air between us is the unspoken question of a business partner, someone from Russia that we're supposed to be impressing. *Look how impressive we're being now*, I think with bitterness. If word of this gets out, it could put whatever plan our father is cooking up in jeopardy. *And then he will kill us.*

I start a silent staring contest with Storm, but I'll lose every time. The merciless winter of his eyes is terrifying. But then a small smile breaks across his handsome face. "You're a very smart young woman, Lucy. I think if your parents knew how brave you've been, how you protected your sister, they would be very proud."

My fingers clench into bloodless balls in my lap. "I think we both know better, Mr. Storm," I tell him frankly. I obey the rules. That's what I do. And in this case I messed up. "And I didn't exactly save my sister, did I?"

"Nolan. Call me Nolan," he says. He places one big hand over my hands. His flesh crackles with a kind of heat I don't understand. "Or Storm if you prefer. She's alive," he tells me in a grim voice. "She'll survive."

But I wonder, how much did they steal from her? And fresh on the heels of that tumbles another, more troubling thought: *what is the price of living?*

O nce we arrived at Storm's we were taken straight to a guest room, where they parked Margot in a queen bed. It looked huge in the little room with its floor-to-ceiling windows across one wall. The walls were cheerful pale yellow and covered in bright paintings with squiggly lines in primary red and blue and yellow. The windows looked up to sky, which I reckoned in daylight transforms the light in the room into fine opals.

The woman with the severe bun slipped in the door. This time her hair was a loose curtain of sable, and she wore a simpler dress, black and tailored down to her knees, a strand of freshwater pearls twisted around her neck. Her expression was strained as she pulled in a cart with water to wash my sister.

"A doctor will be here in a few minutes," she'd said in the kind of voice you save for funerals. I went back to stroking Margot's hair from her face. She'd said nothing, my sister, but then, she hadn't had to. Her eyes were open but sunken, red rimmed. The woman had begun sponging off the makeshift bandages on Margot's belly when I felt an electric zap course through my nerves.

"No." I grabbed for the woman's hand. The last thing I needed was Margot to get hysterical. "Margot has asked me to do it. If you don't mind."

She nodded and stepped back toward the door. I could see pity in her eyes, so bright and clear it hurt. "I'll be right outside if you need me. I'll knock when the doctor gets here."

For the next little while I forgot everything but the feel of Margot inside my skin as I washed her, sang to her. Her raw nerves lay down and got quiet for a while, and we both started to relax. She wasn't that hurt physically, but I'd known that. The hurt was tucked away, inside her body, where you couldn't see it.

A little while later a sharp rap came and a small woman with wiry curls and bright blue eyes walked in. She carried herself like a practical woman, dressed in a turtleneck and slacks, a stethoscope around her neck and a large bag in her hands. Margot's eyes flickered over to the woman before she zoned out again.

At least it was a woman. I think we were both thankful for that.

She introduced herself as she washed her hands. "I'm Dr. Dorian Raines," she said in a clipped, efficient voice. She leaned over Margot and touched her hand. "I'm going to examine you now. I'll be as gentle as I can be." Margot blinked and gave the doctor a slight nod. We both jerked when the hands pressed down on her belly, the pain stinging and intense. It wasn't the pain so much—the doctor was gentle—but anything was too much now. The doctor was quick, though, and within seconds she was removing her gloves and washing her hands.

"You're going to be sore for a few days, but there's very little real damage. I'll bandage these," she pointed to the incisions in Margot's skin, "but you don't need stitches. Whoever did this to you knew what they were doing. They didn't necessarily want to wound you."

Margot's eyes glazed over. The doctor came back with some pills and a glass of water.

"Margot, I need you to listen to me for a moment. The people who did this—from the description Jared gave me—I think they were harvesting your eggs. There's no way to tell unless I give you a thorough examination, and I'm not sure you're up for that right now. Do you understand what I'm talking about? Did they say anything to you?" I felt my sister fight her terror as she took in the doctor's words.

"It's what they were after," Margot said in a cracked voice. "They know when we're ovulating. It's part of Protocols." The pieces began to fall into place as we sat in stunned silence. It hadn't been an accident. All of it had been engineered. My sister licked her lips before confirming my worst suspicions. "We'd just been in the week before."

Horror swamped me. "Why?"

Her voice rose to a hysterical pitch. "They kept taking Protocols, Lucy. Over and over. He knows exactly when we're ovulating, when we're not. He always knows."

The room went dim. I grabbed her hands and told her she was safe now, safe. Storm and his people had come for her and me. We were safe. And as I watched my sister gulp down her pills and sob herself to sleep, I wondered if it was true.

"His name was Clive," I tell Storm an hour later. I study the man before me. His cheeks are raised with dark nubs of stubble. Shadows brush beneath his eyes, but despite that he looks remarkably well rested. Calm. "Our usual Protocols guy. Always giving us these flowers. I reckon I knew Margot had a thing for him but…" I leave off and shrug helplessly. Maybe later I'll be able to trace back and find the thread that might have stopped this, but tonight I'm too tired.

"The easiest theory would then be that he saw what was happening to you and your sister with the Protocols and decided to see what was in it for him. Black market test tube babies."

"Hmm." I shrug and grace our rescuer with a tight smile. "He was the only one who was the same. They kept switching in all these stupid nurses, but he was always there."

The air in the room drops a couple of degrees as Storm considers me. "He could have stolen eggs from anyone, but he chose Margot. He went to elaborate lengths to make her trust him. So what was he really after?"

"I don't know," I tell him honestly. "But doesn't it strike you…?" I start, then let the thought die. I'd just as soon not say it out loud in case it might be true.

Storm knows anyway.

"It's always possible your parents had been receiving threats or interest, but I don't think so. It could have been anyone from the Upper Circle, or Clive himself. Or the other two."

I let out a breath I didn't know I was holding. At least there's that. Still, the timing is too coincidental. All these Protocols just weeks before our Reveal. *And Father's mysterious business deal,* my mind chirps at me. *Don't forget that.*

"What about the other two? I'd not forget if I'd seen them before. Do you know them? Are they True Borns, too?"

The electric cloud around Storm's body increases. I sit

back as his eyes darken. His curt reply says it all. "No."

"So they're Splicers or something?" But when he doesn't answer, I ask, "So what are they, then, some sort of test-tubers?" He sits there, stony and silent. And all at once I understand what he's saying—what he's *not* saying—in one horrifying gulp. *Test-tubers.* The men at the Clinic somehow were *made* to be different, engineered to be monsters. And as my head tries to wrap around that one, I come to the most important thought: *what do they want with us?*

We've never heard of anyone being put through as many Protocols as they've run us through. This isn't just about harvesting some poor Splicer girl's eggs. They've stolen from the daughter of one of the most powerful men in all of Dominion—who conveniently happens to be out of the country. What happened to Margot can't be random.

This was about her, about us. And we can't afford to wait for our parents to come home to take care of things.

"We're not going to have our happy eighteenth Reveal party, are we?"

The words come out sounding as dull and flat as I feel. I walk over to the window and trail a finger across a rain-soaked window. The smeared drop reminds me of birds in flight. Something I'd love to be right now. Free, able to soar away from all these heavy burdens. "They say it changes everything. When they finally tell you."

Storm doesn't answer. He just silently unfolds his long body from the couch and walks me to my room. If I glance at him from the corner of my eyes, I can still see the swirling mass of energy rising like sharp branches from his head. If I didn't know any better, I'd swear it looks like antlers.

8

I don't know what time it is when I wake, shivering and confused. I'd been in my sister's skin, living through her memories: rounds of testing, the long, snake-like syringe invading me, pulling from my body sticky, microscopic lumps. Then I was watching in dull-eyed horror from the bed as Jared ripped the room apart, his face a feral mask. From Margot's perspective, he is a beautiful angel of death. All she can think is how peaceful it will be once he finally turns and rips into her.

That isn't even the part that has me crying.

The dream transports me. I am in Margot's skin. Her hands rest on her bedroom window as she watches a riot mushroom outside our gate. Bodies smash into the fence. Limbs sever from torsos in the panic and press of the crowd. *This is it,* a voice says. Through Margot's eyes I stare at three figures standing just inside the gate, like they're holding back the crush of humanity. It's me, flanked on one side by Jared and on the other by Nolan Storm, a set of antlers rising from his head like a massive crown. Suddenly I'm bodiless, a massive tidal wave ripping through the city street, a tsunami that will swallow everything and everyone in its path.

Wetness tracks down my cheeks. My eyes tiptoe through the darkness until they bump into a strangely familiar sight.

"What are you doing here?" I don't mean to sound so scared as I bolt upright.

Then again, Jared sits not more than three feet away from me, in the armchair near the small glowing fireplace. In my room. Alone.

Arms crossed, he cocks his head and stares like he's heard an insect whine. "Boss was worried about you," he finally says. His eyes are bright green pennies in the dark, pupil all but disappeared.

"He sent you to watch me sleep?" I say it with as much contempt as I can muster. Jared doesn't even bother to reply. He continues to stare at me.

"You were having a nightmare," he tells me, as if I didn't know.

I sigh and curl up my knees. "I've been having them all night." He nods as though he understands. Since he doesn't seem to be going anywhere, I lean over and switch on the lamp to make conversation. "What time is it?"

"A little after one, I think."

"When are we going home?"

"Soon." Jared clasps his hands between his legs, clearly warming to this topic. "Couple days, I guess. Boss wants to make sure Margot is okay."

I somehow resist the urge to tell him Margot will never be okay again, and neither will I. "Will our parents be back by then?"

"Not sure." Jared scratches his chin. "If they aren't, I think the plan is to be a little less remote than we signed up for."

Whatever that means. I take him in then, really look at him. He's changed his clothes but that's about it. The blood-soaked shirt and pants have been replaced by a pair of dark trousers. He's in a powder blue, long-sleeve shirt. I'm shocked it doesn't have a cartoon scrawled across the front. His blond locks are tousled. But more than the blond, ashy stubble on his cheeks and the deep rings of exhaustion around his mouth and eyes, I notice the strange expression. Like a lost little boy.

He gets a good gander at me, too. I must look silly in the oversize white shirt Storm lent me, my hair a nest of dark curls.

Jared clenches the arms of the chair as though he's physically holding himself back. "You are such an unbelievable pain in the ass, Princess. You know that?"

"What'd I do now?"

"Are you really that naive?"

I blink in confusion, wondering what has set him off this time. "What?"

"You haven't so much as asked about it. You haven't said a word."

Oh. The penny drops. I draw my legs up tighter against my chest. Jared jumps out of his chair and leans over me menacingly. "What, you've been raised to be *so polite*," he mocks, "you're just going to sit there and pretend you didn't see it?"

I peer up into his livid, beautiful face. *He's worried*, I suddenly realize. Not angry—terrified. I marvel at the thought. I'd never have imagined that a man who rips people apart with his bare hands would worry much about what others thought, let alone someone he seems to dislike as much as me.

"Wasn't much to say about it, I reckon." Jared peers back at me as though I'm an alien species. Which, if I follow Storm's logic, I just might be. So who am I to sling arrows? I sigh. "You saved Margot. You saved me. As far as I'm concerned, you could be a ten-foot fire-breathing lizard and I wouldn't give a damn."

Jared steps back with a deep intake of breath, looking halfway between trapped and wild. He turns and paces for a moment. Then he sits back down in the chair across from me, hands clenched in his lap. He glances down at his feet, which I see now are bare. His toes are long and white, like the rest of his massive feet. Those bare toes make him seem absurdly vulnerable.

"I've never changed in front of someone before," he confesses. "I mean, a Laster. I mean—someone I was going to let keep breathing."

"Thanks," I toss back. I don't think he hears the sarcasm.

"It confuses me. Part of me thinks I ought to kill you," he tells me slowly. Catching the look in my eye he stumbles on irritably. "Now, cut it out. Storm would snap my neck like a twig if I laid a hand on you."

I gulp past a short burst of panic, unsettled that that seems to be his only reason. "Can you control it?"

"Not always. I'm safe here with my own kind—which you most definitely are not."

But the way he says it, I'm suddenly not sure we're talking about his ability to become cat man.

I flash back to the monster and the albino. "Are all True Borns like you?"

Jared shakes his head. "If you mean do we all have the ability to turn into a jungle cat on two legs, then no."

Can his whole body turn? Curiosity itches at me. But I know how impolite it would be to ask. And besides, he'll just shut down. So instead I ask, "I *mean*, are they all shifters?"

The corners of his mouth turn down but his eyes soften. "I haven't met 'them all,'" he mocks with air quotes, "but of those I have met, all I've got to say is there are no rules. You saw Penny tonight. She doesn't turn into a zebra or whatever the hell she shares her gen-code with. But you can be damned sure not all her genes are certifiably human."

"Oh." I look at my hands. My cheeks flame. With a start I realize I don't want Jared to talk about Mohawk.

"And those two guys at the Clinic who were trying to grab you two. Just one whiff of those guys was enough to tell. Splicers smell all kinds of wrong, but those guys *reeked*." There's a pause before he continues. "And then there's you." I look up to catch him frowning furiously at me. He leans back, like it can help him get me in perspective.

"What about me?"

Frown deepening, Jared bounces a hand off the chair arm. "You know you're different, Princess. And it's not just because you're some fancy, spoiled rich girl. Hell, you don't smell like anyone else. Money can't buy that smell." I assume he wasn't talking about my expensive perfume, which money did in fact buy. I watch his chest rise with another inhale, like scenting me is an instinct. He seems to mean it as a compliment, but I am irritated. Of all of the aspects of myself that I have been trained to control, my scent is not one of them.

"I don't know what you're talking about. And I'm not spoiled."

"Me either. Lie down and go back to sleep, Princess," he grouches, though suddenly I'm not sure which statement he's agreeing with.

I do as he says, if only to get away from those eyes of his, eyes that want to solve me and put me into a neat little box. I turn off the lamp and squeeze my eyes shut, but if anything, my head whirls even more. He hasn't said the words, but they hang between us in invisible parentheses: *True Born*.

My mind chases down the same old arguments. Wouldn't we know? Wouldn't there have been some clue before now… like one of us turning into a tiger or something? Wouldn't we feel it, deep down in our bones?

But then, there's always been something about us.

An image floats behind my eyes. Margot lies in the darkness across the narrow bed, eyes unseeing. Alone. The shot the doctor gave her must be wearing off because the pain is starting to return, pulling through my abdomen in long, aching threads. But it's the pain in her heart that undoes me. I sit up again, blinking back the tears.

Jared lets out an exasperated, "Lucy, go to sleep. You're going to need it."

"I can't," I confess. "Every time I close my eyes…"

His exasperated sigh hisses through the dim room. As he makes his way over to the bed, his hair picks up on the little light there is, turning him into a dim angel. He settles his weight on the edge of the groaning bed and awkwardly rubs my back.

"There. Better?"

I snort dismissively but lie down. His hands slow, the awkwardness evaporating as something else takes its place. Everywhere his hands touch my skin feels like it lights up parts of my body I didn't know were connected.

Like a languid cat, Jared props his back against the

wall and pillows my head on his lap. "There, that's more comfortable," he says as with one hand he trails a finger over the sensitive skin on my neck. I shiver as the sensation burns through me. Ever so light, his fingers wind a trail down my back. I arch against his fingers, lost in the exquisite sensations.

"You're like a little kitty cat," Jared purrs. "All cuteness and claws." His breath stirs the little hairs on the back of my neck. I shiver again, rocking back, and meet the hot brand of his flesh. I'm instantly electrified, even more so as I hear his sharp inhale. I move away as fast as fire, though I can still feel the burning imprint of his flesh against my head.

"Better than a pain in the ass, I reckon," I murmur.

I expect him to get mad, but he barks a soft laugh, stirring my hair. "Very true."

"Jared," I croak.

"What?"

"Do you think we could be *different*, different? Like, maybe, True Born different?"

For a moment he pauses his slow, languid touches. I feel like I've lost something precious and wiggle my back a bit.

"All right, all right, pussy cat." He rumbles a laugh and continues the slow drag of his fingers. I can feel him breathing in the scent of my hair. "My mom used to do this when I was a little kid," he murmurs. Then, "I don't know how to classify you," he admits.

My heart knocks loudly against my ribs. He seems to be talking about more than my genetic code.

"Do you think—do you think that's…why?"

I don't need to spell it out. What happened to Margot has changed everything, possibly forever. The only question that really remains—other than the obvious "why" and "who"—is *by how much*? For a moment Jared splays his hand flat against the skin of my back, almost as though he's measuring his flesh against mine. I tilt my head up, catching the bright green of his eyes. Jared's lips purse slightly.

"Maybe. Probably," he admits.

A ribbon of relief flows through me. I didn't realize how much I needed to know he'd be honest with me.

Jared's fingers inch up and tangle with my curls, pulling them away from my face in long, unhurried strokes. Slowly I relax, my body growing heavy. "You have beautiful hair."

I wonder if he realizes he's said it out loud. I cock open one eye to glare at him. "This doesn't change anything," I tell him. My voice thickens with sleep as the darkness comes to claim me. "I still don't like you." I glimpse the wink of his teeth, the deep dimple beside his very generous mouth. Something tightens in my chest.

"That's as it should be, Princess," he tells me with conviction.

And I slide off into the dark, safe at last.

9

I wake tangled in Jared's legs, heavy warm logs under my head. His arm curls around me, twists in my shirt. I peek up at him. His perfect lips pull up in sleep, making him look like a little boy with a secret. One blond lock hangs down and cradles one eye. As I stare at him, he stirs and stretches, cat-like, before cocking one eye open.

"You make a terrible guard," I grumble, frozen to the spot.

Jared just looks at me, curiously peaceful. "You say that now, but you actually slept through the night."

"And so did you," I accuse.

"I don't sleep. Not on duty." He rubs his eyes.

I snort and roll over, sitting up. "What am I, if not a duty?" He doesn't answer, but lets his hands fall onto his legs as we contemplate each other. This morning they are a miraculous blue. Up close they aren't blue exactly but ocean blue shot with green and gold, and I wonder how they look indigo sometimes. My fingers reach up as if to stroke his face. "Your eyes change," I murmur, unsure I've said it out loud until he answers.

"A lot of me changes," he says after a long beat but doesn't spin snark into his words. We're still close, close enough for me to study a faint freckle near his left eye. He's so warm and alive as I breathe him in, out. For a moment I close my eyes, dizzy with sensations.

A ghost of regret maybe, maybe even a hint of panic, passes over his handsome features. He swallows and suddenly I'm nervous as a cat as he leans back and slowly, like he expects me to jump him, pulls himself off the bed. He looks around the dim room like he's never seen it before and announces, "Let's get breakfast."

It's barely seven when I slip into my sister's room. The room is bright, the drapes wrenched open at awkward angles like someone's clawed at them. Margot's curled up in one corner, snail-like. Her sleepy blood surges through my veins.

"Margot," I whisper. I take her hand. It's clammy and hot with sleep. For a brief moment I panic over fever, but then remember the doctor telling us that Margot's system might react to some of the shots she was given.

I run my fingers through her silky hair, feel it catch between my fingers. The troubled lines of her face, what little I can see, at any rate, smooth out at my touch. After a few minutes I kiss her cheek, cold under my lips like china, and creep out the door.

Jared is leaning against the wall, waiting for me, as I come out of the room.

The hallway is wide and well lit, but closed in with Jared, it feels small. He hides a small smile and claps a hand on my shoulder and points down another hallway. "Kitchen is that way, Princess."

"You're taking this stalking thing to whole new heights," I tell him.

"How is she?"

I shrug. "She's asleep."

"Trust me, that's a good thing."

"And what about when she wakes up?"

His eyes glitter. "Then you get on with the rest."

We arrive in the spacious dining room just as the dark-haired woman comes in carrying a tray of French toast. She barely glances at me, so I am able to catch the fine web of lines that pulls across her eyes as she smiles at Storm, sitting at the head of the table. I peg her at our mother's age, maybe a bit older. Sometimes it's hard to tell with the Lasters. Then again, I think, recalling where I am, she may not be a Laster.

"Thank you, Alma," Storm says, setting down his NewsFeed to look me over. He seems larger today, if that's possible. His black turtleneck sets off the wintry steel of his eyes. The crackling, interlocked energy framing his head is becoming flesh and bone. "Good morning, Lucy. I hope you slept well."

The wooden table gleams, nearly as big as ours back home. Jared comes around behind me as I sit down. I color. "Eventually."

"Good. We have a few things to discuss after breakfast."

I reckon my father might be one of them, Margot too. Jared graces Alma with an all-but blinding smile. She *tutts* and fusses over him before coming around to me.

"Come on, eat up," she says warmly. "You'll need your strength."

I eye a heaped plate of French toast, another beside it stacked with bacon and sausage. I wasn't hungry before, but suddenly I'm ravenous.

I'm halfway through my plate when my hunger leaks away. I feel the familiar pull, now laced with pain and something so dark I don't have a name for it. Wild, maybe. My fork clatters to the plate, and I stare into space for a moment, adjusting to Margot's weight inside me.

Storm scans my face. "Lucy."

"Margot's up." The words are filled with the false optimism of a Protocols nurse. I don't know if they believe me or care. I only care that they don't see it when, scrambling to get to my sister, disoriented by her chaotic state, I stumble against the wall. I should know better by now.

A hand clamps over my arm and pulls me upright. "How did you manage to survive so long without me, Princess?" a familiar voice grouches.

There must be something in my face. Jared stops cold, swears under his breath. His fingers prod me softly until I'm leaning against the wall. "Dammit, Lucy." His eyes bore into mine, taking on that faint green sheen I now realize means he's getting upset. I bat at the arms he's clamped over my shoulders, but I'm distracted by the closeness of his mouth, the look of total concentration stamped over his handsome features.

He doesn't say anything more. Not what I expect. "What?"

"You can't keep doing this to yourself."

"Do what?"

"This. You're letting her torture you."

"Don't say that," I yell, genuinely shocked. "Don't you ever say that." Jared doesn't understand. Even if Margot weren't my twin, my other half, it's my responsibility to make sure she's okay.

Tears burn behind my eyes, leak onto my face. And maybe I'm as surprised as Jared when he pulls my head onto his shoulder and just holds me. He pulls me tight against his body until the tight knot in my throat starts to dissolve and all I'm left with is the hard lines of his muscles beneath my hands. The smell of him. The tingling heat that seems to fill my body whenever he's around.

His hands trace down through my hair, capturing my full attention. Time slows to a crawl. Margot's tug inside me, I realize blankly, has subsided to a small ball of ache, something I can manage. My hands run down his back. I hear a small hiss in my ear. I pull back an inch and instantly regret it. Some part of me feels untethered without his heat pressing into me.

"Why are you doing this?" I croak. He tilts his head in confusion, and I wonder if it's because I've left my hands on his chest.

"Doing what?"

"Being nice to me."

His hands frame my face. He studies my hair, my earlobes, my lips like he's reading something fascinating before answering. "I like pains in the ass," he says with a hint of a smile. "They remind me of me."

I grab his wrist. "I mean it. Why are you all being so nice? Saving us?"

When Jared sighs and steps back, eyes shuttered, I shiver. "That's something you need to talk to Storm about."

My stomach drops. Of course, I remind myself cynically, even the most basic kindnesses being extended to the Fox sisters must have a price tag. I tear myself from Jared's embrace and straighten the fabric of my blouse and skirt.

"Right. Thank you. For a moment there I had almost forgotten. All we are to you is a job."

Jared's eyes green as they narrow and his back turns ramrod straight. "Forget I said anything, all right? Go ahead, let your sister eat you alive. I must have lost my mind thinking that you might be different from all the other self-entitled, grabby Uppers, but seems I was wrong. You're worse."

As he spits the words out he inches closer and closer, and I keep moving back until I'm splayed flat against the wall and his face, his angry, beautiful face is just a hair's breadth from mine. I suck in a deep breath as Jared blinks and shudders. I bite my lip so as not to cry and push hard at his chest. He moves easily enough now, and I stumble down the hall to Margot's room—but now I stumble for another reason. I feel his eyes on me as I retreat, the heat of his simmering anger.

Just another bodyguard, my head tells me. A mean one, at that. The sharp ache in my chest says differently.

I spend the day fussing over my sister, avoiding the rankling in my heart. It has never bothered me before, what other people have thought of us, the Fox family. Me. But Jared's words haunt me. And each time they circle round, I feel them sinking in and deepening like a bruise.

By nightfall Margot is feeling well enough to sit up in bed and chat. Doc Raines visits her again and says she'll do. Once the doctor leaves, Margot all but drags me out of the room. "Come on, Lucy," she says, "I want to catch up with some kids from school and go to sleep."

I go, though unwillingly. Half of me is impressed. I can feel what my sister feels, but I still can't understand what it's like to be her: able to slip off whatever responsibility or duty or danger crosses her path as easily as changing a dress.

I can't rid myself of the feeling that if I leave Margot for even a second she'll disappear. And somehow it will be my fault. But as I close the door behind me and thread my way through the elaborate hallways of Storm's tower in the direction of his office, I can already hear her giggling at some silly thing Deirdre Phalon is saying.

It will be up to me to fix things. *As usual*, I think with a sigh.

"Why are they like that?" I point.

Storm stands framed by floor-to-ceiling windows and crowned with a thorny, mature set of antlers that twinkle darkly in the glass. One ankle slightly crosses the other, like an elegant buck. He focuses on something below, lost in thought. Sad, too, as though he'd be alone even surrounded by people.

Storm cracks the tiniest of smiles as he beckons me over. "It would be pretty difficult to fit through the door if they were more substantial, don't you think?"

I laugh and come over to where Storm is standing. He smells different than Jared, more like spice and cloves and something dark. "Look out there," he says. I follow his outstretched finger. Red drips from on the top of a building, far below. But even from here the letters are huge. *EVOLVE OR DYE.*

"They can't spell," I observe.

"True" — Storm nods — "but hardly the point."

"What is the point?"

Storm leads me to the couch. "Evolution, Lucy. Evolution is the point."

It's not the answer I want. I want to actually know what's happening, why the rabble are after us, why those test-tubers or whatever they were in the Clinic wanted to grab us. I want to know how and when we will be safe. I want to know when my parents will be home.

More than anything else: I want to know what we are.

Storm leans over his thighs. "Shane called your father," he confesses apologetically. "I wasn't able to prevent him. With both of you gone yesterday…"

"Oh. What did he — what did they say?"

"They'll be back as soon as they can. They have some business to wrap up first."

I whisper, "Of course," and try to shrug off a dose of disappointment. But what did I expect? I picture our mother fiddling with her pearls in a hotel room in Paris or Russia or wherever they are. Our father beating his gloves bloody against his palm. Cold, so cold. "Do they know…?" Storm shakes his head. "Are we going home then?"

He regards me carefully. "Do you want to go home, Lucy?"

We'd be in familiar surroundings. Shane and the others would be there. And it's what our parents would want. Above all, there's duty to the family to consider. But would Margot feel safe? I can't imagine so. Something in me digs in its heels and rebels at the thought of leaving Storm's sanctuary.

And there is the other reason for staying, that small voice whispers inside of me. Shoving back the memory of cozying up on Jared's lap, I remind myself that Storm knows things. He has resources at his fingertips—not a given, even in our exalted world—and while his job is to protect us, he tells us the truth.

A glimmer of a plan takes root inside me and begins to grow.

"Do you want to speak to Margot before making a decision?" Storm asks while the cogs and wheels in my head turn. I nod, grateful to have more time to mull it over.

But I know the first question Margot will ask. The same one I need answered. "Thank you. But first I need to…may I ask why you're doing this?"

He studies me for a long moment before answering. "I'm not sure now is the time or place to get into all the details, but suffice it to say, I have a vested interest in your well-being. Yours and your sister's."

"Why?"

He rubs wryly at the spot above his head where the antlers swirl and coalesce in a pale electric blue. "You see these? Did you know not everyone can? You're one of only a handful that I know of. I don't think your sister sees them. At least, I haven't caught her looking at me funny."

Another secret part of me that is not like my sister? Intrigued, I sink down on the couch.

"They're a gift from my father who, come to think of it, was a lot like your father." Storm winks. "A very strong man. A man who arranged destinies." Storm points to his crown. "These don't do much in this form, but they carry a certain significance, like a…family crest, I guess you could say. They signify that I'm one of those people who has…well, I guess you could call it an overwhelming compulsion to make things right for people. *My* people." An uncomfortable silence slips in between us. "You know who my people are, Lucy."

I feel like I'm standing on the edge of a cliff. Like I'm about to hurl myself into an abyss.

"True Born," I whisper.

He nods slowly. "True Borns are in hiding. All over this city and elsewhere. Did you know that Dominion is trying to pass a law to have all True Borns licensed?" My hands shake as I mouth the word "*no*." The mention of my father hangs between Storm and me like a blade. Who else could be behind such barbaric legislation? "We can help, you know. We can keep the city running as long as it can. And we can turn it into a new city once the Lasters are done." His eyes are like lightning as he speaks, incandescent and full of power. But it's what his words imply that raises a lump in my throat.

Once the Lasters are done. Extinct. I don't have time to fully comprehend this before Storm continues.

"Because the True Borns will still be here, Lucy. Do you understand? And the True Borns are *my* people, Lucy." And then: "*You're* my people."

And with those three little words my life is forever altered. Splicer, Laster.

True Born.

I wait for a crazed, overwhelming feeling to rock my bones, but it doesn't. I'm just quiet-quiet, as though I've known the whole time.

It seems the first step in my plan will be easier than I thought. "Will you let your doctor test us, then?" When Storm nods, I go more boldly. "And will you tell us the results, no matter what? We're not yet eighteen."

It's a question loaded with significance, and Storm knows

it, I muse, as he regards me thoughtfully, calmly, before nodding again, this time more slowly. To run the True Born Protocols and tell us their outcome would be to go against the Upper Circle's careful code of not making your results public until the Reveal. It goes against what our parents obviously wish for us.

Under the circumstances, though, it's the right thing to do. We can't afford to embarrass our parents. And I'm not so young I don't recognize that whatever answer lies hidden in our blood aligns neatly with whatever agenda Storm is keeping to himself. Which gets me thinking some more…

"What kind of True Born do you think we are, then? We're not like you. Or like *them*." I sweep my hand to the door. Storm's people are more like the True Borns we've come to know about: people whose genetic mutations are written on their skin.

But Storm is different again, I think, eyeing the wrack wreathing his head once more.

He smiles, genuinely amused. "No one is like me, Lucy. I guess that's why I'm so bossy," he teases. "Then again, no one is like you and your sister, either."

"What does that mean?"

Storm rubs a hand over the stubble on his cheeks. "I'm not entirely sure yet. But I sure as hell am going to find out."

10

The streets are cold and empty as Jared drives me home. It's an unexpectedly dry day, the sky a clear and unusual pale blue. The rabble, the preacher men: all are sleeping or lost in the early morning hours of Dominion. So cold it could snap your bones.

But it's the cold in the car that has me shivering, the cold that stretches between Jared and me.

"You're awfully quiet," Jared says.

I glance over. His jaw pulses as he drives through the deserted streets. I don't answer his unspoken question. It's too painful still, too raw. There are too many questions swirling around my supposedly True Born brain.

How can we be True Born? Is that really why the men at the Splicer Clinic were after Margot's eggs? *What does it mean if we are?*

True Borns aren't permitted in the Upper Circle. Is that why our parents have had us tested over and over again—a vain attempt to get some other result? But it should have been easy enough to know. The True Born chromosome set is unique, identifiable from birth. They would have known from the time we were babies.

No, True Born is too easy an answer. There must be something more to the puzzle of our blood, some missing vital piece that has been carefully swept into darkness.

I need to find out what those pieces are. And who wields them—preferably before our parents bring home their mysterious Russian stranger.

But I recognize I first have to get through today with the mercurial True Born beside me. Mulling over the empty streets I ask him, "Is it over? The unrest, I mean."

Jared shakes his head. I fight an urge to pull back the blond lock of his hair that flops over his right eye. He's changed into a pair of loose jeans, a dark blue sweater over top a white button-up shirt, its butterfly collar resting crooked against the warm skin of his neck. He's dressed up, I realize. I wonder if he's done so because of where we're headed.

"It's just early," he finally says. As though that explains everything.

"But there's been nothing," I argue. "No more bombings, no hostages." That's what Lasters do when they're desperate. There are always hostages—until there aren't, that is.

"Don't be so quick to jump to conclusions," Jared criticizes. His eyes jump left to right. With a queasy rush I realize he's nervous. "Notice how quiet it is? No preachers, no nothing." he says again. "Nothing means trouble."

I grip the door in alarm. "Should we turn back?"

Jared shakes his head and swears under his breath. "No. We keep going." He levels a look at me beneath his full eyebrows. "But we make it quick."

Fritz rides the gate. When Jared rolls down the windows Fritz comes down from the gate pegs to peek in at us. Fresh rust stains splatter the concrete around the black iron bars of the gate. I close my eyes.

Fritz's flattop nods in the window. He eyes me, all but ignoring Jared. "Shane said you'd be picking up some things. We were expecting you."

"What happened here?" Jared asks softly.

Fritz turns hard eyes on Jared. I think he's going to be rude, but then, like the drill sergeant I'm sure he once was, he barks, "Had sum late-night visitors. Had to make sure they knew they weren't welcome."

"Bodies?"

Fritz nods. "Took their own. 'Zem preachers haff got a lot to answer for in ze Kingdom of Heaven," he says in his clipped, efficient Austrian accent. He waves a hand. The gates open and we sail into the opulent, manicured grounds of my father's mansion.

Jared follows me up the staircase to the second floor. I turn back to him halfway up the long, curving flight. He immediately puts his hand up. "Forget it, Princess. I have my orders, and they don't include letting you slip out a window while I've got my back turned."

I shrug. It had never even occurred to me to escape Jared's custody. Storm's True Borns have my sister and the answers I seek. Still, if there was a way to keep him from our sanctuary, Margot's and mine, I would. He's too big, too *pushy*, to be allowed into our rooms without protest. I lead him to Margot's room first.

As always, it's pin neat, like a showroom. The frilly canopy over her bed falls down over the sides and drapes like a veil, a mirror to my own. It makes the room look mysterious, haunted even. I head toward the closet where Margot stows her luggage. Halfway there I become tangled in the view from the window.

For a moment I'm looking through this window from the outside. This is the window I see again and again in my dreams, Margot standing right where I am, and down below, my own body sandwiched between Storm and Jared.

Jared nudges me with a finger. "You having some sort of tantrum, Princess?"

I nod, blinking away the rabble hordes who press their bodies like a mass of writhing insects against the gate. The dreams mean something more to me now that I know about us, about Margot and me—that we are not condemned, like the Lasters, to die of the Plague—*if* Storm is right, that is.

And if we are True Born? We'll be shunned, of course, excommunicated from our family and friends. I can imagine the look on Robbie Deakin's face now, his boyish good looks dripping with disgust.

"Do you think that doctor of yours would tell us if we were True Born?" I ask.

"Sure, why do you ask?"

"Because." I turn.

Jared is an eyelash away from me. My breath catches as I look down at our feet. So close we could be dancing. He tips my chin up with gentle fingers. "Hey, you okay?" Then, "You're not, are you?" Sighing, he pulls me over to the window seat, squashing himself in beside me among the embroidered cushions and decorative dolls. "What's wrong?"

He takes one of my hands in his huge paw and with the other strokes my hair, as he had the night before. I hate it. Kind and caring Jared undoes me, unravels me until I no longer know whether I'm coming or going. Then jerkface Jared comes along and rips it all away. I am tired of wondering which version of him I'm dealing with. I try to pry us apart, but my hand sticks there on his chest. "Don't make me cry," I tell him with a hiccup.

"Why?" The words are so gentle. "Lucy," his breath whispers against the sensitive skin of my cheek. I go into shock when his lips scrape against mine. They're softer than I could have imagined from such a hard man. His lips come down again. I feel my mouth open under his, hear a low, deep growl from Jared as the kiss deepens. I'm dizzy with him filling my mouth. The feel of him beneath my hands: strong, alive, pulsing with life. I think I moan as he crushes me to him, losing himself. My hands tangle in his hair, and I'm pulling him closer, closer, needing more of his warmth, his fire. And then he wrenches me away from him. He stares at me with vivid green wild-eyes. So it's not just when he's upset, I realize as my stomach lurches once more. We're both panting as though we've run a long distance. I put a hand to my lips, swollen now. So sensitive they feel like glass.

I've never been kissed before. Not my own lips, although I've been buoyed along by Margot's often enough. But this kiss, forever seared in my memory, bears no resemblance to the sensations I've experienced through Margot. Jared shakes a little as he gets his breathing under control.

"Sorry," he says.

He doesn't look sorry.

"Don't," I say through my fingers.

"Lucy." I bite down on my lower lip when he pulls my fingers away. Jared stares at it with a mixture of hunger and fascination.

"What?"

"I—" But I never find out what Jared is about to say. Within a heartbeat he's sprung off the window seat and has dropped into a battle crouch, growling at the intruder at the door. The intruder who's aiming a gun at Jared's head.

"Shane!" My cheeks glow red as I hold out my arms in front of Jared. Jared growls louder behind me. My feet leave the ground as he picks me up and shoves me behind him like I'm a package. Shane only grows antsier. "Cut it out," I yell, trying to climb over Jared's arms. "Shane, put down the gun."

Shane backs up and glares at Jared. "Get away from her," he barks.

"Shane!" I shunt around and plaster my back to Jared, who growls again, this time in annoyance. "Stop it. You know Father hired them to protect us."

"I can get rid of that problem right now," Shane says bravely.

I roll my eyes at both of them. "Go downstairs, Shane. Now!" I raise my voice when he doesn't get moving. "You can have your pissing contest another time."

I drag Jared into my room through the bathroom that joins Margot's bedroom to mine. "Cut it out," I seethe.

Jared turns his glare on me and spits with anger. "You call that security?"

"I call that the man who works for my father. Remember him?" I stomp my foot and disappear into my closet, searching for my own bag. When I pop out again, Jared is exactly where I left him. He seems stunned, like he's been caught in a busy hallway with no clothes on. "What?" I call out impatiently.

"This is your room," he tells me.

"Your powers of logic astound me," I drawl.

Jared ignores my barb. "Your smell is all over it. Your sister's, too, but less."

"And?" I tap my foot impatiently.

Jared's eyes glow. "It's like bathing in your scent."

I drop the suitcase on the bed. "I'm not sure you should be saying things like that," I say, feeling shaky. But because I'm curious, I ask, "Is that a good thing or a bad thing?"

He tugs me ever so closer to him. Like the last few minutes never happened. "It makes me feel…calm, I guess."

"Oh." I don't know what that means, nor how to keep up with his lightning fast mood changes. What I'd like is to lock myself in a room and think over that kiss for a few days, all by myself.

He doesn't release me. "You smell different than she does."

"Margot?"

"Yeah. I would have expected it to be more the same, since you're identical."

"And conjoined." I roll up my pants and remove my sock to show Jared my birthmark. "Here," I point out the tidy square of darkness that marks me as my sister's other half. Lock and key.

"Hmm," he says with real curiosity. Heat sizzles from his body. He's close-close again, so near I can feel his chest move with breath. Jared clears his throat and steps back an inch, maybe two. He throws a nervous glance at the window. "Got to get going. Don't trust these streets."

He might have stepped back a mile. It feels like the same distance. And what does it matter to me anyway? As soon as the mystery of our blood is cleared up, Margot and I will resume our life in the Upper Circle as though nothing has happened. With all of these Laster rebellions blazing, Father will need us more than ever.

Still, something burns in my chest as I toss back, "Yes, well. Father does expect you to keep me alive in his absence."

Jared tosses one of my antique dolls across the room. "That's right, Princess. We've got to make tracks before the Lasters try to carry away the spoiled rich girl for ransom," he says coldly.

I suck in a stinging breath, trying to clear my head. Turning my back, I concentrate on my packing, moving the carefully folded squares of cloth from my dresser to the bag with a kind of military precision my mother would approve of. Before I've even secured the straps Jared has grabbed the bag from my hands and started downstairs. And then I am alone for one tiny moment in my bedroom.

I run my fingers over my lips again. They don't feel like they're just mine anymore. I wonder if Margot has ever felt this way and doubt somehow that I could ask her. And the man who kissed me? I recall all the things I harbor against him: his pushy attitude, his bossy ways, and superior smirk.

He's just another merc, I tell myself sternly. Our father paid for that kiss.

11

The remote learning pod comes on with the rising tune of the school's anthem. The screen flashes the Grayguard Academy crest, which might as well be the brand of the Upper Circle, before the smiling face of the school's dean blinks on with a welcome message. The screen flashes to Ms. Hojin's delicate features and the pre-recorded "homeroom" pod plays.

They don't like resorting to the learning pods. They say we learn better in classrooms, in groups where we can socialize. "This is where you become the responsible adults and leaders of society you were born to be," they are fond of telling us during school assemblies.

Beside me, wrapped cozy in a blue blanket, Margot peeps at the screen and barks a dark laugh. She looks better today. Hazy sunlight showering in through the tall windows lights her up, filling her cheeks with color. We're on her bed, snug with one another, although the divide between us is still there, pressing on me like a knife.

"I wonder what Robbie Deakins will say," she whispers as Ms. Hojin's unsmiling face fades from the screen.

She's talking about the scars on her belly, of course, already scabbed over. In a few days there'll be nothing but two slim scars to mark what happened to her.

What would Robbie Deakins say? Nothing. If he even suspected what happened to Margot, he'd probably shove her down a flight of stairs and spit on her when she reached the bottom.

It's a thought that adds to the rising tide of anxiety in me. If this gets out before we know the *why*, before we can defend ourselves…

"Robbie Deakins is never going to know," I reply confidently. My arm snakes around my sister's shoulders, thinner than the last time I held her. "We're never going to tell anybody. And we'll get to the bottom of it so that if anyone ever does…"

"You don't think they'll know just from looking at me?"

I laugh. It's a false laugh, but I don't think Margot is in the headspace to tell. "There's no flashing red lights like with the security scans, Margot. So you'll be a bit antsy at first. It's not like you would even give one of the Grayguard boys the time of year anyway." This is a fact. Except for her strange fascination for Robbie Deakins, my sister has always preferred older boys. Until now, that is. Now she's as fragile as glass, ready to break at the slightest bump.

Her voice fades away. "But the Protocols…"

I hug her tighter. "Well, we're done with that, anyhow. We never have to go back or get tested at the Clinic again."

Watching Margot's eyes fill with desperate hope, I want to kick myself. It has never occurred to me, not once, that

Margot would believe she'd have to go back. Pretend like nothing happened. Go through it all again.

"You know Father will burn the place down because of what they did to you, Margot."

She shakes her head. "No, he won't."

"Of course he will."

"No, he won't," she insists. "Listen to me, Lu. Even if I were to tell Father—and I won't—" She eyes me meaningfully.

"Mar, you've got to tell them. What if they're selling your eggs on the black market? What if there's something bigger going on, something that could affect the whole family?"

Margot grabs the NewsFeed from my hands. "Listen to me for a moment. Do you really think Dominion can afford to have the Clinic shut down? With the number of people in the Upper needing a Splice, and more every day? You've heard them, haven't you? You heard what Patricia Anderson told Mother the other week. More than three quarters of the Circle is expected to fall sick in the next five years. That's… annihilation. There will be riots."

I tap a rhyme on my chin as I ponder my sister's words. Margot is right, of course. Those numbers are just the sort of thing I block out to keep my sanity intact. But Patricia Anderson, who works with the Ministry of Health & Well-being, turns white as a winding sheet whenever she trots out the figures she works with every day. Sure, she scares the   daylight out of everyone at Mother's socials. Sure, she's the kind of lush our mother calls "*embarrassing*." But no one ever accuses Patricia Anderson of making up the math.

"Doesn't matter. We're still not going back."

Margot scoffs. "Why, because we're turning eighteen? Look how many times they've made us walk through

Protocols already."

I shake my head. I don't want to tell her, but I can't let her go through her days and nights being so afraid—terrified of living as much as dying. "We don't need to go back, because I think they already know. I…I heard something," I end lamely as my sister's eyes widen and her fingernails dig into my hand.

"Tell me," she spits out, too desperate for news to be truly angry with me.

I whisper the words, still unsure how to splice us together with this new reality, making us into someone new. "Maybe we are True Born."

Margot's eyes narrow at me. "What have you heard?"

I nod. "Storm thinks we might be. I reckon that's why Father has put us through so many rounds. To be certain." This is the charitable reading of the situation. And we both know that our father is not charitable in the least.

"We couldn't be. They would have known since birth."

"What if we were wrong about that? Maybe we're a different kind, like Storm is, and they just don't have the tests to measure it. You have to admit they've been acting weird. We could be the reason why."

"That's more than a True Born problem. They could have just thrown us out. Are you sure Storm can be trusted?" Margot asks cynically. I nod again. "You're sure. But then why haven't we... *Oh.*"

"What. What?"

Tiny tremors run up and down Margot's body. I hug her tighter. "I reckon Father wouldn't want it to get out if we were True Born." She turns a wry smile on me and taps a cheek with a slender finger, the exact copy of my own. "But maybe that's why they—forget it."

"What, Mar?"

Margot shakes her head. "Just thinking, maybe they wanted to blackmail Father. The—the men at the Clinic, I mean. But they'd already collected scores of our genetic material, enough to blackmail Father to the moon and back."

"If it was blackmail, I don't know why they felt the need to steal from you like that," I tell her honestly, my mind reeling with the possibilities.

My sister is the most open member of the Fox family. And our family's money, power, and connections are very attractive lures for the desperate. It's why our father has taught us to always, always stick together. *Protect the family*, he's fond of telling us. *It's all you'll have if things go sour*. Always think of the family first, ourselves second. And a secret this vast? …I shudder to think on how this could be wielded against us.

Still, I'm not convinced that's the real reason why three Protocols attendants did such a despicable thing to my sister. Margot curls up in a ball and starts to rock. I give her a little hug. "What if they're not coming back?" she wails.

It's not the craziest idea in the world. We've read stories on the Feed. Parents abandoning their rare True Born sons and daughters. Or worse: slaughtering them. But those people aren't Lukas and Antonia Fox.

"Don't be silly, Margot. Of course they're coming back."

On the screen, Mr. Gardiner, our astrophysics teacher, begins to drone on about star formations, earth-type planets, frozen rivers and their crystalline structures. He takes a tangent to talk about current cryostasis nanotech and the next generation of space travelers. Doesn't matter, I think cynically. You can be a goner in space just as easily as on Earth. What matters is what's on the inside. Neither of us absorbs a word.

...

Two days later my sister and I take in our exploding city on the small, foldable screen NewsFeed. A man donning a long green face mask lobs a grenade at a floor-to-ceiling storefront window. It's a posh store popular with the Upper Circle, one of the few still capable of catering to the rich. The camera shakes as a roar of smoke and fire blow out the glass. The Feed jumps to another segment.

Jared had been right. The Lasters were just biding their time.

"That's Keller's," Margot says at the same time that I recognize the restaurant famous for entertaining Dominion's rich and powerful. Beneath scenes of mayhem and destruction, bright yellow words flicker across the screen. *Special Report: Casualties reported at bombing of the Capitol House.*

Most of our school friends have a parent who works at the Capitol House. Image after image plays of smoke-filled streets, rabble yelling and screaming while a handful of riot police crowd in and drag them away. The world has changed forever during a two-minute NewsFeed.

It's no longer insurrection. It's civil war.

The tattered, broken buildings are spray-painted red with the message we've seen everywhere. Beside the popular slogan, *Evolve or Die*, a pair of crude eyes, joined sloppily in the center and slightly cross-eyed, watch over the budding war.

"What do the eyes mean?" I ask. But it's not Margot who answers.

"The preachers have a secret club called the Watchers. Think themselves the judge and jury of justice," says a velvety voice. At the door stands a willowy redhead. Her laughing green eyes nag at me until I remember: she'd come to our father's house with Storm and Jared. Neither of us heard the woman enter the room.

"So we meet again." She leans back against the wall and gives us a smile I wouldn't call kind. Something about the way she moves reminds me of Jared, especially the Jared who rips out the throats of those who upset him. I shiver. Beside me, Margot's heart thumps with fear.

The woman rolls her eyes at us. "I'm not that scary," she says.

I straighten. "Yes, you are."

"Well, anyway, I'm not about to hurt you two. I'm Kira. One of your security detail?"

I'm surprised when Margot pipes up. "Why haven't we seen you around?"

"I've been busy keeping an eye on things around town." She flops down in the white leather armchair beside us and eyes the NewsFeed. "Dominion is going to the dogs."

"Tell us what's really going on?" Margot asks hopefully.

"I think you've seen it all right there." Kira indicates the scene of billowing smoke and chaos.

"But that's miles away," Margot argues. "What about here? What about near our house?"

Kira sighs. "Some fighting in the street. Mostly hand-to-hand. The bombs are some kinda new gimmick. Don't quite know what to say about those." Kira scrunches her nose. "They're bringing in the army tomorrow, or so I hear. But they're not announcing it on the Feeds. They don't want anyone to 'panic,'" she says sarcastically, putting the word in air quotes. "You're safe enough here, for now."

"Right. Because they couldn't possibly throw bombs high enough to do any damage here on the top floors."

"Wow, do they teach sarcasm in charm school these days? Maybe I should enroll."

"They don't accept persons of such advanced age," I reply tartly. Margot gives me one of her "*what the hell are you doing?*" glares, yet I can't seem to help myself. Kira sets me on edge.

Kira tips her head back and laughs, throaty and deep. "I like you, kid," she tells me. "You've got spunk, I'll give you that." In one gliding motion she pops out of the chair and saunters out, looking every inch the predator.

"What the hell was that?" Margot whispers.

"I don't know," I admit. Margot had always been the better politician. It's the reason she got on so well with the many dignitaries that have passed in and out of our lives.

"Well, you better get it under control," she snaps back. "We need these people."

It takes only a second for Margot's words to penetrate. She's right. I can't afford to lose my temper. These people stand between us and the rabble, between us and the Splicer Clinic and their superfreaks.

They're also the only True Borns we know.

Margot's face has drawn in, thick purple smudges marring troubled gray-green eyes. As her panicked heart slows, clarity washes over me: Margot has a lot more at stake in this relationship with the True Borns than I. Her fear spikes like a forest fire, heavy and acrid and overwhelming. So thick it could choke us both.

I take in the chaos brimming over on Dominion's streets. Whatever deluge is coming, the True Borns can help us survive. More than that, they can help us find the answers we seek.

12

"I need a favor."

I look up from my toast. Storm frowns at me from across the breakfast table. "Lucy? I need you to accompany me to a party some business associates are throwing tomorrow night."

It hadn't occurred to me that Storm was addressing me. But as I glance around the table—at Margot's wan, tired face; the throbbing vein in Jared's neck, accenting the deep *V* of his matching frown; Storm's intent, slightly annoyed gaze—I realize I am indeed the subject of this absurd request.

I glance slyly at Margot. She is the one who enjoys the glitter and whirl of parties, the flirting boys and gossiping girls. I'm the twin who'd rather be under my cozy canopy reading a good book. Margot flutters inside me. Her relief at not being asked is profound.

A note of suspicion creeps into my voice. "What kind of business associates?"

"The kind with deep pockets," Storm replies honestly.

"What if I know people? Won't it be strange for me to show up at a party as your guest?"

"I don't think so," Storm dodges. There's something he's not telling me.

"No bloody way," Jared tosses out. Storm shoots him a look that would melt glass. Bowing his head, Jared clenches his fists and holds himself under control. I marvel at the redness of his ears and the deep shock of pink slashing across his cheeks.

"What will be expected of me?" I fold my fingers together before me as though contemplating a business negotiation.

"What do people usually do at these things? Mingling. Small talk. The eating of some little canapé thingies that cost more than most people's houses."

"Do you expect me to dance?"

Storm nods as though this is a clever thing to ask. "Unlikely. I'll need to talk to some people there. But always a possibility, if you're interested." He grins wolfishly.

"Come on, Storm," Jared gripes.

Storm's eyes flash iron. He tosses his head, as though the antlers that exist in some shadowy world have grown heavy and barbed. A tick marches across his cheek and with the smallest move, just a slight lean back into his chair, Storm becomes a whole new level of scary. He gazes at Jared through half-hooded eyes. "Unless you're about to offer to help Lucy get ready for tonight, I suggest you be on your way."

Jared shoves away from the table with a growl and stalks out of the room. I follow him with my eyes. *What does Margot think of all this?* But Margot keeps her eyes on her plate. I feel the walls close in on me, her heavy, panicked heartbeat thudding in my ears like hammer blows.

"Margot," I say calmly. "Why don't we take a walk?" I hold out my hand and lead my sister out of the room. As we pass out of earshot she murmurs, quiet-quiet, in my ear, "You know he's using you, don't you?"

I nod, but inwardly I wonder which of our new True Born friends she's referring to.

It had only been a couple of days ago, but it might as well have been a year since Jared sat in my bedroom and kissed me. The secret sits inside me, heavy as a rock. I haven't told Margot, and now I'm glad I didn't. Jared can barely stand to look at me. He wants me to disappear. An unwelcome jolt goes through me at the thought that he might have been faking his kiss. *What does he want from me?* I run fingers absently over my lips, feel the phantom press of his lips there, hot against my own and then vanished. Like another twin suddenly lost.

An odd sense of déjà vu tugs at me. But this time it's Margot who sits on the bed and watches me ready myself for Storm's party. The dress is beautiful: a teal blue falling to mid-calf and cinched at the waist with a black belt. It's shiny and soft, made of silk, I think. But the real feature is the neckline, which plunges recklessly between my breasts. I feel naked, exposed: nothing like myself at all. Margot stares at me quizzically.

"Is it too much?"

She shakes her head. "No. I was just wondering if I seem half as sophisticated as you."

I smile at my other half. "Margot, every man who sees

you is in love with you." I expect her to chuckle. Instead, my sister throws me a funny look I can't quite decipher, almost as though she thinks I am the beautiful sister, the loved sister. The favored sister.

"What?" I say, moving over to the bed to give her a hug. "Whatever it is, I'm sorry," I manage to spit out just as we're interrupted by a decisive knock on the door. "Who is it?"

"It's Dorian Raines, Lucy. I need to speak with you and Margot."

"Dr. Raines," I say as I open the door and usher her in. "I'm just about to go out for the evening."

"Yes, I know. I wanted to catch you before you leave." She stands at the door and glances at Margot. "How are you, Margot?"

Margot nods. "Better, I think."

"What can we do for you?"

"Dorian, please." She frowns, her bright blue eyes sparking. "Those DNA panels I ran for you," she says, crossing the room to stand before us.

It hadn't taken much cajoling to get Margot to agree to a final round of Protocols. Knowledge is power, I'd reminded my sister. It had been less than twenty-four hours. Barely enough time to run a good Protocol.

"Did the tests fail?" My stomach sinks at the thought.

"No," the doctor says. "The Protocols were by the book. Everything was standard." Doc Raines moves toward Margot and crouches down, eyes blazing. "But here's what's not standard. I've never seen blood like yours. Not anywhere. And I've treated a lot of different people."

I put my hands on Margot's shoulder. "You mean True Borns," I say.

"Yes." She nods.

"Storm said he thought we might be True Born."

"Maybe," the doctor concedes with a shake of her curls, "but at this point I wouldn't say that definitively."

The world drops away from under my feet. "I don't understand," I say. But Margot is much quicker to catch on.

"Not Lasters. Sure not Splicers. But not True Born? *Is* there something else?"

Dr. Raines glows as though she's discovered a lost continent. "True Borns have an incredibly rich genetic diversity. But what each True Born seems to have in common are certain genetic markers, RNA codes that express a certain group of proteins. It's really the only way we have right now of predicting who will likely be immune to the Plague."

I squeeze shut my eyes. *Likely*. Not *certainly*. "And us?"

"You and Margot both have sample markers I've never seen before. It's not quite the same as the True Born Talismans, as we call that class of genetic anomalies. Your blood plasma doesn't carry the same switches that mark the presence of those antecedents—the special links to our evolution that the True Borns carry. This is something far beyond that. It's like"—she puts two fingers to her chin—"a group of people, like a family, all with brown hair and eyes. Then suddenly someone is born who is twice as tall, with bright blond hair and blue eyes."

"So you're saying we're like the tall blond cousins?" Margot jokes with a weak smile.

"No." Suddenly serious, Dr. Raines takes Margot's hand. "I'm saying it's like that moment when you discover an alien species, Margot. Your DNA, Lucy's …I can't even imagine what it points to, what it can do. It's a complete mystery—and utterly mind-boggling."

"The Fox sisters strike again," Margot manages to joke. She twists fistfuls of the bedspread beneath her. "What do we do with this little bombshell?"

"Well, that's why I'm here." Dr. Raines stands and walks over to me. "Typically I'd assume your DNA has the same genetic content as your sister's, since you're conjoined twins. You'd both have developed from the same embryo, which means you both derive from the same set of stem cells. But that's a typical scenario, and we're not dealing with typical any longer."

"I skipped rather a lot of genomics class." Margot feigns boredom. "You're going to have to spell it out for me, Doc."

I cross my arms and eye the doctor shrewdly. "She's saying she needs to run more tests." I trail off, lost for words. An image of the giant and the albino in their white Protocols flashes through my mind. We thought we were so close to knowing. But now…a bitter pill of disappointment and fear eats away at my stomach. I almost can't bear it.

"Thank you so much for coming to speak with us, Dr. Raines. We very much appreciate your candor."

"Lucy, wait," the doctor says as I usher her to the door.

"Lucy," Margot says behind me.

"I'm assuming you'll want more tests, then. We'll let you know."

The doctor shoves an expensive brown shoe in the door, wedging it open. "Lucy, I know this is what they did. Took a lot of Protocols while they kept you girls in the dark. Probably because they saw the same thing. I won't do that to you—I'm *not* doing that to you. I promise you, anything I find out I'll share with you both immediately. It's your body, it's your

DNA, your right to know. But listen to me" — she puts a hand over the door before I can shut it in her face — whatever is going on here, we can find it in your blood. And it's in your best interest to know. You need to be able to protect yourself."

Margot's bewilderment washes through me, and I fight pinpricks of shame. Doc Raines is right — that is exactly what I'd been thinking. But we need to think this through. We don't know if we can trust the doctor. Not yet.

"We'll get back to you soon," I say more gently before I slowly close the door and meet the accusing eyes of my twin.

The moment we hear Doc Raines's footsteps disappear down the hall, Margot yells, "What was that?"

I turn and busy myself at the mirror, putting the final touches to what I'm beginning to think of as my "costume." "That, my dear *big* sister," I mock, "was me being smart."

Margot crosses her arms and glares at me. "How do you reckon?"

I take a shaky breath and sit down beside her. Jared had said the Doc would tell us if we're True Born. It had never occurred to me that there was another choice. Protocols are all well and fine — but I'm no longer convinced they'll give us the answers we're looking for.

"Someone knows what we are, Mar. The Doc can run all the tests she wants. But we need to figure out what they already know."

Margot's eyes narrow. "What 'they' do you mean?"

"I mean" — I take a deep, shaky breath — "what did they see that they would run us through so many times? What do they know — our parents, the Clinic? And why in the Holy Plague fire did they steal from you, Margot? They know something, probably more than the Doc can find out from these Protocols. I'm going to find out what."

My sister gazes at me with luminous eyes, trusting eyes. Her hand slides over mine. I feel it there, beneath, above. Inside. "Okay." She sighs. "Okay, Lu. We'll play it your way for a little while. Just be careful."

Fire ignites the sky outside the window, bathing us in an eerie light.

"Looks like the rabble have come out to play." Margot sighs, biting her lip and staring out the window.

An explosion rocks the building, sending up an orange flare outside Storm's office windows. I jump, the heels of my elegant leather shoes scudding to a stop before Jared and Storm and Kira. They watch the war outside with the rapt fascination of children.

"How close was that one?" I ask. Two heads whip around to stare at me in surprise, followed by Storm, who clearly is not surprised. Jared's mouth drops open.

"Catching flies," I tell Jared pointedly, although secretly I'm pleased.

Storm fiddles with a gold cufflink as he appraises me. "You look very nice, Lucy."

I step into a small curtsy, perfected from years of use. "Thank you." I clutch my small black beaded purse closer and examine the trio. They are all three dressed up, even Jared, who wears a tux like it's a bathrobe. Beneath the fitted black shell of his jacket is a pristine white shirt with a thick white collar and a bow tie. He tugs at it impatiently, as though he'd like nothing better than to tear it off and wrestle it to the ground. Even his boyish locks have been tamed back into casual waves with some sort of product that leaves his hair glinting like shiny gold. But it's his eyes that I watch: there's a look to them that spells trouble.

Unlike Jared, Kira could pass for Upper Circle. Aside from the gun she leans down to strap to her thigh and the bloodthirsty expression on her perfectly made-up face, she's done up in a black sequined halter dress that falls, smooth as silk, across her collarbones. She turns slightly, revealing a smooth expanse of skin where the fabric drapes into a tiny "v" at the small of her back, her hair tumbling down her back in perfect auburn waves.

For some reason, though, Storm's fancy clothes make him look a cut above. I've always marveled at people who can turn themselves into dignitaries as easily as shrugging on a coat. Then again, I have the feeling that Nolan Storm is as rich as they come — and that he's redefining what important looks like in our exclusive little world.

"You all look very nice, as well," I murmur shyly. "Do I get a gun to round out my outfit, too?"

I can feel Jared freeze from across the room. Storm just laughs. "Self-defense lessons are definitely on the agenda. But unless you know how to fire a gun…?"

I toss my head. "That's what mercs are for," I quote an oft-used phrase in our exclusive little world.

"Another time, then. Shall we?" Storm offers me an arm and escorts me down the hall to the private elevator.

"No one answered my question," I argue. One of Storm's thick eyebrows tick up. "How close?"

"No more than a mile, I'd say. Likely they took out the North Dominion power station."

I gasp, genuinely shocked. Blowing up the power station means that half the city that still had power will be plunged into the dark and cold tonight. There's no saying whether it could ever be rebuilt. "Why would they do that?"

Storm's teeth gleam in the dim hallway, bright as buttons. "Because they can."

"Kira says there's some cult called the Watchers." He doesn't offer any explanations. "Don't we deserve to know?" I ask, huffing in annoyance.

Storm ushers me into the elevator. Jared and Kira wedge themselves in uncomfortably beside us. They all look like they'd rather eat nails than tell me anything. But somehow I know this is important. And so do they. I stare at him expectantly until finally Storm sighs, deep and wild.

"I'll fill you in on the way."

"They call him Father Wes on the street," Nolan Storm begins from the backseat of the van. Jared smolders at me through the rearview mirror as he drives. Kira sits shotgun. Nervous, especially with Jared's eyes following every insignificant movement, I fiddle with the neckline of my dress. It just seems to make Jared angrier. I pull my concentration back to Storm. "His real name is Jerry Westfall. I understand he was a mechanic up until about seven years ago when the car industry crumbled. After that he converted to the faith and took up a post at Southside Mission."

"Is Father Wes responsible for the uprising?"

"Not alone, by any means. But our latest intel suggests that right now, at least, he's the guy running the show."

"There are others?"

Storm nods. "At least three other major preachers in midcity alone. But none of them capable of advanced strategy. Westfall has ties to the Mafiosas. Worse, we've heard he presses kid gangs into his service."

I shudder, thinking about the dirty boy again. I'd heard of the kid gangs. They were rumors, tales passed around at school to shock and scare. They say that lost Laster children come together like packs of wild dogs. Young orphans ready to beg, steal, and kill to survive, they terrorize the surviving shop owners, organize heists that would put a lifetime criminal to shame.

To me they're just stories. I've never seen a kid gang. Still, I can't help but think of the young boy holding up his sign, following me with eyes burning with hate.

Evolve or die.

"What does that mean exactly?"

It's Jared who answers, voice tight. "It means we're totally screwed."

I turn to Storm. "Is that true?"

"Let's just say that the situation is more challenging and unpredictable than I'm comfortable with."

"And these Watchers?" When Storm doesn't answer, I give him my best Upper Circle glare. "We're turning eighteen soon. Old enough to live or die. Don't we have a right to know what's happening?"

He sighs. "You're right, of course." Sighs again. "The Watchers are the most unpredictable element. They take their orders from Father Wes, but as far as I can tell they're all zealots, and therefore completely capable of going off script if they believe something strongly enough."

"What do they want?"

Storm rubs at his face. "We aren't entirely sure, to be honest."

"Word on the street is they're looking for some kinda savior," Kira supplies. No one needs to ask *what from*.

I swallow past the growing lump in my throat. "Do you think they could have had a hand in what happened…at the Clinic?"

"Doubtful." Storm shakes his head. "But we'll find out," he promises.

"Those freaks at the Clinic." I stumble on the words, unable to put a proper name to the horror that was the men at the Clinic. Jared and I meet eyes in the rearview mirror.

"Yet another party with a stake in this whole mess. I'm just not sure who they work for or whose interests they represent."

"Just not yours."

Storm pats my hand and smiles down at me. "No, not mine."

At Storm's gesture, my eyes flicker to the rearview mirror. Jared's indigo gaze follows me through the dark of the car. The van jolts as Jared swerves and lets fly an inspired curse. We've neatly missed a body on the streets, a woman by the looks of things. I stare at the long, almost elegant thinness of the wrist bone jutting out from a heap of flesh and cloth.

All that separates us, that poor woman and me, is an accident of birth.

13

Dread squeezes me as we arrive at the brightly lit mansion. It's the Senator's mansion. Tucked up in the highest bower of the city's northern hills and walled away with a concrete security fence, high voltage wires and men with machine guns, Senator Mitchell Kain and his family live like royalty. I've been here before, of course, many times. Senator Mitchell Kain used to bounce us on his knees as Margot and I held hands and giggled. He's been a senator a long time, thanks in large part to our father's ardent support. Mitchell Kain knows our family very, very well. Owes our father much.

Senator Kain's footmen and valets wait at the bottom steps to escort the arriving guests. Bodies are frisked for incendiary devices, guns, neurotoxins. The high-pitched tinkle that passes for society laughter reaches us from the car. The mansion's windows are undressed, showing off crystal ropes hanging like nooses from the chandeliers.

I gape. "What are you thinking? My father is going to kill the both of us."

He shrugs. "I take it you know where you are."

I consider throwing a fit. But what would that accomplish? Margot isn't ready to go home, and Storm is the only protector we have at the moment. I decide to swallow my worry.

That Storm would waltz me into the home of one of our father's closest friends had, sadly, never occurred to me. I'd pictured us sitting all cozy on some little settee with some minor statesman and batting my eyelashes until he revealed a contact of some worth to me. Someone I could follow up with on my own.

Clearly I have underestimated the man standing at my side. I'll have to improvise.

"Do they know?" I ask.

Storm regards me calmly. "Know what?"

"You know."

"That I'm True Born? Yes, I should say it's fairly obvious to most people."

"Then—how did you get an invite?"

Storm's eyes glitter as he points at the sparkling chandeliers. "You see all those pretty firecrackers, Lucy? You know what's keeping all that wealth afloat these days? Money. And you want to know who has the money? Me. And you know what else I have that these rich, fat cats want? True. Born. Talents." He leans back like a king, resplendent in his suit and tie, and glances up at the opulent windows of the mansion above. "The world is changing, Lucy. The men and women in that house may not want to admit it, but they are aware of it."

I nod, suddenly keenly aware that Storm's civilized

demeanor is a thin disguise. I would never mistake him for Upper Circle now—can't imagine how I would. And it isn't a matter of manners or breeding: Nolan Storm is just too elemental, too raw, like the weather he's named for, to ever be a true part of the Upper Circle.

The Upper Circle doesn't like things too real. They like to pretend there aren't things like sex and death. Everything about the Upper Circle is about the civilized, cold veneer— which might go a long way to explain why our parents are so popular.

I sigh as the footman opens my door. "This is going to end badly," I tell him.

"Probably," Storm concedes with a nod.

At least he's honest.

We have completed less than one full circuit of the room, swampy with the crush of bodies, but thus far even Mother would be proud of Storm's Upper Circle manners. All around us the rich flash diamonds and gold cufflinks. In and among them move the black-and-white-suited waiters, trays loaded with drinks and *hors d'oeuvres*. Along the right side of the ballroom are buffet tables overloaded with food while most of Dominion starves. Before me, Betts Gallagher is terrifying in her blood-red sequin dress that hits the floor with a four-inch train.

"Darling, whatever are you doing here? Where is your sister?" is followed by the double take. "And who is this?" The greeting ends with air kisses and a shrill note of uncertainty. Beside me, Storm's jaw tightens. Jared scowls at a polite distance behind me. Kira, on the other hand, is all charm and smiles.

But it's the crocodile before me that I can't afford to turn my back on. Betts Gallagher is the gatekeeper of our little world. When our mother feels kind, she calls Betts the "only true friend of the Fox family," and "a true arbiter of social taste." When she's gone sour on batty old Betts, she's "that menacing, busybody dragon lady," and sometimes, "that bony old hag."

"May I present Mr. Nolan Storm, Betts? Mr. Storm, this is Mrs. Gallagher, a dear friend of the Kains and my own family, as well. Mr. Storm is a close business associate of our father," I prevaricate.

Betts raises one carefully drawn-on eyebrow. "Oh? And how are Lukas and Antonia?" she asks, all fake innocence. She even glances over my shoulder as though she expects to see them. But Betts likely knows more than I about our parents' whereabouts, and we both know it. "Will they be joining us this evening? I don't recall seeing their R.S.V.P."

The other thing Betts Gallagher happens to be is Mrs. Senator Mary Kain's, our hostess's, best friend.

"Mrs. Gallagher." Storm leans low over Betts Gallagher's hand. A smile hovers around his lips that would have most ladies' knees knocking together. "I have had the pleasure of conducting business with your husband, Gerald. It's an honor to meet you at last."

Betts's false eyelashes flutter. A real blush peeps out from underneath her severely rouged cheeks. But Old Betts won't crack that easily. "Oh? And just what is your business, Mr. Storm?"

"Construction. Or, more precisely, reconstruction."

I watch as a light bulb flickers on in Betts's scarily organized brain. "Ohhh. You're the backer for the core and fringes projects," she coos.

Storm's dimples deepen. "Guilty as charged, ma'am."

As Betts all but gushes over Storm, I look past them to the rest of the room. The walls are hung with gilt-framed portraits of ancestors that, according to our father, Senator Kain probably made up. The OldenTimes band strikes up its first song, a peppy number filled with horns and strings. From across the room Senator Kain's ice-blue eyes rake over me. He breaks away from his cluster of suited admirers.

We are secret keepers, my sister and I. We know, for instance, that Senator Kain is a notorious womanizer. He and Betts had an affair at one point, and we've seen him trying to stuff his hands up our mother's skirts a time or two. But what really tipped us off was last summer, when Kain tried turning Margot's internship in his office into a different kind of internship altogether.

"Is that you, Margot?" Kain peers at me with his sharp eyes. His carefully manicured salt-and-pepper hair swoops down perfectly across his patrician brow as he looks over my cleavage. "I hardly recognize you, all grown up."

"Lucy," I correct the Senator as he pulls me into a too-tight hug. His hands linger on my waist a few seconds too long for propriety. Jared's eyes scald my back. I pull away from the Senator as soon as I'm sure it won't give offense and tip back my head with a plastic grin.

He returns it, brittle and wolfish. "Where's that gorgeous sister of yours tonight?"

"Oh, right where I left her," I tell him honestly. "She's having a quiet night in."

"Your father and Antonia are still abroad, aren't they? Who's your fella?" He looks around the room, everywhere but at the man at my side, Storm. The wily old lech.

"Senator, may I present to you one of Father's associates, Mr. Nolan Storm?"

Storm offers a hand. "Senator. I believe we've already had the pleasure."

"Yes," Kain says slowly, sizing up my escort like a gunslinger. "I believe I vaguely recall. Beg your pardon, Mr. Storm." Kain stretches out his hand as though he'd rather do anything other than shake Storm's hand. But even he can't seem to find a reason not to. "I meet a lot of people. And how is that, *er*, project going, Mr. Storm?"

"Extremely well, Senator," Storm counters blandly.

"Well" — Kain nods and looks around the room anxiously — "make sure you say hello to Mary. Enjoy yourselves." With a final squeeze of my arm and a leer down my top, the Senator backs away.

"What the hell was that about?" I seethe through a frozen smile. How am I to gather information if all of our father's most important associates are running away from my escort and me?

Storm just takes my elbow and escorts me over to a waiter holding a tray of champagne flutes. He hands one to me before taking one for himself. His glass clinks against mine as he sips.

"What kind of game are you playing, Storm?"

He evades my question. "You're doing well," he murmurs.

"Kain doesn't like you. It's obvious. So why is he doing business with you and pretending he isn't?" I smile like I'm having a ball, a little trick we girls perfected years ago.

"Not everyone feels they can afford to let the world know they're working with the True Borns, especially in your circle."

"Yes," I say with some bitterness. "Appearances are everything."

Storm regards me curiously. "It's a game, Lucy," he says.

I snort as a reply. I'd just as soon call it what it really is: a Upper Circle insult.

Storm has other ideas. "Where do you think the senator would be if his constituents knew he and the rest of Dominion's government, not to mention the State, have given up on them? A collapse in the order is imminent. We know it. They know it. They also know Father Wes and his ilk are about two seconds away from a full-scale riot, and soon it's going to be obvious that the senator and the rest of the government aren't going to do a damn thing to stop it."

I can't completely stifle a horrified gasp. "But why?"

"Because they can't. If they bring in the army to defend the Upper Circle, they expose themselves as the complacent death dealers they are. And they don't have the resources to fix the mess they're making. Believe me, we are their last resort."

I stare into the ruggedly handsome face, the eyes alight with a vast intelligence and that eerie, unearthly power. He's beautiful, so haunted with power it takes me a second to realize exactly what position Nolan Storm has put me in, and by extension, my family. Our father may have hired Storm to protect us, but he surely didn't reckon anyone would know about it.

"It was supposed to remain a secret, wasn't it? Oh God, Father will kill me." I groan. The room lurches as my stomach flips over. I set my untouched champagne flute carefully down beside me. I stare down at my feet, at the beautiful dress I'm wearing, a dress my father would never approve of, the heels a little too grown up, the hair too untamed. I am not dressed like his perfect little girl, the girl who fulfills her duty to the family. Nor am I acting the part.

"Relax, Lucy," Storm breaks in gently. "Your father is not a stupid man. He knows what side he needs to be on. If he didn't, he wouldn't have hired us in the first place."

"You don't know him," I say, my breath coming hard and shallow. "You don't understand."

"I do." He tips my chin up. His eyes sear mine. "I will protect you and your sister."

"You can't protect us," I tell him. Because he still doesn't understand. He can't know the depths of our father's hatred and distrust of the True Borns, nor the extent of his reach.

And I have just very publicly aligned him with the True Born leader.

Head buzzing with anger, I head to the ladies' cloakroom and sag against the wall, grateful to be alone and at peace for a moment. I stare into the twelve-foot mirror adorning one entire wall of the room. How could I have screwed up so badly? Our father will be so disappointed in me. My moment of self-pity doesn't last long. The door opens and through the mirror, lined with gold-rimmed tissue boxes and puffed folded cotton towelettes, Mary Kain saunters in.

Mrs. Senator Kain chooses to look inconspicuous amongst her wealthy friends and neighbors. Her sapphire blue gown is severe in its simplicity, but I'd reckon costs a small fortune. She wears no flashy jewelry but a large diamond encrusted ring. Under her ash blond hair, her patrician face barely carries a line. A perk to running the Splicer Clinic. I used to think this made her elegant and thoughtful, more conscientious than most of our set. I know better now.

It was Mary who caught Mitchell Kain trying to break in Margot as his new intern. That's the day we learned the truth about Mary Kain.

"Lucinda Fox." She says the words with a softly accented sigh, a remnant of her southern heritage. Her tone, though, is sharp enough to cause a flesh wound. "What on earth are you doing here?"

"Mrs. Kain." I curtsy and bob my head respectfully. "I am escorting Mr. Nolan Storm this evening. Have you yet had the pleasure of meeting Mr. Storm?"

She stares at me for a long moment. Margot convinced me long ago that Mary Kain is the military mind in the Kain family and the real reason Senator Kain has been in power as long as he has.

Eyes wide, she throws her gambit on the table. "You have the nerve to bring one of those people *here*? Has your family taught you nothing? What will your father say? How will Antonia ever show her face again?"

I surprise myself by answering, "Isn't that a little hypocritical, Mrs. Kain?" I push a piece of hair behind my ear and regard her reflection calmly. Mary Kain comes to stand close behind me. "I believe Mr. Storm is an important business associate of Senator Kain's, as well as my father," I add.

Mary Kain's face twists into an ugly mask. "You know nothing, you little minx," she snarls at my reflection. "You enjoy playing your little games. This is a silly cry for your parents' attention."

"I'd never," I splutter in shock.

But Mary Kain swings the axe again. She's so close her

breath is hot on my neck. "You think I don't know what happened to your sister? You think we aren't aware of *everything* that goes on in this city?" She isn't referring to what happened to Margot last summer at the hands of her husband.

She *knows*.

I turn to stare into her brilliant blue eyes, eyes that could chip away at your soul if you'd let them. So cold she could be made of ice. "If you know *everything* that happens, then why haven't you been able to stop the insurgency? Why did you let Perry be attacked? Your own *son*," I add meanly.

Blond, dimpled, bland Perry Kain is also a senior at the Academy. I hadn't seen him during the evacuation, but I'd heard through Margot's grapevine that Perry and the rest of the boys in his class had gotten stuck in the men's change rooms when the bombs were being lobbed.

Her hand snakes out, so fast it could be a whip. The sting is fast and hot across my face, a lightning strike. "Do not *dare* to speak of my son."

I slowly bring my hand to the pulsing hot flesh of my cheek. "I won't tell my parents about this," I say, enunciating each word past my thick tongue and cheek. "But if you ever, and I mean *ever*, mention anything about my sister to anyone, I will make sure that Senator Kain's support is revoked for good. And not just by the Fox family." I give her a cheeky little smile.

Mary Kain, though, is no flincher. "You dare threaten me, little girl?"

I make sure I don't waiver, despite the tears that threaten to spill. "No ma'am. I don't make threats," is all I say. Then I walk away, head up, shoulders back. Just the way our father taught us.

Before I can reach the door, her voice, dripping with

cruelty, chases me down. "Ask yourself. Why would a child need to go through Protocols more than three times? Why *have* your parents just up and left? What kind of a child causes her own parents to run away? I hope you and your sister enjoy your Reveal, you foolish little girl."

My legs threaten to buckle. I'm too upset to care when Jared catches my arm and escorts me to a dark hallway, cussing under his breath the whole time.

He pushes me against a wainscoted wall in a deserted hallway. I shiver and say nothing as he examines my cheek under the pot lights. "Holy Plague fire. Who hit you?" he says, halfway between gentle and pissed off.

I try to pry his fingers away, but I get caught on them. "You were waiting for me."

"That's my job," he says, ignoring my attempts to get free. "Who hit you?" he repeats with a few pounds of steel.

"Mary Kain." My cheek throbs furiously beneath Jared's gentle fingers. And maybe Margot has more two-way awareness than I thought, because now that I'm away from the senator's wife I can feel her, wide awake and trembling. I shut my eyes.

"Ohhh, hell." When I open them again, Jared is still staring at me, not angry, but with a question in his eyes. "Margot's awake," I tell him, as if that answers it.

"I'm more concerned about you right now, Princess. Being a real pain in the ass, aren't you?"

I grant him a weak smile. "You said you liked it."

He smirks. "You know, the best way to get back at that old bitch is to enjoy yourself."

"What are you talking about?"

"C'mon, I think I can shuffle you around a dance floor."

"Won't Storm mind?"

Jared shrugs as he regards me carefully. The careless boy is back. "Do you care if he does?"

I consider the matter for exactly ten seconds. "No. But—I have a better idea," I say, steering him toward the dance floor.

Stars of light float over the gleaming wooden floors of the ballroom, bathing us in ruby. The band plays something old-fashioned and wistful. Tucked into Jared's arms I almost forget the throbbing skin of my cheek, the awful, sinking feeling of knowing how dead I am when my father gets home, the sick feeling crashing into me, again and again, as I realize how hated we are.

"She knew," I whisper into Jared's ear.

Jared's hand tightens around my waist. I become hyper-aware of my dance partner, the tightly coiled power in his hands, his legs so close to mine. His breath is a hot tickle against my flesh. "Knew what?"

"About Margot." My bodyguard says nothing, just dances me across the ballroom silently. "I need your help, Jared."

I'm loathe to admit it, but it would be helpful to have an ally in this little recon mission of mine. Still, I'm surprised as anything when he murmurs close to my ear, sending sparks skittering down my back, "What do you need?"

I feel Jared's eyes land on me, hot and knowing, even as he laughs at something the lovely, frosty blonde he's dancing with has said. He turns back to her and smiles as though she's the only woman in the world. I can practically feel her legs grow weak. He's talented, I'll give him that.

He's "cut in" on a half dozen couples now, each one chosen for what they might reveal. So far, Jared told me, he's learned that dove white is the "in" color for Reveal debs this season and that Milly Fitzwaters, who rides horses every Saturday, would *really* like to show him around the barn.

And me? What have I learned?

I turn back to the senator with sweaty palms and a bad comb-over I've been flirting with for the past ten minutes. It's not like me to try to dazzle. Putting on a fake laugh and pretending Old Sweaty is delightful while I try to provoke a certain line of conversation is not something I'm comfortable with. I'm the one who hangs back and makes sure our mother and father's wishes are carried out. I'm the one who watches Margot do this, though clearly I was paying attention. Still, I take a certain amount of perverse thrill at waltzing around the room with this latest partner, seeing him begin to loosen up.

And every time I let loose a laugh or a delighted smile, each time I lean in closer or flip my hair over my shoulder the way I've seen Margot do a thousand times, I catch Jared's eyes, tracking me with the intensity of a hunter even as he charms his way through the ladies. It somehow makes the laughs more real, the sparkle in my eyes genuine. After years of thinking only Margot could charm a room, it turns out I'm not half bad myself.

The gentleman finally stops moving and politely claps while I resist the urge to wipe my hands on my dress. In moments Jared is before us, his eyes thick and hard with menace—as they have been at the end of every one of these dances. The gentleman's former partner has not been returned to him, of course. "Thanks for that, chum," he says, casually dismissing the man before sweeping me up into another dance.

Nose quivering, Jared grumbles under his breath, "That guy smells like a perfume factory."

"Yes, Gordon is quite aromatic," I reply, my eyes on the room.

"You really seemed to be enjoying that one."

I level a look at my partner in crime. "I'm that good."

"I'll say." Jared whistles under his breath.

"Though I reckon it takes one to know one," I toss out breezily. Still, I notice my hand automatically tightens on Jared's shoulder as he turns me through the throng of dancers.

Jared pulls me half an inch closer as he leans down to my ear, sending a train of electric sparks up and down my spine. "What do you mean by that?"

"Looks like you were really enjoying yourself there, that's all. I hope you managed to learn something useful," I puff.

A cocky grin lights Jared's face. "Ohh, Janet is quite a gal."

My chin goes up. I reply stiffly, "I'm sure."

Jared's grin grows as he looks down on me. "You could say that I'm learning all about the voracious appetites of the Upper Circle."

"Eww." My nose crinkles. Laughing, Jared spins me. Deep and rich, it soaks into my skin, warm like whiskey, and stops me in my tracks. I peek up at him. Somehow the moment stretches on, the matching grins on our faces frozen.

It's Jared who breaks the moment first. Clearing his throat, he sweeps sharp eyes around the room, which has become infinitely more crowded since we began our little recon game, and marches me backward across the room.

"So what about you? Any luck with Gord-o?" Jared nods at the youngish senator, now immersed in conversation with another suit.

I shiver delicately. "There seems to be some divergence in opinions as to who really runs the show at the Splicer Clinic."

"Go on," Jared says, steering me away from the crush of bodies.

"On paper, at least, the Kain family is majority shareholder of the Clinic. But from there, things get a little murky. Gordon seems to think there's someone else floating the operation."

"Why?"

"Because of Nolan Storm."

A green sheen floats over Jared's eyes as his perfect lips twist. "Relax," I bite out. "What he was saying was that it was incredible that Storm was here. Everyone in this room knows that Senator Kain is considering letting Storm do more than provide silent backing on the reconstruction projects," I say, mentally flipping through the conversations I've had over the course of the evening.

Jared pulls his head back in confusion. "So?"

I take a deep breath, knowing he's not going to like this. "So it's a widely held opinion in the Upper Circle that the only reason the Kains would stoop to allowing a True Born into what they consider a 'family business' is if they were experiencing serious cash flow problems."

"Incredible," Jared huffs. "I should have known these stuck-up fat cats would—"

I tug at his arm. "Don't you see what this means? It makes sense now. Those weird True Borns… maybe there's a silent backer for the Clinic."

Jared's face is hard when he looks down at me again. He dances me to the fringes of the ballroom. I swallow past a knot of disappointment. "Do *you* think they're behind it?"

"Probably not." Jared shakes his head very slightly. My

heart sinks, it was a long shot, but I had wanted to be right. "Rich cats like them?" He nods in the direction of Senator Kain on the other side of the room, surrounded by cronies, "Oh, they'll play dirty, all right. They'll make sure they don't know anything about it so they can deny any of the charges. But I reckon I'm talking to someone who knows all about the sharks, am I right?"

I don't like the accusation, but before I can chew him out Storm appears from the crowd, his luminous antlers curling well above the heads of the other guests, and comes to stand behind Jared's shoulder.

"May I have this dance?" Storm asks in a silky voice.

Jared barely looks at me as he steps away. "Sure. I was about done here, anyway," he says before melting into a sea of black suits. My chest squeezes at the insult as my head reels with confusion. Why does he have to be that way? Sweet one minute and cruel the next, like the man who changes to beast. I shouldn't let it, but it wounds me. I take a ragged breath and tuck the hurt away for later, when I'm alone.

Storm dances with me for a moment before asking, "What happened?"

Which part? I wonder to myself as I try to shake off the sting of Jared's lightning quick rejection. "Mary Kain happened," I grumble. Storm chuckles but waits for me to go on. "She knew about Margot, Storm. I know it isn't proof but… What if they're behind what happened?"

Storm doesn't blow me off, for which I'm grateful. "One thing you can count on with those two is that they're thinking about the greater gain. And what kind of gain would they have if they alienate your parents so badly the Foxs stop propping up the ship? Your father could have Dominion, hell, the state, at a standstill if he wants to."

I look up at Storm hopefully. "Okay, so what if they aren't behind what happened… Do you think they have something to do with those freaks at the Clinic?"

"Well, now," murmurs Storm, and for a brief second I catch sight of the antlers, bleeding into reality like cobwebs bathed in light. "That's a different story. I'll keep digging on those two." Storm twirls me with a smile. "Look at you, Lucy Fox. For a first mission you've done a bang-up job rattling the suspects into revealing important information."

My answering smile dies on my lips. "Is that what this is? I'm on a mission for you?"

"Would it be so bad if you were?"

The song ends. We clap politely with the other dancers. A group of men come up to Storm and start talking about reconstruction plans for the city. I stand there a moment, bored and ignored, and decide to head over to the drink table. I've made it about halfway when I'm halted by a giant of a man who looks at me like he's been waiting for me.

Taller than Jared, and swarthy, the stranger wears a suit of an unusual cut. Eastern European, I think, noting the butterfly cuffs and the longish trunk to the black suit jacket. In fact, the cut is almost military, I think, adding weight to the scarred and pocked face, one eye covered with an eye patch. He has short, slicked-back hair.

"Excuse me." The man bows slightly to me. "Perhaps you would be so kind as to honor me with a dance?" He holds out a white-gloved hand.

I don't have an excuse formed so I feel honor bound to accept his request. When I take his hand, he beams down at me from his impressive height and wheels me over the floor.

"My name is Richardson."

"A pleasure, Mr. Richardson."

"Oh, the pleasure is mine, Miss Fox." I detect the slightest hint of an accent as his slightly uneven teeth gleam in the darkness.

"Have we met? You seem to have the advantage," I say uneasily.

"Yes, I do, don't I?" he returns thoughtfully. My nose tickles with the faint scent of wool and gunpowder. "I know your father."

"A business associate?"

"Not really," he tells me. His expression doesn't change. I begin to panic. I try to pull away, but Richardson holds me fast and gazes at me curiously, like I am a bug under glass. I look around frantically for Storm or Jared or anyone I know.

An invisible cord pulls tight inside of me. Margot floods me with alarm. Safe enough, but something has happened. On instinct, I cast my eyes to the window. Something perches on the windowsill. I blink, wondering if I've imagined it: a feathered beast man with immense golden eyes. When I open them again, he's no longer there. With a squeeze of my shoulders Richardson ends the pretense of dancing. "Why don't we go for a stroll?" he says.

"No thank you." I shake myself loose and turn my best ice princess glare on the man. "I'm tired," I tell him. "I'm going to rejoin my friends."

I pivot on my heels, turning my back on the man with the eye patch. But as I march through the throngs of expensively dressed guests, a huge shadow drifts past the open balcony. I take a few steps toward it, curious. The door is open, but

I don't see any tuxedoed men wreathed with the obligatory cigar smoke.

I'm nearly there when I'm caught up in the gaze of two unearthly round eyes poking out from an inhuman face. Its lips curl down in a perpetual frown. It blinks once. Its nose is human but curved, thin, ending in a point like a beak. Feathers line its throat in soft, downy white waves while darker brown feathers shoot from his cheeks, where sideburns would normally grow. He—it looks like a he—has the sleek and self-contained appearance of a hunting falcon, a bird that hunts for its human handlers.

I nervously look around the room for the machine-gunned mercs hired to look after everybody, but to a man they are mysteriously absent. Behind me, the crowd restlessly stirs as they sip their drinks, talk and dance. No one is around—not Storm, not Kira. Certainly not Jared. I'm on my own.

That's when I hear it: a murmur that grows into the thick cacophony of a crowd, shouts and yells punctuated by gunfire.

The mansion is under attack.

14

Flashes of orange light cut through the trees. The falcon man jumps onto the stone balustrade behind him. I creep closer only to catch a fleeting flock of smells: ammonia, saliva, and blood. He jumps backward, and I scream, sure he'll be busted on the pavement fifteen feet below. But when I arrive at the balcony, he's already spiriting away in the darkness. And instead, Kira's sequined form steps into the light.

"Why, hey there, Lucy. You make a new friend at the party?"

"What's going on?" is all I have time to ask.

Kira pulls off her heels and flings them into the darkness. "Find Jared and Storm and get to the car. Now!" she yells as she dashes off after the falcon man.

I backtrack into the party, which has become a scene of chaos. Women scream, and I watch as men in their expensive suits drag them off toward the exits. Waiters rush to the kitchen, trays all but forgotten, as the band starts shoving their instruments into bags. Something loud rocks the Kain mansion. The crystal chandelier above me jumps and chimes, its heavy pieces knocking heavily against each other. I watch as a shard sheers off and falls to the ground, shattering in a thousand pieces. A woman to my left screams bloody murder, and I just stare at her. Both of us are covered in glass. Tiny shards poke from her arms and face, drawing blood here and there as though she's been bitten by a thousand bugs.

Suddenly I'm dragged toward the back door by a man cursing a blue streak. I bat at his arms, and he rounds on me, fierce eyes lit with green fire.

"Do *not* provoke me right now, Princess."

"Let me go." I try to tug myself from Jared's unbreakable grip. "You don't need to manhandle me."

"What were you thinking?" he yells as we reach the tall doors leading to the kitchen and thread our way through the deserted rooms to the back door. "Do you really think it's a good idea to just disappear with some strange guy? And now look at you. I swear, Princess, how did you manage to survive until now?" He surveys the glass still embedded in my dress, showering my hair.

I don't have time to reply, so I simply glare. A minute later we've exited the mansion and make our way to the left side of the mansion where the Kains' massive garage is located. Jared drags me across the carefully cultivated greenery of the massive backyard, now wet with dew, so that I stumble every few feet. We're nearly there when my phone buzzes against my leg. I pull it from my dress pocket. *Margot*, the phone buzzes insistently.

"Don't even." Jared glares at me, his eyes narrowing to slits.

I ignore him and press answer as he looks up at the sky and says something very unfriendly.

"Margot?"

"L-Lucy?"

"Margot, are you okay?"

"M-mag…tree, Lucy. Ma—" Margot's voice dips and fades.

"Margot, you're breaking up."

"You've got to watch out." Margot is nearly breathless with panic. "Tell them they have—bombs, Lucy—heading right for you."

"Okay," I say, more to soothe her than from any real fear and slip the phone back into my pocket.

"You about done?" If looks could kill, Jared would have murdered me twice over, I think as I watch him gnash his teeth.

"Margot says there are bombs going off downtown. They're heading toward us."

A flash of guilt crosses Jared's face, but he just as quickly covers it up with more glowering.

The shadows are thick and strange in the garage as Jared leads me to the car. I catch the swish of a tail and the gleam of bright, shiny eyes. "Hee haw, guys," drawls a familiar voice. "What's shaking?"

Mohawk wears a bright red tank top and black running shorts with bright orange stripes up the sides overtop her printed body. The result is a colossal clash of colors and styles so gaudy it qualifies as art. "Some superfreak appeared," I tell her, ignoring Jared entirely. "Kira went after him."

Mohawk tilts her head like she wonders if I'm joking. "She'll be okay."

"Will she?"

"Storm told me to extract you. We need to locomote. *Vaminos.*"

"But what about Kira?"

"Get your butt in the car, Lucy," Jared says in a steely voice. I jump in the back as Mohawk dashes around to the driver's seat. Jared climbs into the back beside me but keeps his distance. Cold anger pulses at me in waves.

"It's the rabble, isn't it?" I barely get the words out before the first bodies reach the mansion. Lasters, most in dirty shirts and shoes held together with sticky gray electrical tape. They are mostly young men, but here and there are older men, the occasional woman, a handful of stray children. Wild looks on their faces I'd just as soon call hatred. I hear a scream as one young man, brandishing a shovel above his head, barrels toward an ultraluxury car. He smashes the driver's side glass before moving to the front of the car and smashing out the lights, the dash, denting whatever he can. But for now, at least, he ignores us.

I strap myself in as Mohawk pedals the gas. But before we've even backed up five feet, we're surrounded by a sea of rebel Lasters.

The Preacher man, the one from outside our house, lights onto the top of an Oldworld Mercedes. Mohawk leans on the horn and blasts us backward. There's a yelp as we run over someone's feet. But by the time we've cleared the garage the preacher has seen us. His mouth moves as he points a bony finger at the van windows. Heads whip around to follow his finger. They advance on us like a clockwork army. I slam my door lock down. Mohawk curses and floors it backward. A body sails over the hood as we veer around and forward into the crowd. In the second before Mohawk pulls away, I'm distracted by a Laster, spray painting two joined circles in bright, candy-apple red on the front of the senator's mansion.

We race through gobs of people, Mohawk continually laying on the horn, until we reach the copse of trees that signals the end of Kain's property. Mohawk pulls over, engine still running. A tug at the door almost has me jumping out of my seat. "Relax, kid," Jared bites off, reaching around me to unlock the door. Storm piles into the back.

"Go." Storm is grim as he stares straight ahead.

Mohawk has barely touched the gas when an eerie crackling fills the air and fountains a bright pink and candy red explosion against the night sky. The car shakes and makes a whining sound, as though it's spinning its wheels. I cry out and grasp the door handle. Behind me, Storm yells at Mohawk to go faster. It doesn't take a genius to figure out that whatever has been detonated is trying to pull us in, like an immense vortex, a magnetic black hole.

"What's going on?" I scream.

"Floor it, goddamn it, Penny," shouts Storm. The SUV comes to a standstill and begins a backward slide. I hear a ripping sound. Storm bellows. My stomach lurches. Tossing his head wildly, Storm pulls his spotless white shirt off, his tuxedo jacket already in tatters on the floor in front of him. His head tips back, and his eyes roll into endless, molten silver as he bellows. The car shudders, and a moment later he's ripped the door open. I stare, slack-jawed. Jared bares his long teeth, his glowing eyes restlessly changing color.

"Christ," Mohawk spits out. "Lucy, don't move a frigging muscle, you hear me?" I nod, mute with terror as the SUV suddenly lurches forward. "And you—" She spins in her seat and narrows her eyes at Jared. "Keep it together. Stay put, for crying out loud!"

What feels like a battering ram heaves at the van, propelling us forward. Pressure builds all around me. Through the side mirror I see the outline of Storm, halfway between beast and man, alight in a wash of white as he pushes the van from behind. Shirtless, he looks like an unearthly being, a god. I can't tell where he ends and the electric, snapping lightning begins.

Two Lasters come from behind and rush him. Caked in mud and yelling murder, they don't seem to be affected by the tugging current of whatever has detonated. One raises a thick plank and swats at Storm, connecting with his back. Storm turns as though he's been hit with a plastic child's toy. A sound I've never heard before erupts from him as he picks up the man who hit him and with one hand pulls his head off. I gasp, shutting my eyes against the gore. Then, with a mighty push, I feel the tension from the bomb stretch and pop, and suddenly we are moving forward with speed again.

A spill of pink floats down from the sky like a wilted feather. Even from here I can tell that the Senator's mansion has been decimated. Large sections from the roof and front have gone missing, like someone has taken a bite out of it. Mohawk doesn't slow down or stop to collect her boss. I sit forward and pull at her seat. "Wait. Storm."

She shakes her head. "He'll catch up. I'm guessing he'll need some time to run it off."

"Run what off?" I ask. But neither Mohawk nor Jared, silent and grim, answer.

We turn onto the main route heading back to Storm's keep. I tremble as I take in the destruction: entire half-blocks have simply disintegrated, nothing left but scorching holes in the ground. Incredibly, against reason, one crater had already begun growing a tree, matured past the height of a sapling.

"What is that?" I whisper.

"What's that, kid?" Mohawk asks, visibly more relaxed despite the incredible swath of destruction the preacher's kin have cut into the cityscape.

"Margot mentioned something about a tree. I didn't understand, but there it is. What kind of bomb would grow a tree?" I muse aloud. A look passes between Mohawk and Jared through the rearview mirror, instantly sobering me. "What are they?"

"Don't know," mutters Mohawk.

Jared throws himself back onto the seat. "Just drive."

My words are quiet-quiet, but the accusation is loud and clear. "And Storm isn't just a True Born, is he?"

Jared peers out the window, ignoring me. "Drive," he tells Mohawk again.

At first I think much of the downtown core has been spared. But as we inch closer I see how wrong I am. Dominion's streets are clogged with Lasters who've either been fighting or avoiding fights. Splicers' fancy cars clog up the roads, trying to escape the chaos. I even hear the wail of sirens—a sound I haven't heard for a while.

"Must be bad," I mutter, taking in the tattered ribbons of a storefront awning, blown-out windows. Chunks of debris litter the streets, some in mounds as tall as houses, and what appears from a distance to be burned out husks riding on top of them. As we drive closer I realize the husks are ragged, bloody corpses missing heads. One street is particularly dark, until I realize the entire block has been erased. Streetlights, cars, houses: everything just vanished into darkness.

"Why would the rabble do this?" I choke on tears. "Why would they level their own city?"

I'm so taken with the scene on the streets that I don't at first notice Jared, shaking with fury, lean forward. He clamps his jaw tight, like he's trying not to bite me. His face flushes dark red against his blond hair. But it's his tone that scares me the most. It's deceptively calm. "Well, now that's the problem right there, isn't it, Princess?" he purrs. I pull my hands in tight to my body, not daring to move or breathe.

"Cut it out, Jared," Mohawk throws back.

"No, I want to know how she defends calling them 'rabble.' They're *people*, Lucy. Starving people, dying people. Something you wouldn't know anything about, would you? And you wonder why they'd dare burn it all to the ground?" Distaste rolls off him in waves, like something I can taste on my tongue. Jared's fingers, bone white, crush the upholstery behind my head. "Look at me, dammit." He digs those fingers into my shoulder, causing little pinpricks of blood to appear. Caught completely off guard, I turn to him in confusion. That's what all of this is about? One word? A knot of anger forms in my chest as I look back at him.

"They aren't acting like *people*, Jared. Starving or not, where is the humanity in destruction and murder?" I hear Jared's sharp inhale, brace myself for his response.

Mohawk jars the car to a stop and turns to push Jared back one-handed. "Sit down and shut up," she barks. "We're almost at headquarters."

And amid the darkened, wrecked city, Storm's tower glitters darkly.

15

The ride up the elevator is frosty. I head straight for Margot's room. For once I'm not shadowed by Jared. The ache in my chest grows heavy even as the cord pulling me to my sister grows stronger. I rap once on the door before opening it.

I don't know what I had expected. Maybe to find Margot wilted in a heap on the floor, waiting for me to look in on her. Maybe shivering in the closet. Instead, she stands at the window facing the darkness of Dominion, lit by the curling tendrils of exploded bombs. She turns, relief etched into her face, and something harder, firmer. I was wrong: Margot may be rocked by what has happened to her, but she's strong. Far stronger than I've given her credit.

We embrace, two halves fitted together again. Her hair smells like sunshine. I can feel us both begin to calm now that we're together again.

"You're safe," I say, just as Margot whispers, "You're okay.

I was so worried."

We pull apart to stare at each other. In some unfathomable way, the gulf that has opened up between us since she went missing is more pronounced than ever. Her worried eyes travel over me restlessly. It's hard to hide from my sister. "What happened to you?" she asks, her tone accusing.

I move to her closet and pull out the luggage I'd packed for her just days before. "Get packed," I say in response. "We're going home."

"What? No."

"Margot." My voice is filled with steel. "We can't stay here any longer."

Margot sinks onto the bed. "What happened?"

"We need to speak with Father and Mother… And we need to go home. That's all." I cross over to the bureau beside the bed and start emptying her underwear drawer into the bag. Margot puts a hand on my arm.

"Lucy," she says, so gently I could break.

But I refuse to think about Jared. Refuse to cry. It's easier to think about the damage Storm has done. Not for a single second longer will I be a punching bag or a pawn. "He's using us, Margot," I say with bitterness. Anger helps me to shut down the tears threatening to leak.

"Yes, but we already knew that."

"You don't understand. He really used me tonight."

"I heard."

"What?"

"Robbie Deakins called me. He was there."

"What?" I turn and gape, forgetting Margot's socks for the moment. "I didn't see him."

"Well, he and his parents saw you. Apparently a Fox sister

showing up with Nolan Storm was the talk of the town."

"He didn't say hello."

"His mother wouldn't let him. Said you were going to be in 'wicked trouble' for bringing a True Born to the Kain party," Margot puts the words in air quotes.

"Those hypocrites! You know they all do business with Storm, don't you?"

"Yes. I do. So why are you so mad?"

It explodes from me. "Because he didn't tell me what he was up to. I was just…waylaid."

"Could you really not guess what it would be like?"

I sit on the bed beside my sister. "I suppose I didn't really think it through. I'm an idiot."

She nudges me with her shoulder and gives me a quick, wry grin. "You're not the one who went off with a lunatic who cut pieces out of her to sell on the Black Market."

"Oh, Margot," I say as pain, fresh as knives, blooms between us. "And then the rabble came. And a superfreak was there."

Margot's face turns the color of chalk. "What happened?"

"Kira went after him." But as I begin to tell Margot the story I realize I don't know what happened to Kira. Is she alive or dead? Had she survived the bombing or—whatever that was? I can't think past images of Storm, turning into a vision of my worst nightmares, his shirt in shreds and his eyes glowing with that unearthly light.

And with intense clarity I recall Margot's call.

I narrow my eyes on her. "How did you know?"

Margot worries her fingers. "What do you mean?"

"The bombs. How did you even know they're—whatever they are? How did you know they were coming for us?"

Margot peels back the curtain and peers out at the night.

"I could see them. You can see a lot from here."

"How did you know they weren't regular bombs? How do you even know what they are?" I accuse. "Do you know what he is?" I don't have to say his name. The look in her eyes tells me she knows more than she's letting on. "Why aren't you telling me what's going on?"

"I don't know anything for sure," she says defensively. "Honest. The bombs were so bright, Lu. They were like paintings in the sky. And I just…it's like I could feel them."

"What are you talking about?"

My sister gives me a funny look, like she can't believe I'm asking such a stupid question. "Come over here," she says. Her finger points into the darkness. "See that?" I look. Two blocks away a streetlight illuminates a massive, leafy tree growing in the middle of the street. It's too exotic to be native of Dominion: broad leaves shoot up into a prehistoric canopy at least two stories high.

"I saw one of the preacher's boys lob a bomb there. When it detonated, it felt like a fist squeezing my insides. I thought I was going to die."

"Oh."

"But then, maybe a few minutes later, I heard all this shouting and got up to see where the fighting was. I was worried they were going to bomb this place next. And there it was." She turns serious gray eyes on me. "Lu, it's grown a good seven feet in the past hour."

"That's not possible." I shake my head.

"But you know how I really knew? I mean sure, someone could have dropped the tree there when I was taking cover. And maybe it was one of those genetic accelerants they've been trying to use on the crops, although really, I've never seen something grow so fast. Maybe it was a trick of the light. But I knew what it was, Lu. No one had to tell me."

"How?"

"Because, sister dear. It's the same feeling I get whenever I'm around them. Especially Storm. Same feeling I've always had." Margot swallows, her voice dropping quiet-quiet. "Just like that shiver I get whenever you're near," she whispers.

It's late. I listen, dry-eyed, while Margot sheds the odd tear. The NewsFeed is oddly silent on the attack on the Kain mansion. No mention of it makes the bulletins except to say that a "band of disgruntled followers of a popular street preacher led a protest today through the streets of Dominion." No one talks of strange bombs, or whole streets given way to darkness and trees. There's not even a whisper of casualties; no reports of deaths, although I reckon that's the least surprising thing of all. They stopped mentioning numbers with that sort of thing long ago. Too many were dying each day, and they had to curb the panic.

When the report is over, we look at each other. She feels it, too. If the NewsFeeds aren't talking about it, what else haven't they told us? We live such sheltered lives in the Upper Circle. But surely someone will notice an entire downtown block gone missing?

But then, the Lasters are dwindling so fast. What if this cover-up has been engineered to prevent an even worse riot situation?

I get to thinking about what people know and what they don't know, the secrets we all keep. Mary Kain knows what they did to Margot in the Splicer Clinic, which means that Senator Kain knows, too. And who else: dull-eyed Perry Kain? *Everyone*? I haven't told Margot yet, afraid of what she might do. Terrified of what she might not do.

By the time Margot and I are packed, Storm has returned, a bloody Kira in tow.

We make our way to his office. Beside me, Margot is dry-eyed but trembling. As we are invited in by a booming voice and come face to face with this Nolan Storm, her trembling gets worse.

"What happened?" is the first thing out of my mouth.

Kira stands beside the couch as Storm bends over her arm with antiseptic and gauze. Her face is a mask of bruises, mottled and swollen purple across her cheeks and around her eyes. A long purple line decorates her neck. Sequins hang off her dress in torn strips, the right strap dangling. She only glances at us as we march in. Storm doesn't even look up as he stitches a jagged gash.

"We can come back." I motion to Kira.

Just a flicker of his eyes, and he has taken us in. "If that were true, I doubt you would have brought your luggage with you," he drawls, nodding to the matching bags set behind us. "Why don't you just tell me what's on your mind?"

I take Margot's shaking hand. "We're leaving."

"I gathered that." Storm cuts the thread and begins winding white gauze around Kira's forearm as she sucks in her pain. "Do you think that's wise, given the events of this evening?"

This is not the same Nolan Storm I have become accustomed to dealing with. I don't understand what I'm seeing. It's as if two people share the same space, one superimposed upon the other. The human Nolan Storm hides underneath a mantle of power that shimmers from him, extends so far out from his body now that he is almost blinding to look at, fierce, terrible. Deadly.

"I don't know. Is it?" I answer curtly.

Storm nods. "Kira," he dismisses the limping True Born with a nod. "Sit down, ladies," he commands as Kira skirts past us, her eyes flickering to mine for only an instant. I can't be sure but there is the ghost of a smirk on her lips. I sink down on the couch beside Margot, but it's me Storm stares at with those unearthly eyes. "Why don't you tell me what's going on?"

I don't waste any time. "What are you?" Not *who* are you. "You sure as Moses aren't human. And you aren't True Born, either, so don't try to pretend."

He crouches before me. "How would you know what True Borns are?"

My voice cracks as I whisper back, "We've seen them. Fins on backs. Furry hands. What Jared is. Shifters, I guess. Mohawk—I mean, Penny. Not you."

"Yes, me too."

"No."

"Yes, Lucy," he says my name gently, but his eyes are still violent, rivers filled with death. He runs a hand over the back of his neck, as though the antlers, more impressive than ever, have become a heavy burden. "A different kind, yes, but True Born. But you need to know what True Borns are to know what that means."

I open my mouth to argue. Margot twists my hand. A not-so subtle command for me to shut the hell up. "I want to hear this," she cuts in.

Storm sits on the couch opposite us and leans over his knees. "What do you think happened when the Plague came in?"

"A massive increase in pollution," I tell him, rattling off the lessons we've learned in school since we were small children. There had been breaches in nuclear energy plants. Ocean's worth of radiation leached into the environment along with everyday manufacturing debris, plastics, mercury. All that pollution eventually led to increased metabolic rates and genetic anomalies, resulting in the evolution of an ancient earth-class disease now busy chewing its way through the human population.

"You're about half right."

Margot crosses her legs and tucks a piece of hair behind her ear. "What then?"

"We *evolved*. That's what species have always done to survive massive changes in our environment. That is also the reason why humans are so susceptible to the Plague."

He says it so casually. *Humans.*

"But here's where evolutionary theories diverge. The Plague isn't just a reaction to our environment, although I'll grant you, it sure sped it up. It's a symptom of something else, something much bigger—an evolution that began eons ago. And though this current era is marked by a sudden shift… Wait, I'll show you." Storm jumps over to his orderly bookshelf and pulls a giant tome from a shelf taller than the rest. He thumbs over to a full two-page photograph of a stone slab and lays the picture before us.

The slab has been sculpted into a frozen scene: behind a winged man stands a tall, ruler-straight throne made for giants. His are the wings of dragonflies, intricately patterned. In one hand he holds a lightning bolt like he's about to throw it. In the other, a snake. Before him is an audience—men in headdresses and huge, sleek jungle cats with human eyes and collars around their necks crouch at his feet—and all around the scene someone has sculpted very detailed, realistic tropical trees. The back of my head prickles with premonition. I feel as though I'm about to drown.

"You know what this is?"

Margot answers, as breathless as I feel, "What?" My heart pumps furiously as my eyes race over the carved images again and again, trying to make sense.

"Our history ties us to the past. Our future is in our blood. You know what the True Borns are, Margot?" Eyes huge, she shakes her head. But it's Storm's eyes I can't look away from suddenly. Fathomless pools of molten gray, steeped in something I don't even understand, something I'd as soon call alien. "This. The resurrection of gods."

I tamp down a nervous giggle. "These are just pictures, myths," I argue, reading the caption beneath the image. *Bas-relief of Neo-Babylonian tablet, circa 1122 BCE, found at the temple of Esagila, depicting the supreme Babylonian god, Marduk.*

As I stare down at the image, something about the cat pulls at me—worse, reminds me of Jared. Suddenly I'm not so sure anymore.

Storm continues in a voice as soft as silk. "Marduk was First. He was First Born of what they called the True Born gods. And from his body the humans were made. But his first children weren't human, Lucy. They were *us*."

Slowly, as though not to startle us, Storm heads back

to his bookshelf. This time he takes down something I've never seen before, a dark cylinder covered in symbols and weird writing that looks like chicken scratch. "Marduk had in his possession a covenant. Call it a pact." He cradles the cylinder before setting it down before us. "Marduk's people declared him steward of the land, of man and beast, and when he decided it was time, he passed it to his children, who passed it to their children. Right down the line. To me."

I squint up at an eerily bright Storm. "You're saying your ancestor is an ancient Babylonian god."

His answering smile dazzles. "Marduk didn't just belong to Babylon. He was the chief deity for Mesopotamia and beyond. But he went by other names, too, over the ages. Cernunnos the Horned One. And yes, I'm telling you this being was my great-great-great grandfather. Am I saying he was a god?" Storm shakes his head. "No. I wouldn't go so far. But I am telling you that since Antiquity, no one had any idea what to do with people who could transform into animals in the blink of an eye. People born with the strength, agility, and power of nature coded into their very DNA—even in that era, when what seemed like strange and mystical events occurred every day. They worshipped Marduk like a god. And one day they all just disappeared from the face of the earth. Look." He flips to another page in the book to a painting of ruins covered in moss, hanging down like bunches of grapes.

"What is this?"

"The Hanging Garden of Babylon, one of the ancient wonders of the world." Margot looks at the page with fascination as, with a lifted eyebrow, I urge Storm to continue. "Marduk created it for the King of Babylon. No one knows what it looks like because it disappeared one day. Just as

Marduk did. And all his True Born children. Until now."

I feel my sister's eyes on me, heavy and dark. *The trees,* she mouths.

I turn my attention back to the stone tablet. It's so unbelievable, but Margot is right: there it is. In Dominion trees are scarce enough, scrawny and thin since there's so little real sunlight. There are no trees like the one that has suddenly sprouted in the middle of Elizabeth and Perth Avenue. Even among all the fancy houses of the Upper Circle, with their greenhouses and gardens, I have never seen its like. Yet there it grows: the same tree that grew from the bomb thrown onto the streets below Storm's tower. Only, this tree is etched onto a dull stone tablet in the middle of a glossy page, recorded over two and a half thousand years ago. Caught like an amber fern.

The trees in Marduk's throne room. The tree, growing quickly and mysteriously in Dominion's street.

I bow my head. The silver-edged clock on the wall ticks frantically. Storm has them everywhere, these clocks, all nearly identical. School clocks, big and round, with dark letters and plain faces. I wonder why he watches time.

"If it's true," I ask, "what do you think happened?"

Storm fingers the etchings on the cylinder. "I wish I knew."

"I thought you said this guy was your ancestor. Don't you know about him?" In the Upper Circle, pedigree is practically printed money.

"I don't really know what happened. For all I know, the True Borns went extinct. Or into hiding." He smiles at us gently.

Margot pinches her leg. I rub my flesh where she has hurt herself. A call for me to take a leap beyond the world of clocks and genes. And what will I find there? Something more frightening than men who turn into lions and horned gods?

And more frightening still: what will be revealed in our own blood, my sister's and mine?

"Do they know? The rabb—" I catch myself. "The people fighting with the preacher men. Do they know what you are?"

Storm's body language is instantly alert, tense as trip wire. "What do you mean?"

"*Evolve or die*. Did they get that from you? From the True Borns?"

It had never occurred to me to put it together like that. But now that I have it seems so simple, so true.

Another smile, this time with a deep dimple. "No, not from me. But it's a thought that has intrigued me now and again. No one knows my origins, our origins, but my people and me. And now you. I'd like to keep it that way, if you don't mind." Storm gets up and walks over to the bar, pouring himself a generous dollop of a rich, caramel alcohol.

"So the True Borns came from your ancestor, but you're still different from the True Borns," I say, wishing I didn't sound so accusing.

Nolan Storm's face darkens as he takes a sip of his drink. "I'm telling you that the True Borns are a race resurrected from the ancient line my ancestor began. That line created the bulk of humanity. And I'm telling you that particular genetic expressions from that ancient line are being reasserted. And I have been marked to lead them," he says pointedly. He takes another sip, his glass punctuating his words as he swirls the dark amber liquid. "What I'm saying, ladies, is that all your teachers are wrong. True Borns aren't an expression of genetic regression. True Borns are the reassertion of strong genes that existed a millennium ago. Genetic *progression*."

His huge frame blocks the light in the room as he gets up and stalks over to the window, taking heavy steps. He looks fatigued, his shoulders drooping. And I suddenly wish I hadn't been so stubborn.

"Storm," I venture, halfway to an apology, "thank you for trusting us with this information. We will be very careful with it. And we—we appreciate all you've done for us," I tell him.

Storm turns his head and stares at us. "Do you really think it's safe to leave, Lucy? Do you really think I could just let you walk out of here when your safety, the safety of your sister, is my prime concern right now?"

My shoulders sag. He's right. How could I drag Margot out onto the streets right now, into our house, empty of all but a couple mercs, when the rabble are in dissent? How could I take us away from the protection of Nolan Storm and his True Borns? Even more importantly, *why*?

I know the answer. It's the small, selfish voice I wish I could drown out. The one that tells me that I need to run away from the relentless disapproval in Jared's eyes. All that anger over one little word. And what of it? My own anger starts to bubble inside of me. Margot squeezes my hand. And just like that, the decision is made.

"Okay." I blow out a breath I didn't realize I was holding. "We'll stay a little while longer," I say, already knowing I'll regret this. "Just until we hear from our parents."

I don't catch so much as a glimpse of Jared until the next day when Margot has finally managed to heckle Storm into letting us go for a walk. I'm about crawling out of my skin by the time we're ready, coats on, boots on, scarves pulled tight. And then I turn around and he's there, leaning against the wall, regarding me with a shuttered expression.

My heart knocks against my chest as he slowly uncurls himself from the wall, arms folded, and swaggers over to us. "If you're ready, let's go," he says quietly to Margot. Me he ignores altogether.

Outside, it seems like every wall in Dominion is covered in the same red graffiti. Two eyes, crossed in the middle. Here and there the new slogan of the preacher men is written in sharp, careful letters. *Evolve or die.* Margot pulls me over to a wall where instead of red the eyes are worlds colored in blues and browns and white.

My sister takes a few paces back, tilting her head at the wall art. "What do you reckon it means?" I shake my head. Margot walks up to the wall and traces one of the worlds. "It's beautiful, though, isn't it?" I shrug, feeling painfully shy around the True Born shadow behind us. "Let's keep going, Mar," I call to my sister.

We round the corner to Main Street, where most of the most functional shops in Dominion still exist. *Did* exist. There are only a couple of shops on the street that still have windows. Most are now just the charred skeletons of stores: blackened timbers and scorched bricks. Someone has already scavenged through the wreckage, too, it seems. The sidewalks are littered with wrappers discarded from packages, broken glass, the odd glove or sweater tossed carelessly and abandoned. My eyes fill with tears. Beside me, Margot takes my hand, both of us overwhelmed with horror.

"Who could do this?" she whispers, quiet-quiet.

Jared comes up behind us. "We can't stay here." He presses on something in his ear and murmurs a description of the chaos.

"This happened last night, didn't it?" I say, picking up a brick that had come loose from the building. "The preacher men and their followers did this. Didn't they?" Jared eyes me uneasily, but he says nothing. "How can you defend them? How could you possibly defend people who would tear down the world?"

Something sparks in Jared's eyes as he takes a giant step forward. "Let's get something clear. They've torn down *your* world. How many Lasters do you reckon can afford to shop on Main?"

"Does that excuse their violence? Does that make it okay for you, somehow?"

Jared's jaw twitches as he stares at the swath of destruction running down the street as far as the eye can see. "No," he says. When he turns to me, I can see it in his face: the bleak acceptance of a violent world. And something else: maybe, just maybe, he can see my point of view. His next words prove it. "No, it doesn't. Nothing could excuse this."

Jared turns and takes a few steps toward the blown out glass of what used to be a tailor's shop. "Jared." My voice grates out, harsh and angry. But whatever I was going to say is forgotten as I spy a figure standing across the street.

It's the boy who chased me down the alley. The preacher's boy. I can just make out the defiant lines of his face. His shirt is torn and grubby, and it hangs off of his gaunt frame so that he looks like a dressed-up skeleton.

Jared has spotted him, too. He starts walking toward the boy, but when the boy makes our bodyguard he breaks into a run and disappears around the corner. I catch up with Jared, who stops dead center in the street. "Did you recognize him?" I ask as adrenaline spikes through my veins. "The boy from the alley."

"Yes."

"I reckon he's one of the preacher's boys. We saw him with Father Wes."

Jared pivots abruptly, taking my arm and dragging me back to where Margot waits.

Surprised, I struggle in his grip. "Wait, aren't we going to go after him?"

"No."

"But, Jared—"

"No." He sweeps his eyes across the rooftops, the streets, looking for something. Or someone. "Margot, get over here by your sister," Jared barks. He doesn't let go of my arm as he leads us away from the gray and acrid street.

"Your move." With a wide grin, Margot teases the young man sitting between us.

Of course, it's easy for her to smile. My sister has just spent the better part of an hour trouncing Storm's man Torch and me at the elaborate board game spread out before us.

Across the room, Jared's golden curls are bathed in the soft light of a lamp where he lounges on the sofa. For the past hour or more he hasn't taken his eyes off me, as though I'm about to disappear in a puff of smoke. And though I've managed to ignore him, I haven't been as successful at keeping my concentration—which could explain why my sister is doing all the winning.

Torch shakes his head. "I can't believe you. That's the third time in a row. Nobody's that lucky."

"Who says it's luck?" Margot throws her hair behind her

shoulder and shrugs. "Some people are just better at Gamon than others."

"Argh." The young man laughs, but I notice he can't stop smiling. Another victim of Margot's blinding charms.

The door opens, and Mohawk sails in, her tail twitching. "Oh, Malcolm, sweet pea," she coos in a high falsetto.

"I told you never to call me that." Our companion blushes.

Mohawk flips a mini disc at Torch, who catches it and rolls it between his fingers. "Storm wants you to run specs on this surveillance footage."

"Okay, when does he want it by?"

"Yesterday."

Torch sighs and pulls himself from the table. "Looks like you'll have to finish trouncing me later, Margot." He grins shyly at my sister before walking out of the room behind Mohawk.

We have been abandoned to our sulky bodyguard.

Margot glances over at me. She folds up the game and yawns. "I'm beat," she says to the room more than to me. "I think I'll head off to bed now."

I don't like the gleam in my sister's eye. "It's early," I tell her.

"So?"

"Mar—" I grab her wrist before she can leave. "You okay?"

She places her other hand on mine, a hand so identical to my own I can't tell whose is whose. "I'll be fine. You take on too much, you know," she tells me with an odd smile. A second later she's gone.

And then I am alone with the predator.

I pack up the rest of the game slowly, deliberately putting

every piece back into its rightful place before stowing it on the shelf. I don't know what to do next, but Jared solves that easily.

"You let them win," he throws out. "Why?"

"No, I didn't," I reply quickly. I busy myself with cleaning off the table, removing Margot's water glass and taking it over to the bar sink on the opposite side of the room.

I hear a creak of leather and am compelled to look over. Jared leans forward, his hands draped across his knees as he stares intently at me.

"Why, Lucy?"

"Why what? Don't be ridiculous. And what does it matter, anyhow?" I run the glass under water and set it aside to dry. I wipe my hands. I'm still trying to figure out how to make a graceful exit when Jared's tall, lithe form appears between the narrow galley of the bar, blocking my exit. My heart starts to thunder so loud I wonder if he can hear it.

He places a hand on either side of the bar, locking me in. "And why won't you admit it?" he asks.

I'm so startled by his new, gentler tone that I hazard a glance. My breath catches in my throat. Jared's eyes have changed to that sumptuous green, huge and mesmerizing, the pupils dilating like a cat's. I can't seem to look away as he inches forward, until he's standing all but a hair's breadth away from me. So close I can smell more cinnamon on his breath, the scent of him.

I want to move away, but instead I stand my ground. "You have a lot of nerve."

"As do you. Why do you let her win? Why are you always putting her ahead of yourself?"

I clasp my hands tightly together so he can't see me trembling. "You don't understand."

"So explain it to me."

"I can't."

"Can't? Or won't?"

"Both," I blurt out.

A beat of silence stretches between us as he considers me with a thoughtful, almost hungry look. "You don't trust me."

"It's not that," I'm quick to say. And it's the truth. Trust has nothing to do with it—at least, not trust in him. I don't feel in control with Jared. When I'm with him, I feel I'm standing on a precipice and will go into free fall just by standing next to him.

"So tell me." His breath is soft on my cheek. I'm trembling so badly he'll have to notice, which is the last thing in the world I want him to do.

So I do what will distract him most. I tell Jared the unvarnished truth about the Fox family. "You think we're spoiled rich brats but we're not, not really. Our family is…very strict. The rules that govern the Upper Circle, all that etiquette and protocol? It's doubled on us. The Fox twins… We have a lot to live up to. Our family's reputation is at stake every time we take a step. Our father is an important man. What we do reflects on him." I briefly muse over the Russian who will be coming to stay with us, Father's most important guest.

Jared screws up his face in confusion. "What does that have to do with letting Margot always get her way?"

I shake my head. "No, you don't understand."

"Then explain it to me. Please. I really want to know." Jared's hand comes up and rests on my shoulder where it burns like a hot coal. He doesn't seem to mind or even notice.

"Margot is…different than me." Jared snorts. Apparently this is no great surprise for him. "The restrictions we live under—I don't mind them much. But for Margot? They make her crazy. She ends up acting out. Does rash and stupid things. I have to protect her, and the family. And despite all that—or maybe even because of it—she's *better* than me." He looks like he's going to interrupt me, so I continue. "Margot is better at dressing up and flirting and impressing a crowd. Margot is the Fox family's crown jewel, and it's my job to keep her that way."

A scowl appears on Jared's handsome lips. "How does letting her win at Gamon protect her, or your family?"

"Because she needs it, Jared. More than I do." Unable to find the words to explain, I bite my lip in frustration.

Jared drops his gaze to my mouth. "Why don't you get to have any needs?" he whispers.

"Wh-who says I don't?"

A long minute stretches between us as we contemplate each other. My heart knocks against my ribs until I'm dizzy. But still I don't move, not even a muscle, as Jared gazes at me with the concentration of a hunting cat about to pounce.

He licks his lips as his head tilts down toward me. My body goes wild. Frissons of electricity travel up and down my spine as the True Born leans down. His voice is silk in my ear. "You're not with your parents now. No restrictions. How does that make you feel?"

Like I'm jumping out of my skin, that voice inside me whispers. Jared's hand is still on my shoulder, his lips just inches from mine. I gulp and try to take a step backward, only to find I've inched closer.

Panicked, I tell him, "It makes me feel…like I'd better take a trip to the Splicer Clinic."

16

From the safety and warmth of the car, I sit and contemplate the squat building. It looks the same as it has every time we've come here. Now, instead of emanating a hue of healing and care, the Splicer Clinic has taken on a sinister varnish.

Beside me, Jared has thrown his arm around the back of my seat. He stares moodily at the Clinic roof. Looking for cameras, I reckon.

"We don't have to go in, you know."

"Yes, we do."

"I don't get you, Princess. You talk about needing to protect your family. So why are you putting yourself in jeopardy—and me, too, I might add—to go back inside there?"

Angry, I turn on him. "You didn't have to come."

"Oh, yes I did."

"Then let's get going." I throw open the car door and step out into the darkness and cold without a backward glance.

The Clinic would have closed hours ago. Still, the building feels more deserted than usual. Jared's steps sound rapidly behind me. Seconds later he grabs my hand and tugs me into a shadow.

"What do you think you're doing?" he asks.

I point at the door. "Going inside."

Jared rolls his eyes. "Do you think you'd like to go to jail for breaking in, Princess? 'Cause I hear they don't hand out tiaras there."

"Well, what do you suggest," I return briskly.

He tugs me along the side of the building, deep with shadows. "We'll go in the way we got in before."

When we finally turn the last corner and arrive at the delivery bay, I'm not certain we're in the right place. Boxes and crates are broken all over the bay. The contents of garbage bags litter the ground in corners, likely eaten by animals. Gloves and plastic tubing and old, rotten noodles. It's as though a storm has come through and blown everything up in the air, only to set everything down again in the wrong place.

It feels wrong. And apparently, it smells wrong, too. Jared wrinkles his nose before we even get to the door.

"Sacked," Jared tells me, pulling me tight against the door while he pulls out the electronic hacking device and connects it to the door. Within seconds its tiny light turns green, and Jared nods at me, his eyes lighting up the darkness. "Stay close to me. Don't touch anything. And for God's sake, Princess, let me lead."

It's my turn to roll my eyes. But I say nothing as Jared takes my hand again, its warmth enveloping me with a sense of calm I reckon I have no right to feel, and leads me into the building that contains some of the darkest memories of my life.

The hallways are deserted. Here and there stray bits of shredded paper dot the floor. We follow the trail to the main records room, which stands ajar. "Wait," Jared tells me. He sets me firmly to the side with that dark look that tells me to stay put. Seconds later, he bobs his head back in and bids me to enter.

This is where they feed the Protocols results into massive machines. I've never been in here before. But even I know that the burned and trashed monitors, the frames for the computers scorched beyond recognition, is not standard operating procedure. The air smells acrid, as though there's been a recent fire. Someone has destroyed the records.

"Did Torch do this?" I narrow my eyes in suspicion.

Jared whistles at the inestimable damage. "Not as far as I'm aware." He moves over to one monitor in better condition than the rest. Flicking it on, the monitor splutters, lines crisscrossing on the screen before pulling up the submenu.

"Do you think it's still connected to the mainframe?" I ask.

Jared glances at me as I move in beside him. "Only one way to find out." He taps in our name. F-O-X.

The cursor blinks. We wait for what seems like an eternity before the machine comes back: *No results found.*

"Try our first names," I suggest. Jared types in my full name. Nothing. Then Margot. Nothing again.

Jared shakes his head. "I think the mainframe is fried."

"Wait." I curl my hand around his, stalling him. "What about our chart numbers? We were in here often enough that I know it. Try FLA10122," I rattle off the number I'd committed to memory.

Jared dutifully types it in. *No results found.*

"I think they're all gone."

"Everyone?" I breathe. But I can't believe it. I can't believe that thousands of records have been obliterated. Just to make sure, I type in: D-E-A-K-I-N-S.

Seconds later, Jared and I find ourselves staring at a column of names. *Robert, H. Robert, H. Sr. Adelaide, S.*

"Wait, wait a minute," I murmur, a sick feeling creeping along my spine. I type in a new name.

Phalon, Deirdre appears on the screen. I suck in a breath as panic threatens to overwhelm me.

Not all the records have been erased. Just ours.

"Maybe your father's behind it," Jared says. I've been so lost in thought on the drive back to Storm's that his words barely register.

"Pardon, what?"

"Your father. You know, scary guy, intense stare, bad manners?"

"Don't make jokes," I say weakly. But we both know it's a possibility. Who but our father would have the resources to have the Clinic shut down, the records destroyed? Who else but our father would have an interest in keeping the truth about us girls a secret?

I sigh, suddenly exhausted. Jared looks at me across the

dark seat dividing us. "Don't give up," he says with a small smile.

"Easy for you to say. You know what you are. And you won't be excommunicated for it."

The smile slips from Jared's face. He turns his attention back to the street, still littered with rubble from the Laster's insurrection.

"Why would you even care?" he murmurs.

"What?"

"So they turf you out. Who'd want to be with those pretentious, hypocritical snobs, anyhow?"

I sniff. "Those 'snobs' are my family." I don't bother explaining any further. There's no point with Jared. It's not just our lives that would be ruined, our livelihoods lost. If word gets out that the Fox twins are True Born, our father's career would be ruined, as well. Our entire family would be devastated. *And it would be our fault.*

There's not a sound on the street. Not a soul, not even a body. It's as though all of Dominion has rolled up for the night.

It sets my teeth on edge as much as the man beside me. Still, years of ingrained manners won't let me be rude. "I want you to know how much I have appreciated your help," I say as graciously as I can muster. "I know you've gone out on some limbs with me. Thank you."

Illuminated by the dashboard lights, Jared nods. "You're welcome. And for what it's worth"—he steals a glance at me—"I think you've got rare courage. It would be so much easier to pretend that everything is okay."

I don't know how to respond. Nice Jared, kind Jared, isn't at all what I expect. Beyond that, it's so comforting to have an ally in this other than Margot. The tightness in my chest that has been eating away at me since the Records room eases somewhat. Whatever happens, we'll find the truth, I promise mentally.

"What do you think we should do now?"

Jared shrugs, the collar of his plaid coat tickling the ends of his curls. He graces me with another smile, this one a touch shy and mischievous. "I think we should take our minds off things, have a bit of fun."

It's full late by the time we get back to Storm's. No one is around. Storm's tower is as dark and deserted as the Splicer Clinic's. I expect Jared to say good night and disappear. But the moment the elevator doors open, he drags me through the hallways, back to the games room.

I stand in the doorway as Jared switches on a lamp. "Get in here and close the door," Jared tells me, shrugging off his coat as I waver, uncertain, at the threshold. "Well, don't just stand there, Princess. I haven't got any engraved invitations, you know." When I still don't move, Jared comes toward me, arms outstretched like he's afraid of startling me. "Come on, Lucy," he says, his voice like silk. "Don't you know how to have fun?"

"I know how to have fun," I return defensively as Jared shuts the door behind me and pulls me gently into the room. *But I don't know how to have fun*, I realize as Jared divests me of my purse and coat and bids me to slip off my shoes.

He walks over to the control center on the shelf and flicks a switch. Music saturates the air as Jared moves a table to the side of the room.

I eye his labors uneasily. "What are you doing?"

"Making room."

"For what?"

"Dancing." He cracks a smile.

"Dancing? Now I know you're teasing me." I twirl, heading for the door, but Jared catches up to me in seconds.

"None of that Upper Circle garbage. We're going to do some real dancing."

But what Jared calls "Upper Circle garbage" is all the dancing I've ever learned: formal dances, dances with partners and string orchestras. Not something like the lively beat jumping from Storm's control panel into my bones.

"Come on," he teases, takes my hand, leading me deeper into the room. "I've just called you brave. Don't make me a liar."

I grimace but let Jared move me around to the beat. After a few minutes I get lost in the song, in Jared's mouthing the words as he twirls me out then reels me back in. Off balance, I start to fall but Jared catches me. I'm giggling, I realize, putting a hand over my mouth. I can't remember the last time I giggled.

"See, there? That's nice." Jared grins so wide his dimples become craters.

"What?" I say, still giggling.

"That." He tangles me up in his arms and dips me back. My hair brushes the floor, and I giggle harder. Jared pulls me straight again. He's close. So close. My hands fall across his shoulders as I try to keep myself upright, blood pounding through my body. He moves my body left and right, an intensity filling his face I've never seen before, making him look young, beautiful. Free.

A stray thought filters through my brain: *is that what I look like when we're together?* Because that's what it feels like—like I can do anything. I may have been born into the

Upper Circle, but oddly, it is only with this True Born that I feel the world is mine.

We're but an eyelash apart from one other. I reach out, unable to help myself, and trace the scar by his mouth. Jared's eyes tighten, and an exquisite sense of power rushes through my veins. I'm drunk on the bubbling joy as he murmurs, "See? Isn't this so much better than that Upper Circle stuffy stuff?"

"What have you got against the entire Upper Circle, anyway? What did we ever do to you?" I mean to tease, not provoke. But as usual, when it comes to Jared, I've blundered into something I don't understand. He comes to a halt but keeps my one hand in his, his arm around my back.

His eyes glitter darkly into mine. "You ever been hungry?"

"Sure." I shrug. "Three times a day."

"I mean *hungry*. As in, a day away from dead, hungry?" I shake my head, sure I won't like where this is headed. "I was on the streets for a few years, you know. And not in one of the gangs. The gangs don't take True Borns. No one does."

I'm about to protest—I don't even know what, maybe just tell him that we're not all bad—when Jared's fingers fall across my lips, silencing me.

"So one day I steal from a garbage can behind this big, stately home. I'm just looking for scraps, because I know if I don't eat soon I'm going to die, when all of a sudden there's a gun at my head."

Jared's fingers come away, and I step back half an inch, as though that extra space will give me some distance from whatever horror Jared is about to reveal. "I thought they were going to kill me. So imagine my surprise when I'm taken in by the rich man of the house. He gives me clothes, a bed, a bath. He gives me all I can eat."

He pulls me over to the couch and has me sit beside him. But for some reason he doesn't let go of my hand and I'm glad. "His name was Peters. He offered me a job."

Jared describes his life in the big house, the training regimen his new boss puts him through. He thought he was being trained to join the security team.

"Little did I know how men like Peters make a living. And when they brought me to the ring with that animal—"

I blink. For a moment, I think Jared has lost his mind. "What animal? What are you talking about, Jared?"

Jared rubs his jaw and grins ruefully at me. "Why am I not surprised? They trap big game animals and pair them up with True Borns who are thought to be their genetic antecedents. Then they're forced to fight to the death. They were wrong about me. I'm no lion."

I stare at him in shock. "You killed a lion? With your bare hands?"

"And when they run out of animals, they pit the True Borns against one another."

I gasp. "Why didn't you just leave?"

Jared's laugh is ugly. "Are you really that naive?" I bristle, but say nothing as Jared continues, his tone softening as he explains. "They had guns. We didn't. If we didn't fight, they shot us."

But my mind continues to rebel. "Surely that wasn't the true Upper Circle, Jared. Upper Circlers wouldn't do something like that." What I mean is that those people, the people who I have grown up with and who raised me, are not capable of such horror. One look at Jared, though, and I can tell he believes my comments to be about the wealthy, as if I believe that somehow a Mercedes and a merc make a man morally superior.

Jared's face is a bland mask as he stares back at me. "Senator Kain had a man in the ring, Lucy. I saw him there several times."

The blood runs like ice in my veins. "It can't be," I say weakly, picturing the man who used to bounce me on his knee as a child. Yes, the Upper Circle has always felt fake—but never evil. "How would he not have recognized you at the party?"

"I was only fifteen," he says, matter-of-factly. "Besides, who would have recognized the True Born killer thug wearing a well-made suit and circulating with the Uppers?"

I cover my face with my hands, more ashamed than I have words for. When I think about Jared trying to help me there, of what it must have cost him, I want to cry. All those times I've been angry at him for hating the Upper Circle, when by rights he should hate me, too.

"How did you get out?" I whisper.

We are interrupted by the chiming of notes, counter to the music, somewhere near the door. It's my parents' ring. We stare at each other as the notes sound, over and over.

Jared's mouth is a thin line as he nods in the direction of the noise. "You'd better get that."

I stand, shaky, and move toward the phone. As I hit the playback button my mother's face comes on the screen, telling Margot and me to call them in the morning. A second later, Jared's phone goes off. I watch him check his message as I let our mother's words drift past me like smoke.

I don't pay attention until the very end, just as my mother tells me that school is reopening.

17

They've told us not to call while they're away. It's a rule our father dreamed up one day when he was in France on a big deal, our mother was in France on a big shopping spree, and Margot wanted permission to go on a weekend trip with some of the kids from school.

Now we are expected simply to wait: to make no decisions for ourselves, to behave ourselves, but at all costs, we are not to bother them. The perfect diplomat's daughters.

It's a different thing altogether when we've been summoned to call.

"Lucy?" Our mother's grainy image appears on the tiny screen until I unfold it to its larger, 4x5 dimensions. "Lucy!"

"Mother," I call out and watch with fascination as the frown on Antonia Fox's perfect face deepens. "Where are you and Father?"

"We're away on business," she snaps, reaching up to clasp her pearls. "I understand you're staying at that True Born's house. Honestly, what's gotten into you both?"

"Mother, I can't explain over the phone. But please, just trust me."

Our mother cocks a hand to her hip. "You get you and your sister home, Lucinda, and I mean today. When your father gets home… Where is your sister? I want to speak with her." She looks behind me, searching for a glimpse of my twin.

I sigh. Our mother has always considered Margot to be the better sister, owing to her popularity, her outgoing nature, and ability to get along with just about anyone. Maybe it's because she's a normal teenager who likes to go out and have fun. Unlike me. "Margot can't talk right now, Mother." Right now, Margot is somewhere in Storm's keep taking one of her daily hour-long showers. I feel her distress as she scrubs her skin away in the scalding hot water. My skin itches sympathetically.

Our mother's frown deepens. "What do you mean she can't talk?"

"She's in the shower."

"Well. Since you're here, the academy reopened. They called last night," she ambles.

"Yes, I understand," I cut her off quickly. "Tomorrow?" And when she nods I ask, "Where's Father?"

"He's around here somewhere." She waves her arm. In the background I catch glimpses of rich red oriental carpet stretching like a sea to a doorway framed by dark wood paneling. A hotel dining room, five-star, I think as I size up the decor, recalling the number of conversations we've had while one or another of our parents sat in one of these.

"Are you planning to come home anytime soon?"

"Your father was hoping to wait until the troubles die down," she replies airily.

"I don't think you can afford to wait that long."

A glint forms in our mother's eye. "Mitch told your father the same thing just yesterday. I must say, I could hardly believe half the things he was telling Lukas. Didn't your father warn you to be on your very best behavior?" She leans closer to the screen, as though afraid of being overheard. "We'll be bringing your father's business partner home soon. There had better be no more gossip floating around, Lucinda."

"Mother," I start. I want to ask about the Splicer Clinic, but she looks off to the right, a smile lighting her flawless skin, a twinkle in her eye for someone off screen. Someone not our father. She turns back only for a second to tell me, "Got to go now, kisses!" Then she's gone, leaving me with a dead screen and an ache in my chest.

Twenty minutes later Margot hangs back while I stand before Storm. He looks calm enough as he sits at his desk and regards us. But the fine lines above his head waver in and out with sharp blue electric sparks.

"I take it you've heard?"

Storm leans back in his chair and nods, an air of defeat settling around his shoulders. I don't believe it for a second. "Of course," he replies. "Your father was quite explicit, shall we say, with his directions last night."

"I'm so sorry," I say, biting my lip in mortification.

Storm stands and pushes away from his desk. He has never looked larger. Or more impressive. He comes around and puts a hand on each of our shoulders. "This is not your fault, Lucy. Nor yours," he tells Margot. "This is a difference in opinion as to the proper handling of a security detail."

Margot twists her hands in her lap, vividly uncomfortable. "What are we going to do?"

Storm holds out his finger and whips out his phone. He presses a button. Alma's voice fills the room.

"Yes?"

"Tell Torch and Jared to pack."

"Certainly."

My guts twist. "Where are Torch and Jared going?" I ask uneasily. But somehow I already know.

"I can't let you go home without a security team. Your own guys are fine, but I want extra insurance."

Jared? Staying in my home? My stomach lurches. "Why?"

In the blink of an eye, Storm's horns lengthen and thicken. "Because I need to keep you safe. It's what I do," he says, clearly frustrated. But I'm now fairly certain that the "role" he's referring to has nothing to do with our father's paycheck. Nolan Storm has his own agenda.

I stare out the window, avoiding his gaze. "I don't think this is a good idea."

"Lu," Margot says. Panic rises within her like high tide.

"Margot," I reply stubbornly.

Storm folds his fingers together. "This isn't a negotiation, Lucy. You either go with Jared and Torch or you both stay here where I can keep you safe."

They both stare at me, waiting. I bite the inside of my cheek, feeling blood rise to the surface. "Fine. But—just—tell them to behave. Our parents are *not* going to like this," I say in frustration as I shoot over to the door.

Storm chuckles, though I don't know what he finds so funny. "I'll tell them. One more thing." His voice stops us in our tracks. "I'm going to have Dorian visit you with your test results. You should expect a call in the next couple of days."

I guess that means we're going to get those blood tests after all.

Hours later I sit on the edge of my canopy bed and try my parents' number for the fifth time. No answer, just like the first four times. I leave a message. "Mother, it's Lucy. We're at home now, and we'll be heading to school tomorrow. When are you and Father coming home?" I've gotten just the last word out when the recording cuts me off and the line goes dead.

I stare around me, holding back what I think are childish tears. The room no longer feels like it's mine, nor does the house. It feels like strangers live here, strangers that bear no relation to the sudden twists and turns our lives have been taking. The painting on the wall of the black cat toying with a red string; the lovely antique china doll on the display shelf; the tiny glass globe hanging from the ceiling, an exact match to the one hanging in Margot's room: were these ever truly mine? The photo on my bedside table of my twin and me is the only thing I recognize, and even that seems wrong. In the picture, Margot wraps an arm around my neck. Her smile is bright, beautiful, confident. Free of shadows. My own smile is smaller, more uncertain, my eyes shadowed by doubts.

I keep hoping things—*me*—will snap back into place once we're a bit more settled, but I have the sneaking suspicion they never will. Even if we find out what we are, we've already learned we're not the same as everyone else.

I get up to find Jared, who I discover in the opulent living room with its tall mahogany grandfather clock presiding over the wide chintz couch covered in bright sprigs of poppies and wingback chairs meant to relax kings and presidents. Jared doesn't look very relaxed, although he's in his typical uniform: loose, worn blue trousers, a bright red and white plaid button-up over a white shirt with a 3-D dinosaur mouth roaring at anyone who walks by. His tousled hair looks like he hasn't owned a comb since before the Plague.

Jared breaks off what looks like an earnest conversation with Fritz as I walk in. "Well?" he asks in a clipped military voice. I shake my head. "You're kidding, right?"

I trade understanding glances with Fritz. "Well," Fritz adds gruffly. "I'm sure zey are very busy. I haff got to get back to ze gate tower. Thanks for the tips, Jared." He says this with such sincerity, I can't help wonder what tips Jared could give an ex-merc with over twenty years of combat experience. As Fritz's flattop disappears through the wide arch separating the living room from the main entrance, I busy myself examining the figurines in our mother's display cabinet.

There is nothing innocent in the frozen, painted figurines. If anything, they remind me of my family: so arranged and superficial, so brittle, they'll crack with a glance. A little shepherd sits on a bench playing a flute; a shepherdess in a pink frock and a crook with an oversized pink bow leads home a tiny ceramic lamb. Our mother inherited these from her great-grandmother, she's fond of telling us. And one day they will belong to us, a legacy to pass down to our daughters. Unless, that is, I have launched each of their pretty, painted faces at Jared's head.

I have tuned out Jared so successfully I don't hear a word

he says. "Are you listening to me?"

"Pardon?"

"I said, did you speak to your father?"

"No, he wasn't there."

Jared runs a frustrated hand through his hair. It stands at attention as he glowers at me. The second he'd set foot in my home Jared had been in the foulest of moods. Gone was the boy who comforted me, danced with me. Now he treats me like the enemy. "Did you even speak with your mother?"

"I told you I didn't."

"Well pardon me for not being sure we speak the same language, Princess."

It's just this small slight that makes me snap. I pull myself up and in my haughtiest, diplomat's daughter voice look down my nose at him. "I may be a lot of things, Jared, but one thing I'm not is a liar."

"Okay. Fine. So we'll just—"

"No, *not* fine." I poke my finger at his chest, all the pent-up frustration and anger and fear tumbling out at once. "I will *not* be disparaged any further, Jared True Born. If you don't have anything nice to say to me, stop talking."

He pauses for a long second before looking at me from beneath his eyelashes. A slight smile ghosts his mouth. "Jared True Born, huh?"

"Well." I step back. "No one has seen to proprieties and given me your last name."

The air between us crackles with tension as he continues to look down at me, and I glare at his chest. "I guess it hasn't really mattered since we're just the hired guns."

"Do *not* start—"

"All right, fine. Sorry." I can see how much it hurts for him to say the word. "We'll have to go to Plan B."

I raise an eyebrow. "And that is?"

"Same as Plan A. You're stuck with us until they get back."

"Fantastic," I grumble, throwing my hands up in the air. My fingers itch for a figurine.

"Disparaged, huh?" He just about chuckles the word, so softly I think I've imagined it.

"Pardon?"

"Nothing, Princess," he says, moving toward me. I back up a step, but I'm far too slow for his True Born reflexes. He's already leaning down to my ear, murmuring, "It's Price," before wheeling around and walking out the door.

18

The night before the school reopens I don't sleep for dreams: long, rolling seas of dreams that leave me shivering in fear. Through the decaying streets of Dominion sweeps a tidal wave. It leaves a crimson wake littered with body parts. Preacher man perches on top of a car, laughing at me. I stand fixed inside the gates of my home, flagged by Jared on one side, Nolan Storm on the other. Jared *Price*, my subconscious adds. Margot is alone again, framed inside her window like a ghost who can't come out to play. I shiver and stare at her hand, trapped and fluttering against the glass like a pale moth.

A woman with large, milky white eyes, coated with the cataracts of the old and sick, walks up to the gate. She's young, I reckon, only a few years older than me. Ash blond tresses flutter down to her waist. The pale skin of her cheeks ends in a pointed, pixie-like chin. She's slender to the point of skinny; curveless like a boy, accented by a skin-tight black catsuit. Her sightless eyes are intent, watchful, as she raises one hand and reaches for the locked gate. It falls open at her touch. Her voice flows through my head. *I see the threads.* She reaches for something as she steps through and slowly, calmly walks toward us. No, not a thing – a *who*.

Something has changed. The school pretends it's the same: the same dented steel lockers, the same slick marbled floors, the same classroom smells of old wood and burning dust. Still, something is off.

You can't tell there was an attack. They do too good a job of vacuuming over the violence. But it's there, like a stain in the air. Some of the classrooms are locked, their doors battered and scarred. The shattered glass has been replaced and all traces of the explosions, the bullet holes, have been swept and washed away.

Still, the school feels haunted. It's been an academy for over two hundred years, standing for well over four, but this is the first time I have felt its ghost.

Margot sends me a heated stare from the desk beside mine. She pinches her thigh and I rub, nodding slightly. When the bell rings, Margot lingers at the door while I approach Mr. Hobart, our Genomics instructor. Laugh lines crease his face as he turns to me. "What can I do for you, Lucy?"

This is the next important step in my plan. I've been practicing my question for the past hour, but now it rushes out in a tangled mess. "Is it even possible—I mean, how could a genetic sequence jump so far back into its history that it practically evolves? I mean—that makes no sense, does it?"

He nods. "You're asking about the True Born genetic mutations, aren't you?"

"Yes." I swallow. "I mean, isn't it against evolutionary biology that a species could evolve by regression?"

"Great question." He flips a book up in the air and catches it, his signature move. "Under ordinary circumstances I would agree with that claim. But with the levels of pollution found in all aspects of our environments and bodies, I think our DNA decided that if we didn't adapt, we'd go extinct, so some of our genetic sequencing chose very specific strands to replicate for survival. It appears that some of the DNA needed to survive our new environment just so happened to have existed before. Likely, this is because most animals lived without the sanitation and cleanliness that we humans have grown accustomed to, grown soft over. My personal theory is that all of us contain the DNA of our antecedents. We just don't all have it triggered. But, to be completely honest, we haven't collected enough data to be certain. So far, not many True Borns will allow themselves to be tested."

So it is possible that Storm is right. They may not know. *Or they could be hiding the truth.*

"The way you're talking—it almost sounds like you think our DNA is alive and aware, like people," I muse.

"That's an interesting thought," he says with a shrug. "Something to pursue." The last of his books disappear into his knapsack, and he walks me to the door. Margot waits just outside.

I pause at the threshold. "*We.*"

"Pardon?"

"You said, '*we* haven't collected enough data.' Sir, I was just wondering who 'we' is? Who says what tests can or can't be done on True Borns?"

"The government regulates everything, Lucy."

"But who, exactly?" They never talk about the True Borns. Not if they can help it.

"All True Born issues are handled at the state level. And if I'm not mistaken, it falls under the portfolio of the Minister of Health."

An icy shiver whips through me. "Senator Kain's portfolio?"

"Yes, I think that's right."

I nod, only vaguely aware of Mr. Hobart's hasty retreat and parting words. "I have to dash, Lucy, but we can continue this next class if you like," as Margot tugs me to our next class.

"Catatonic," she whispers, furious at me.

"Thinking," I reply a little too sharply as we sail, lost and adrift, through the wide halls, only to be swallowed by a sea of identically clad bodies.

At lunch I sit alone with Margot at one of the long oak tables in the dining hall. I feel hot eyes on us. We're being unfriendly. On a typical day we'd sit with Deirdre Phalon and Jenny Smythe, three tables away. This is not a typical day.

Margot keeps her head down, nibbling at the salad and baguette I purchased for her since she wasn't up to standing in line. Margot taps a code on her knee. I look around to see who she's talking about. In this way we keep up with the tidal life of the school. I rap a finger once on the table, pointing toward the washrooms at the far end of the school. She nods, taps once in response, indicating she'll be fine staying put.

I'm not more than a few minutes, but by the time I walk

back to our table, Robbie Deakins is leaning over my red-faced sister. I pick up the pace, arriving just as Robbie leans too close to Margot.

"Hey!" I manage to startle Robbie so badly he jumps. Margot's eyes, big and haunted, bore into me.

Robbie Deakins exudes the kind of sexual confidence that, until just a few weeks ago, had Margot very intrigued. He's charming, sophisticated. Worse, he and my sister have been waltzing around each other for a year now.

"Luce," he says in his casual way. "Where've you guys been?"

I shrug. "Around. Where've you been?"

He barks a laugh. "Avoiding my pops, that's where."

"Why, what's up?"

"Well"—he leans in conspiratorially—"you know how this insurrection is because of the preachers, right? Well, my pops is on the warpath. He's going to 'clean up the streets of Dominion by any means necessary.'"

"What, has he got you enlisting in the army or something?"

"Practically." He turns to Margot with a laugh. "But you never returned my call," he tells her, picking up on some thread of conversation I missed.

"Busy," Margot evades with a shrug.

"Well, when you get over being busy"—he gives her a cool look—"give me a call. Let's hang out or, I know—you can make it up to me by making me your date for your Reveal."

I roll my eyes. "Robbie. You know we can't."

Our father would never let Margot or me bring a date of our own choosing to our party, not even someone on our "safe" list. Not for this milestone. When they tell you, it's public. You need to be aware of your public face. Robbie knows this.

Robbie thinks the world of our father.

"Hey"—he flashes a pearly white grin at us—"never hurts to ask." He leans back to look me up and down, his shirt and collar bunches like grapes at his neck. "You're keeping pretty interesting company these days, Luce."

"Just doing my *duty*," I shoot back with a tight smile.

Robbie leans over and kisses Margot on the cheek. She flinches, and I feel her momentary shot of panic, but it subsides as he skips off toward a rowdy table of boys.

"Sorry," I breathe in our quiet-quiet way. Margot shakes her head. We float there for what feels like a long time, utterly alone amid the noisy din and press of bodies in the long, cold room.

At the last bell we skip down to the large entrance floor, its floors shiny again, and are confronted by rows of security. Home security, not school. Many are the mercs we've seen chauffeur our friends to school every day. Some new faces. My sister stops in front of me at the bottom of the stairs. I cast around for Fritz or Shane, but in the sea of buff bodies I spy only the tall, thin True Born I saw on the day of the attack, just a few meters away. He nods to me as I step carefully toward him.

"You think I'm going to pull a sword, Miss Fox." He bows slightly and smiles a faraway smile. "Or maybe, as the saying goes, bite you?"

"No, sorry—I just didn't want to disturb you."

He waves this away. "No bother. What can I do for you?" Up close, he has the rangy build of a fighter. His skin is not so much blue as clear, so translucent you can see the blood circulating underneath, as though his skin is the surface of a pool. It's his eyes that are the most interesting, though: a blend resting somewhere between a washed out yellow and green, a color our mother would likely call "savannah."

"Have you—" I break off, question forgotten. I feel the eyes pinned to my back even before the True Born tracks his attention to someone standing behind me. That crackling, burning presence that won't let me be.

"Jared"—I turn and look down my nose at him—"what are you doing here?"

"Coming to fetch you, your Highness." He graces me with a mocking bow. The True Born raises an eyebrow at us.

"Whatever." I roll my eyes and turn back to the tall, thin man with the strange green eyes. "Here's my ride. I'd better go. Thank you anyhow."

He nods, solemn, before giving Jared a thoughtful look. "True Born," he mutters.

"What was that?" Jared says, his hand clamped on my upper arm as if I'm a rabbit about to bolt.

"I did not know the Fox family kept True Borns."

Jared gives the man a big, lazy grin. "They don't," he cheerfully tells the guardian as he whirls me out the door.

Outside, the whirring of choppers fills the air like dead weights. I press my hands to my ears as one chopper sets down on the building across the street. Grayguard disallowed choppers on their own roof some time ago. Jared grabs my hand and shoves me into the Oldtime car before disappearing around the other side. Margot is already inside.

Our eyes meet before flickering over the scene outside. More than one family has sent two or more escorts, and from the sheer numbers of men with escort badges, I'd say a few of the families who've been lax about security in the past have changed their tune. A dozen academy security lines the perimeter of the school. More, I'm sure, behind and above. Their semi-automatics are drawn, a sure sign they're expecting trouble. But there's something different about the way they're standing, a pattern that catches my eye and nags at my memory.

"What are they doing, Jared?" Forgetting my annoyance at the True Born, the question has flown from my mouth before I can take it back.

But he surprises me by answering. "Standard military op." He nods to the front line of bodies. "Stagger lead guards with rear. If you're hit with artillery or dirty bombs, the leads will act like shields, allowing the rear to retaliate and disarm the attackers."

Margot inches her way to the front of the seat. "They're expecting another attack?"

"It's a likely scenario," Jared answers a little too cheerfully.

Fritz frowns at Jared through the rearview. They don't like it when we know things. They prefer us to exist in ignorance.

"Then why did they reopen the school?" Margot asks.

Jared turns around in his seat. "Don't you want to get smart so you can marry a rich Upper Circle jerk?" he mocks. I roll my eyes. Now his insults are just getting lazy. I can tell he's losing energy for the fight.

"I wouldn't need to be smart to do that," I murmur. I'm not sure he's heard me until he turns back around in stony silence.

Increased security is everywhere: snipers crown the tops of buildings, shops have their metal shutters down, caging them in. And everywhere I turn a painted pair of red eyes stare back at me, *Evolve or die*, written sloppily beneath the mystifying pictogram.

...

As we step out of the car and enter the house, Jared calls to me in a steely voice. "Lucy, a word."

Margot shoots me a worried look as she and Fritz melt away. But, traitor, she heads for the stairs. I send her a reassuring half smile. I can handle Jared Price, the smile says. Although whether or not that's true is another matter, I think, as I follow him into the living room.

He waits for me to enter, then saunters over to me like a predator. His eyes are green, a sure sign he's worked up.

"We're going to get a few things straight," he snarls. I nod and clasp my hands in front of me, patiently waiting for him to get to the point. It unbalances him. He stops, as though his prey has done something unusual, and tilts his head back to look at me from beneath hooded eyes. "What are you doing?"

"Looking forward to hearing what you have to say, of course," I shoot back with my most charming smile, one I've learned from my socialite mother.

Jared's low growl fills the room with menace. "You stay away from that True Born," he snipes.

"I was just about to ask him if he'd seen Fritz."

"I don't care what you were doing. You stay. Away. From. Him."

"Why?"

"He's a stranger. You don't know him. We're not a solid tribe where you can trust any one of us. He may be different, but he's not like you. And he's not going to tell you what you need to know."

How did he know? My nose twitches. I rub at it,

momentarily closing my eyes. I *had* wanted to speak to the True Born. I wanted to get friendly, perhaps even strike up an acquaintance that would allow me to throw out an awkward question or two without being rebuffed. Clearly that part of my plan won't pan out, I realize as I stare back at the moody man before me, face alight with some kind of fire. I look down at my feet as Jared's voice turns softer, almost compassionate.

"Storm and I can answer any questions you might have."

I decide to take him at his word. "When did you know you were True Born?" I fire back.

His breath hitches. "You don't waste any time, do you, Princess?" But when I just continue to stare, Jared tells me, "I always knew. Always. As far back as I can remember."

"How? How did you know?"

The dismissive shrug of his shoulders is not the answer I'm looking for. "I just—*knew*. I guess it's the same as knowing whether you like girls or boys." As I ponder that answer, Jared leans against our mother's chintz-covered sofa and crosses his arms. "And I was early for a shifter."

"What does that mean?"

"It means"—he leans closer to me—"that I changed into a panther kid and scared the pants off everyone."

"How old were you?"

"Twelve. Why do you want to know?" Jared's face clouds over. I feel a pang, imagining Jared shifting for the first time. He was so young. Just a kid, really. It makes sense now, why he's so threatened by the outside world... True Born is all he's ever really known.

"How old are most when they shift?"

"Most True Borns discover their—uh—*gifts* just past puberty. There's a reason why you all have your coming out parties at eighteen."

"Is it possible to not know, do you think?"

Jared rubs his chin, but his eyes shadow with suspicion. "I couldn't say."

"What about those born with fins and such?"

"Most of those are killed at birth."

"Oh."

"I think you should go to your room now and do your homework like a good little girl," he tells me quietly, reducing me to nothing more than a child in his care.

My eyes skate over his tousled blond locks, his shoulders covered with a ratty old sweater, his moth-eaten shirt covering what my hands remember to be a spectacular chest, pants that only accentuate powerful thighs. I wonder what draws us, because I can tell from the rapid way his chest rises and falls that, even now when he's so busy pushing me away, he's drawn to me. Memorizing me and filing me away in that mysterious brain of his. But I won't give him the satisfaction. I quickly turn and all but dash out of the room.

And me? Can I forgive myself for recalling with searing memory what it was like to be kissed by him? The memory of dancing with him, my chest pressed tight against his, haunts my dreams. I'm so aware of Jared I can tell when he walks into the house.

I try to forget his jibe about me being a little girl and head up the stairs. His eyes burn into my back as I puzzle over his answers. But I know I will turn his words over and over again as the dark claims me for sleep. And I know, equally so, that his confessions don't bring me any closer to finding out what Margot and I are.

19

I awake the next morning to a sharp rap on my door before Margot peeks her head in. "Lu? You aren't ready for school," she accuses.

Usually I am the one who shakes Margot awake after one of her marathon half-night phone sessions. But that Margot is well and truly gone, I realize as I take in my sister's pin-neat uniform, hair pulled back with a simple brown headband. Even her eyes are serious this morning.

She looks like me.

"Lu, you've got to get up."

"What's happening?"

"Father's on the phone."

I leap out of bed and race down the stairs to the phone, ignoring the fact that I'm wearing blue pajamas and my feet are bare. Father's face fills the small screen. He grips his black leather gloves impatiently. *Uh-oh.*

"Lucinda," he barks, "what are you doing in your pajamas?

Isn't today a school day?"

"Yes, Father. My alarm must have shorted. We're not late yet." I can't see much more than his head and shoulders in the screen, but it is enough to gauge the situation. He's dressed in one of his best charcoal gray suits. A violet handkerchief pokes from his suit pocket like a stiff doll. But what I notice most is his sharp and disapproving expression.

"I have already spoken to your sister," he tells me, his words loaded with meaning. "I understand that several of the True Borns are staying with us."

"Yes, Father."

"Well," he says with a sigh, "I suppose there's nothing to be done about it for the present. No matter. Your mother and I will be home next week."

"Yes, Father."

His eyes are sharp enough to cut glass. "They're behaving themselves?"

"As much as you or I," I say with honesty. Which is not to say they are necessarily behaving themselves. But our father accepts this as gospel.

"Fine. Oh, and Lucinda," he says. He rarely uses my full name, but when he does, he stretches it out like a complicated threat.

"Yes, Father?"

"Our guest will be with us. Be ready to properly welcome him." The words are as loaded as a gun.

"Of course, Father. Send us a message, and we'll be sure to have a suitable meal ready."

"Good." He reaches for a button and vanishes into a blank screen.

My heart leaps in panic. I shudder at the thought of

someone exposing us before our father's "very important" business partner… Even if that doesn't happen, how much freedom will I have to get the answers we need while we're busy entertaining this mysterious stranger?

Margot lingers at the door behind me. "Did you hear that?" I ask. She nods, her eyes clouded. I can feel throbs of panic between us. "Everything is going to be fine," I tell her with a small smile.

"Is it?" she asks with trembling lips. "Is it ever going to be fine, ever again?"

"Yes," I say confidently, stepping forward and soothing my hand through her silky brown hair. In the light of day it's streaked with red, a fiery sunrise touching rock. She doesn't believe me. I know this, accept this, even as it breaks my heart.

Torch bounces up behind Margot. "Hey, Margot, there you are," he says in an excited voice, his boyish features pink with pleasure. He comes to a crashing halt inches from her. "What's wrong?" he asks, casting a professional glance around the room. Despite how close he stands to Margot, close enough that he could whisper sweet nothings into her ear, she doesn't cringe. She's not ready to bolt. Instead, she fills the cord between us with a sweet sense of safety. *Interesting.* And I wonder how much has been transpiring right before my eyes while I've hared after the mysteries of our blood.

"Nothing's wrong." Margot turns to Torch with a carefully blank expression. "Our father called to let us know they'll be home next week."

"With *company*," I add through gritted teeth.

"Huh," Torch says, quickly hiding whatever emotion he might be experiencing.

A creeping sense of embarrassment washes over me as I

look down at my baby blue pajamas. "Well," I say with fake cheer, "I suppose I'd better get ready for school."

I'm only at the second floor landing when I barrel into Jared, who's leaning against the wall in a classic Jared pose, arms and legs crossed. He grabs my shoulders, preventing me from running away.

"Whoa. Haven't we been in this position before?"

I keep my eyes on his black shirt with its yellow and orange lettering, *Bad Kitty*. "I've got to get ready for school."

There's a teasing note in his voice as he drawls, "Yes, well, I think many a young lad would love it if you showed up in those jammies."

A smile creases Jared's eyes, sky blue this morning. He pulls on one of the thin straps of my top. My skin ignites under his calloused fingers. And maybe he notices, because he pulls back and gulps a deep breath, releasing me.

"So your mom and dad are on their way home, huh?"

"How did you—never mind." I shake my head. I know better than to ask.

"Hey, did you sleep at all last night?" He grabs my chin and forces me to look at him.

"Sure. Some."

"Want to tell me about it?"

"Not really." I glare up at him and pull my chin from his hands. My dreams are my secret, the one thing I don't even share with Margot.

But Jared just laughs. "Been dreaming of me, have you? Don't answer that. Hurry up, though. We're leaving in twenty minutes."

Besides, I think as I glide past a glaring Jared, the dream is always the same, a variation on the first. Jared and Storm flank me. The blond woman comes forward, her sightless eyes trained on me as though she sees me with some other sense. Margot screams and batters at the glass while wave after wave of bodies shatter against the gate.

I see the threads, the blond woman murmurs, over and over again. She reaches out to stroke my cheek. But last night, just as her fingers brushed my skin, her mouth opened into a round "o." She glanced down, surprised. A hook protruded from her chest. A winding river of blood flowed down her chest, trickling from her mouth as she gasped for breath, a fish pulled from water. Storm tilted his head back and roared as though he would tear the world apart.

If this is what being a True Born is, I think darkly, I would almost rather be a Splicer.

I'm testy and out of sorts as we head for gym class across the quad that spans the back of the school. The air is white, as though the sky has been eaten by a cloud, and chilly, too—almost too cold for our short-skirted gym uniforms and calf-high socks. Ten-foot fences topped with barbed wire stretch around each side of the quad, broken only by a single gate guarded by a man in an academy uniform. He holds the standard-issue semi-automatic loosely before him. They don't post many men around back, since it's far more difficult to get to and even harder to breach.

Some of the girls titter as we pass the beefy guard, his muscles flexed tight against the drab navy blue fabric of his uniform. He doesn't look our way, doesn't move an inch from his position.

A month ago Margot would have teased him mercilessly. She would have batted her eyelashes and asked if she could feel his bicep. Today she doesn't even look his way. The realization of just how much my sister has changed jars me. I take her hand and squeeze. She squeezes back, the bond between us filling and stretching with something infinite and sweet. A second later she presses two fingers into my wrist. We stop. She flicks her other finger to the fence, to a group of buildings just off the school grounds that shades the paved back alley. There stands a boy.

He's in dirty, cut-off shorts too cool for this weather. I reckon his shirt used to be white at one point, now permanently grimy, as is his face. I recognize the dark clumps of hair, the bright eyes that pierce us with the hungry, lean look of a young wolf.

"What's he doing here?" Margot whispers fiercely.

I shake my head and tug at my sister's hand. Dread washes through me, some mine, some Margot's. I force it down, swallow hard.

I glance around. The guard is still there but not paying a lick of attention to the boy. Probably thinks he's just another hungry Laster. Sometimes the kids of people who used to work for one of our families come to the school looking for handouts when things go sour. Security ignores those cases. But this isn't one of those, and there's no one outside except us girls, about ten of us in all, sashaying to the far side of the yard for a game of quadball.

He disappears. Casting my eyes around the courtyard, I see nothing amiss. The guard is still there, lazily snapping at his fingers and staring into space. I try to take a deep breath and relax as my sister and I step up to play with the other girls. But the back of my neck prickles with dread.

Something isn't right.

Not a minute later I'm distracted by the sound of fingers trailing heavily across the metal eyes of the fence with a distinct sound, like a snake's rattle. It's the boy, who comes toward us with a gleam in his eye I'd as soon call unfriendly. I move back, pulling Margot with me, but he shadows us. He keeps one hand on the fence the entire time, as though he can touch us through the metal links.

I hear Margot's indrawn breath. And a pop of shock courses through me as I stare into the hollow eyes of a dirty, smiling Preacher man.

20

Most Lasters look old before their time, especially if they're hungry a lot. This one is something else. Preacher man's face is dissected into lines that frame his mouth and eyes as he grins, slow and lazy. He wears a coarse brown poncho, cinched together with rope, that falls to calf-length. Beneath this pokes faded pants and sneakers that have seen better days. On his head is a faded orange ball cap that hides the thinning hair. But there's no mistaking this man.

Preacher men like to set themselves apart. Most go around in Old Timey black suits and white collars. This one is different, but I reckon I've known that from the first time he clapped his eyes on us.

"You know who I am." It's a question but not, said in slow, unhurried tones. I reckon we're struck mute, horrified. The boy bounces his hands off the links of the fence beside the Preacher man, annoyed. But the Preacher ignores his young sidekick to study us. "No? I'm Father Wes. So delighted to meet you ladies." He rocks back and forth on his feet.

Frantic, I look behind me. The guard doesn't move, won't even look our way. Has he been paid off? The girls are too far away now to be any use to us, too busy with their shrieks and laughs. Margot pulls my hand, a sure sign we should flee. A second later, I see them, too. Tall men. Big men. The burly one wears a white shirt as streaked with dirt as the boy's. His chest is unusually thick with muscles, his face flushed red under a cap of brown curls. The other is a dark mountain of a man, midnight skin against a brown sweater that strains across his arms and chest. He cracks his knuckles and one side of his mouth ticks up in a smile as they amble toward us...*inside* the gate.

"I reckon you want something from us, Preacher," I say, bold as daylight.

"Very perceptive of you, Miss Fox. May I call you Margot? Or Lucy?"

"No, you may not," I reply sweetly.

His head tips back to laugh, rocking again on his feet, back, forth. "Oh, I do so enjoy a fiery spirit, Miss Fox. Very well. Shall I tell you a secret?" he says in a stagey whisper and leans in to the gate. Close up I can see bloodshot streaks in his mad eyes. He reeks of corn syrup and pure alcohol and B.O.

And we're trapped. We have nowhere to run.

"How do you know who we are? What do you want from us?"

Father Wes raises his arms wide. "Same as everybody! I want to *evolve*, ladies."

Evolve or die. The words shiver through me. But now the simple phrase is packed with a whole new significance. "I don't see how we can help you with that, sir, and we'd like to be on our way."

He chuckles for an answer. "Oh, now, you're going to make me give away my secrets for free. Although, I reckon I'm a bit surprised no one has told you."

Margot twitches. Her panic makes it hard for either of us to concentrate. I close my eyes for an all-important second, willing myself to relax before I speak again.

"Why don't you say, then?"

He chuckles again, telegraphing something to the men who halt a foot behind us. "I reckon I owe you that. Before the Plague I used to be a mechanic. Did you know that, Misses Fox? Used to build all sorts of things. Machines to clean things, machines to make life easier. Cars. Engines. Then the Plague came and took my family. My wife, two of my sons. And I fell into despair." Father Wes bows his head, his fists clenched.

Beside him, his boy remains unblinking, unmoving. More how I expect one of the lost ones to act. Father Wes, on the other hand, is like one of those preachers you sometimes see on the Feed. Preachers with a crowd of Lasters at their feet, everyone looking for the same miraculous cure the preacher is hocking.

"Then I was visited by the Almighty," Father Wes continues. "He came to me in a vision, He did, and He told me to visit a witch, a very special witch who had something important to tell me. So I used up the last of my money to find this witch. I bribed everybody I came across to give her away. Eventually I found her. Sweet little thing. And she did indeed have something to tell me." Father Wes hooks his fingers through the metal links. His eyes blaze with a ferocious light.

Fear makes my voice gravelly and odd. "What, then? Since you'll make us listen anyway."

"She told me there were children to be born. Two children, born of one skin, one flesh. A door and its threshold. Special children in a world where children would be special."

Margot and I share a sidelong glance. "You mean us."

"I do."

"What's so special about us?"

Preacher man smiles like a crocodile. "These children will be our salvation, the witch says to me. Our way forward out of the Plague that had struck us down. Once the Plague has purged the world of evil men these children would be revealed in the light of the Almighty. Says we can draw a path to the future with their blood. For blood is the answer, blood is the divine holy river, the Flood that shall deliver us."

It's in the blood. Evolve or die.

"How do you know it's us?" Margot pipes up. The preacher man scrunches up his face like he's hearing bird song. She clears her throat and starts again, more loudly. "How do you know this story is about us? There must be hundreds of twins in the world. I reckon it's a little too easy to think your mystery twins are going to be right here in Dominion, don't you?" Margot looks to me.

My head bobs in agreement. "Right. Absolutely."

"You're questioning the workings of the Divine?" Father Wes leans in, his voice rising. "You're questioning the Almighty?"

"N-no." Margot retreats but ends up in the belly of the mountain man. She shrieks and tries to bolt but he grabs her shoulder. His fingers dig into her flesh with one hand, and with the other he circles her neck, cutting off her oxygen.

"Stop it, you're hurting her!" I scream. Margot's face flushes red. I claw at his arms with one hand and pluck at the invisible arm that chokes at my windpipe with the other. Sparks dance across my eyes, the brightness that comes before the darkness. I cling to consciousness by a thread.

And through the fog I hear the Preacher man's cackle. "You're right, of course," he drawls. "But the Almighty likes it when we try to figure things out for ourselves."

A shadow turns the air cold. I barely see the knife as the burly man slashes a long line down my forearm. It takes a second before the stinging takes root, like a nightmare you can't claw your way out from. Father Wes says something, but I can't hear him through the blood pounding in my ears. The air stirs with the scent of my blood, which drips carelessly to the ground. Burly man fiddles with a little vial to collect drops. I have enough sense to roll over, using my other hand to put pressure on the wound.

A low growl shakes the air from behind the two men. Our breath comes back in a rush as mountain man releases Margot and steps away from me. We both sprawl on the ground, which is how I catch a glimpse of the monster behind our would-be captors.

This time there's no pretense of the human. They've been gone such a long time all I have to go on is half-forgotten books. But Jared is what he is: a panther on human legs. Thick black fur sprouts over ears that lay almost flat back on his head. His face is symmetrical and perfect, the long, flat bridge of his nose ending in a perfect snarl and long whiskers. The unearthly green eyes never leave his prey as he crouches on two legs. His hands are wicked claws, his arms coated in a fine mat of hair that looks soft to the touch. But there's no doubt: this man-beast, at least seven feet tall, is going to kill today.

He screams and the air rips to shreds. Jared wouldn't hurt us intentionally, but it wouldn't hurt to get out of his way. I reach over and tap Margot's leg, willing her to run. She stirs, eyes opening with a dreamy expression as she rolls over and takes Jared in.

One-handed, I drag Margot a foot before she catches on a rock. Something rips, probably her tall sock, and she leaves behind a smear of red. From this vantage point it's easier to track what's happening: Jared remains still as a picture in a low crouch. Burly man considers him like he's an interesting bug. Then mountain man reaches into the waistband of his black pants and pulls out something shiny.

"Jared, gun!" It's all I have time to yell before the air crackles with gunfire. I look to see if Jared has been hit, but he's not there any longer. My head swivels frantically, searching for him even as I yank at Margot's arm. At least the shot seems to wake her up a bit. Margot grabs at her head and pulls her legs in to her chest. Progress.

Preacher man and his boy stand there, grim faced, as mountain man waves his pistol around. "You missed, moron," Preacher man spits. "Did you get the samples?" The guard has vanished from his post. I can't see the other girls, either.

In the next heartbeat hell breaks loose. Jared lands on mountain man with a satisfying *thwump*. They tumble down in a pile of black on black, rolling on top of one another. The gun goes skittering across the pavement. I don't realize Margot has seen it, too, until she pinches her cheek, and I follow her eyes to the little black object. *Would it be so hard?* her eyes plead. Burly raises an enormous foot and stomps on the tangled heap of men. A masculine cry is followed by a string of swear words I've never heard before. Out of the corner of my eye, Margot shifts and stretches out as though she's injured. Stretches again.

I have my eyes on the men, so I am surprised as anyone when a pair of feathered legs appear before me. I blink.

"Who let you in here?" I slur at the figure I wish I'd never set eyes on again.

It's the falcon man from Senator Kain's party. He stares down at Margot's body with huge, glassy eyes. In daylight his nose is so narrow and hooked I wonder how he can breathe. He raises his arms. Soft-looking feathered wings trailing beneath skinny biceps that I know are far stronger than they appear. He looks like he's going to jump. His feathered legs end in electric blue running shoes with fluorescent yellow stripes on the side. In the blink of an eye he cracks one into Burly's chest, knocking the man a good five feet away. A huge red wet spot appears on Burly's white shirt. For a moment I think he's been shot until I take in the shattered glass lying on the pavement. Good, I think to myself. Preacher man will not get his sample today. Burly shakes off the hit and slowly sits up. Blood spurts from a massive gash over his eye, his nose, a cut on his lip. Margot moves again and stops.

A shadow towers over us. My eyes travel up the lightweight, severe suit, the unruly ends of non-descript brown hair and a black silk eye patch. Standing with one foot on the gun. And a hair's breadth from Margot's fingers.

"And just what do you think you're doing?" Richardson says to Margot with a slight upturn of his lip. The falcon man has knocked Burly down again, whose neck now cricks at a sickening angle. Then the birdman turns his attention on Jared and the midnight man. I reckon the Preacher and his boy saw which way the wind was blowing, because they seem to have melted away. Richardson picks up the gun and fires it between his falcon man's arms and legs.

He doesn't care, I realize. He'll hit them all. Making a split second decision, I rush at Richardson and hang off his other arm, but I'm too late. A grunt, then two, as the gun explodes. Richardson shakes me loose, and I fall. My screams echo through the yard like they've come from someone else.

Falcon man drags the corpse of the human mountain off Jared's stunned form. I'm preoccupied, watching for the telltale heave of Jared's chest, so I'm taken by surprise when Richardson grabs my arms and pulls me to my feet.

"Don't fight, Miss Fox," he murmurs hotly in my ear. "We're not here to hurt you."

A burst of light fills my peripheral vision. Richardson and I both turn. Five feet away, Torch melts through the metal links of the fence as though they're made of ice. As he steps through the burned fence into the melee he shimmers like a mirage in the late afternoon sun. Scorched links poke through his clenched fists like brass knuckles. He swings one of these at the falcon man, who steps back from the black-clad corpse. Torch grabs one of the man's feathered wings. Falcon man shrieks something inhuman and tries to pull away. The stench of scorched feathers gathers in my nose. A section of falcon man's wing falls away in Torch's grasp.

Richardson keeps me in a painful grip with one hand and raises the gun calmly at Torch with the other. As Richardson pulls the trigger I grab for his arm but I'm too late. The bullet goes wide. Richardson fires again, again. Torch runs and leaps at us, dropping into a crouch as he makes impact. He kicks the legs right out from under us. I tumble to the side as Richardson drops and snaps into a crouch like a world-class merc.

"Walk away or you die," Richardson tells Torch in a flinty voice.

"Go ahead. I've got backup," Torch replies with a smirk.

I can't tell if he's bluffing or not, but right about now I long to see Mohawk's zebra stripes kicking ass. Shouts echo from a distance. I hear the tattoo of shoes on concrete. Swat? Security? Richardson curses. He picks up his scorched birdman with one arm and shoots at Torch once more for good measure as he backs through the deserted sentry gate.

For just a moment we are alone in the quad. Jared lies, half naked and bleeding, in a pool of blood next to a black-clad corpse. Torch drops next to Margot, who has curled up in a ball and is sobbing. And then we are surrounded by riot gear: faceless visors and semi-automatics, nozzles beaded on us. The buzz and whirr of helicopters fills the air.

Torch raises his hands above his head as he winks at Margot. "I tripped security on my way over," he tells us. "*All* of it."

21

We ride back in Storm's shiny black van, splattered with Jared's blood. It slips over my fingers as he lays with his chalk white head in my lap. I run sticky fingers through his blond hair, his and my blood all over everything, until he lifts a corner of his mouth and smiles smugly up at me.

Seconds before he passes out, he whispers, "Knew you had a thing for me."

Back at Storm's tower they run Jared into a small room I've never seen before. For a long time I pace the floor. When I feel woozy, I sit on the bench outside and watch the door. Every few minutes I think I see the doorknob turn. No one comes out. I have too much time to think but not enough room inside me to do so. Someone comes by with a fresh compress for my arm. The bleeding has almost stopped, just a thin trickle on a razor straight line. The pain sets my teeth on edge.

Father Wes's words haunt me. *In the blood. Evolve or die.*

Rumors of blood cults have been around for ages. Around the school we couldn't help but hear the gossip; girls who swore they knew preachers who'd overcome the Plague, men with followers.

What do you call a Laster who survives? the joke goes.

A rich man.

Sometimes survivors sell their blood in little vials strung around necks like talismans. Sometimes they'll sell bits of braided hair to be worn in sachets next to their skin. *Do you know how much salvation costs?* we heard Sally Morgan screech one day as she produced one of these supposedly magic vials between her pale, skinny fingers.

Sally Morgan didn't make it to twenty.

This is different. Father Wes isn't selling salvation from his own skin. I'm not even sure he's peddling salvation. Father Wes has something more dangerous to sell to the rabble: *prophecy.* But where I'm still foggy is how it could have anything to do with Margot and me.

My mind snags on the painted circles that have been popping up with all the graffiti. One circle intersecting with another, red as blood. Crossed eyes. *Watchers*, Kira called the preachers' cult. And what are they watching for? It's unthinkable but the words whisper and twist through my fried brain anyhow. *They're looking for us.* Twins. Joined twins. Sisters who once shared a single cell, blood, DNA.

Shared one egg, one cell, until we started to split. Like two circles slowly coming apart.

I crouch over my knees, trying to gulp in air that won't come. But this time I can't blame my sister. This time the panic is all mine as I realize I've stumbled upon what I've been searching for: the truth.

An hour later Dorian Raines comes out of the room, Storm a thundercloud in her wake. He disappears, but she stays to stare over me, hands on hips, as though deciding something before she speaks. Her mouth has become a severe line, her springy curls frizz all around her head, hell-bent on escape.

But she's gentle when she finally speaks. "He won't rest until he knows you're all right." She nods toward the door. "But at the moment I'm more worried about you." She tucks my chin in her fingers and examines me. "You look like you've been hit by a car. Has someone looked after that cut?"

"I think the bleeding has stopped."

"Well, let's clean it up before you go in there. And what's this?" She tilts my head. "Looks like someone backhanded you." I'd forgotten falling to the pavement when Torch jumped Richardson. No wonder my face felt like concrete. She eyes my cheek with professional scrutiny. "Make sure you get some ice on that as soon as you're done in there. And don't stay longer than ten minutes on pain of death."

I nod as she patches me up right there in the hallway, and then I slip, quiet-quiet, through the door.

The room smells of blood. Tangy, iron, overwhelming. I want to open the window, but I don't want Jared to get cold. He's shirtless, probably pantless, too, I gather from the white sheet and comforter pulled up over his legs. His left shoulder and ribs are bandaged, red fading through the white, like death warmed over.

The patient cracks an eye open as I approach the bed. His chest rises with a deep inhale. "Thought I smelled you," he says.

"Somehow that can't be a compliment," I mutter.

"C'mere." I approach the bed. "Closer," he growls, "I'm not going to bite you." His forehead puckers into a frown. "Someone put their hands on you." His hunter's eyes sweep over me and harden. My hand flies automatically to my cheek as he spies the bruise. Color floods back into his face. "She told me you weren't hurt."

"I'm not. I'm not hurt." I shake my head. "Not really."

"Margot?"

I shake my head. "She's fine. She's with Torch. Malcolm."

Jared relaxes a fraction and studies me. His fingers trail over the bandage that runs from my wrist to my elbow. "But you're not. Not really. Liar." I open my mouth to say something, anything to let him rest easy, but I can't. Sobs break from me like a sudden storm. I stuff a hand in my mouth and turn away. "Hey, now. Lucy. Lucy, look at me, dammit, because I can barely move."

I don't know why I'm crying. Maybe it has something to do with the image of his pale lifeless face I can't seem to scrub from my mind. Or that helpless feeling I can't shake—we were swatted around like bugs out in the schoolyard. Maybe it's the stress of knowing there are more than one group of people trying to get to Margot and me, for whatever reason, and the lengths they'll go to get what they want. Life has always been cheap in Dominion City. That doesn't mean I can live with being responsible for anyone's death.

Most of all, admits a small voice inside me, *I can't bear the True Born beside me being hurt.*

I take a deep breath and wipe my eyes with the backs of my grimy hands before I turn back to Jared. I'd not bothered to wash or change, and I'm still covered in the schoolyard, patches of me soaked in Jared's blood.

"Are you going to be all right?" I whisper when I've finally got myself under control again.

"Me? Hell, yes," he grumps. A shock of blond hair falls over his eye. My fingers itch to smooth it away and watch it fall again. He doesn't move to touch me but I can feel his attention, like tiny caresses, everywhere on me. "Do you have any idea how hard it is to kill some of us?"

I clasp my hands tightly in front of me. "Have you come close?"

He stares at me, blinking slowly before answering with a shudder. "Only once, but it wasn't by violence. I told you that story. Here, sit down before you fall down." Jared scoots over on the bed, wincing. I perch beside him, my hip pressing against his. Instant warmth floods me. Bits of stress fall away from me like raindrops.

"Do you know how I came to live with Storm?" I shake my head and stare at him solemnly. It isn't the first time I've wondered at their history. The only person in this world Jared seems to respect is Nolan Storm. And after what he told me he went through, I'd as soon say Jared doesn't come by trust easily. "I come from a Laster family." My mouth falls open. "Surprised? Yeah, so were we. Especially when my father and two of my brothers came down with the Plague while I started sprouting fur."

"Oh. What happened?"

"Mom went crazy when my dad and Keiran died. She and her relatives decided I was a devil. They decided to burn me out of the house."

"I don't understand."

"They set fire to my bedroom. With me inside, sleeping." Gripped with nausea, I hold my stomach and lean forward. "Hey, you're not going to faint, are you?" Jared eyes me with concern.

"How could—how could—" I sputter.

"Someone put it in their heads that it would cleanse the family line. Like it was a curse that could be lifted. Don't worry, my mother made sure my other brother and sisters got out before the house went up."

"You think that's what would worry me?" A faint blush creeps over Jared's cheeks that I decide to ignore. "How did you get out?"

"They hadn't yet figured out that I had skills other than growing fur. I busted the window and made a three-story jump."

"Did you—were you hurt?"

"Cuts, mostly. Then I lived on the streets for a spell. Like I told you, most of the kid gangs are Lasters, you know. Won't take True Borns. I wasn't very good at living on the streets. Maybe the True Born in me is a pack animal. I got sick. I was starving to death. And then I was fighting in the rings. When I escaped, I came across some Laster who'd seen me fight. He brought me to Storm."

"Jared," I start to tell him I'm sorry but he cuts me off.

"Don't ruin it. Don't say a damn word. Just let me figure out that you're okay."

Despite myself I smile as Jared's arms wrap tighter around me.

"You smell awful," he tells me crankily. "Take a shower or something, would you? I can't stand smelling that guy's hands on you."

"It was the man from Senator Kain's party," I muse aloud. "Do you remember him? He and his bird friend tried to take me there. This time he said he wasn't there to hurt us. How do you think he knows when and where to show up?"

Green fires over Jared's eyes as he glares. "That's a question I'd like answered, too. Hand me my shirt," he says, scooting me off the bed.

"Where are you going?"

"I need to talk to Storm."

"Wait a second," I argue. "You can't get out of bed."

Jared grits his teeth at me as he pulls his legs down off the bed so I'm standing between them. "Princess," he says, "do you have any idea how quickly a True Born like me can get over a little bullet hole? Hand me my shirt."

I wonder whether now would be a good time to break the other news. "There's something else." I try not to let my eyes wander over his very naked, very sculpted chest as I hand over his shirt. He drapes it over his injured shoulder. I help him with the other side, my fingers brushing the hot flesh of his chest and shoulder. "Um," I start, distracted. "We need to find a witch."

Of course, there had always been the Plague stories: the witch who threw out a curse at the lover who spurned her, causing the first case of the Plague. The old lady who walked around pointing at everyone who was going to catch it. I'd always been particularly creeped out by that story. It sounded a little too much like me. I used to lie in bed at night and wonder if I was a witch, too. And that would be bad.

They burn the old lady in the story.

But for my family, the real tragedy would be that our father would not present me to society. He'd never be able to marry me to one of his associates. I would be cast off and alone. As if I was a True Born.

So when we met a real witch I was stunned. It was at Bettina Ford's thirteenth birthday party. After the games and spun sugar cakes, Bettina's mother brought a tall, dark-haired woman into the chaos of the party room. In among striped helium balloons and curly pink streamers that tickled you from the roof, the witch stood out in a dark cloak that covered her from head to foot.

Her beautiful dark eyes cast around the room and landed on us sisters for a second too long, then swept back. We thought nothing of it at the time. We were used to people staring at us, so close to mirror images in matching burgundy dresses.

"You." She pointed at Bettina, and had her sit down. All the other girls sat down around her. The witch pulled Bettina's hand from her lap. She ran a long finger across Bettina's skin as she said things about what Bettina liked, what she didn't like, what would happen on her vacation later that year. Bettina's white-blond hair fell around her face as she stared, enraptured, at her own palm. At the end of the reading the woman's dark eyes fluttered with tears. She pressed a small gold coin none of us recognized into Bettina's hand and said very softly, "This will help you when the vacation comes to a sticky end." The witch read for a bunch of the other girls, but neither Margot nor I approached her, and for her part, the witch avoided making eye contact with us again.

The Ford family was on vacation in Rome when the Plague hit them. It was odd, but sometimes it strikes a whole family at once. It ate through Bettina's family with its diamond teeth, leaving her for last. She ended up wandering the streets alone, sick. She had nothing but the coin the witch had given her—an old, old Romany coin—which was just enough to pay for the hospice where she died two days later.

I push the story of Bettina Ford to the back of my mind as I tell Storm and Jared what the Preacher man had said.

When I finish, Storm hits a button I can't see on the wall nearest the door. "Alma?"

"Yes, Storm."

"Can you please bring Torch and Margot in here?"

"Of course."

"Lucy, sit down, please. You'll do no good to anyone if you're not healthy."

"I don't want to si—"

"Sit," he commands before eyeing Jared. "You, too." Jared sits beside me, gingerly sliding back into the cushion. His heat surrounds me, vital and close.

Storm paces the room like a restless stag. In the glass reflection, his horns knot into a thick and heavy crown.

Eyes drooping with exhaustion, Jared adds, "Someone's got to be tipping them off."

"Not necessarily. At least, whoever is sharing information doesn't necessarily have to be a True Born." Storm pours himself a glass of water from the standing bar. "Who is in a better position to know where you are? The preachers' people are everywhere. They are on the streets. They camp outside your house. He has a thousand spies, all of whom are desperate." I consider that for a moment. Silent, pinch-faced Lasters, peering into our father's car from their parked car hotels. Scavenging near the gates while our mercs train their guns and shoo them away. Camping in the bins near Grayguard…where clearly the guards can be paid off.

"Everyone would know to look for us at school," I throw in.

Storm nods, the frown spreading down the corners of his mouth. "Exactly. And could follow you easily from your home."

Jared's voice cuts through my terror. "And now Father Wes knows he has True Born tails."

"Are they? True Borns?"

"I don't know. Did you get a good whiff, Jared?"

Jared winces and shakes his head. "They were too far away when they shot me."

"If they are?"

"If they are…we're in an even bigger mess than we thought."

I ponder this. "What kind of mess?" I ask. As a shiver of fear crawls up my spine and a shadow of fear takes root in my heart, I'm fairly certain I'm not going to like the reason why the man with one eye and his owl friend are following us.

22

Margot sucks in her breath. "They're back early."

Our house is bathed in a brilliant yellow glow, windows glowing like fireflies winking through the darkness of the city. It still looks cold. I grab for Margot's fingers. Fritz swings his semi-automatic onto his back and reaches out to shake Jared's hand.

"Misses." Fritz nods at us. "Your parents haff arrived home ahead of schedule with an important guest."

"Of course. We'll go in through the side door and get cleaned up before greeting them," I say smoothly as I eye our bodyguards. Just like that, as though I've flicked a switch, I am back on again, doing my duty. It's exhausting, but strangely welcome. Jared still looks pale, but his jaw is clenched with determination. I sigh, realizing they won't go anywhere without a fight. "Fritz," I add, "could you please entertain Jared and Torch in the guard room until we're able to present them to our parents?"

"Of course, Miss Lucy." Fritz nods and indicates with the thrust of his neck to follow him. I meet Jared's glare head on. Panic buzzes from Margot. But there's nothing I can do, and we all know it.

We arrive downstairs twenty minutes later, greeted by the sound of strings, the clinking of glass. I reckon they've pulled out the good crystal. Cut glass etched with fine patterns, made from the hands of the world's greatest artisans. *Crystal worth more than your lives*, our mother likes to say.

We stop at the threshold to perform our usual look-over. Margot has thrown on head-to-toe black, a long sweeping arc of black that makes her gray-green eyes pop out. She's swept and pinned her hair to one side. I've robed myself in a conservative, tailored charcoal gray with pinstripes. Just the sort of thing our parents will approve of. Margot plasters a bright, fake smile on her generous lips as we cross the threshold into our parents' world.

"Ah, there you are," our father says. "Your mother and I were beginning to despair." The words are light but the accompanying frown tells us we are in disgrace.

"Our apologies, Father." Margot reaches out to give our father a kiss on both cheeks before crossing to embrace our mother on the other side of the living room. I take my turn, noting the extra security, strapped with big guns and bad attitudes, positioned on either end of the room.

"Girls," our father breaks in while I fill my nose with our mother's expensive perfume, "I want to introduce you to Mr. Leo Aleksandrovich Resnikov. Mr. Resnikov will be our guest for the next few weeks as we hammer out the final details of an important business deal."

Margot and I curtsy to the figure we have already glimpsed

sitting in the wingback chair, our father's favorite. But when he stands with a mocking smile, my heart stops.

Not Richardson, my scrambling mind tells me. But near enough to be kissing cousins. This man is as tall, shoulders sculpted in the severely tailored black suit and white shirt. His bow tie has come undone and hangs limply on both sides of his collar. Our mother must itch to retie it, I think as I study him. His hair is longer than the other man's, streaked with a distinguished gray at his temples, just a bit messy. But where Richardson has an eye patch, this man, Leo Resnikov is intact.

Leo Aleksandrovich Resnikov bends into a slight military-style bow. His eyes rake over first Margot, then me, with a proprietary gaze. "I see you did not lie, Fox. Your daughters are as beautiful as you claimed." Our mother gives her guest a tight smile and gestures to one of the maids, who wordlessly fixes us the drinks our father prefers we enjoy on such occasions. "And how interesting," he continues, gazing at us in rapt fascination, "to have such identical beings in your care." He comes closer, folding the cigar he holds in one hand behind his back as he walks around us. The maid hands us our drinks and disappears.

"They're good girls," our father returns. His words drip with layer upon layer of innuendo. I briefly seek Margot out. She meets my gaze with a shuttered look of her own before we both look away. We're in trouble.

"Father," I say, clearing my throat. "A party from our remote security team is here to give you a report."

"They can give their report in the morning," our father says with a dismissive wave of his fingers.

"Yes, Father, but they are here now. Would you like them to spend the night in the guardhouse?"

Our father's eyes glitter unhappily. "I see no reason for us to put them up for the night. I will see to them in a while."

I nod, knowing better than to say anything further. Margot seats herself beside our mother on the white sofa. I stand behind and drape a hand on Margot's shoulder, feel her heart slow.

"Quite remarkable," our guest continues. "How do people tell them apart?" he says as though we are not in the room.

"On the contrary, Mr. Resnikov," I boldly say, "we are quite different." As different as Resnikov and Richardson, at the very least.

Our mother clears her throat and fingers the elegant diamond choker around her elegant neck. I am to consider myself warned. When I hear Fritz arguing with Jared all the way down the hallway, I can't decide if I'm delighted or terrified. Then he appears, grim and unhappy, at the arched doorway. At least he's wearing a shirt, I think to myself, even if it does have blood spatters all over it.

"Mr. Fox," he calls out, "we need to discuss some urgent security matters."

Our father meets Jared in the hallway. Leo Resnikov takes it all in, papering over the embarrassing incident in the hallway with conversation and a wave of his elegant and manicured hand. Still, the occasional punch of voices tells us that Father and Jared are having *words*. Father returns a few minutes later, eyes glassy with anger. He reaches for his leather gloves, waiting for him on the mantle, and squeezes the life out of them as he sits back down.

"Lucy? A moment please," drifts a strangled voice from the hallway. I remain rooted to the spot, our father's eyes locking on mine. "Lucy?" Jared says again. I take a single step.

My father's hands are on my shoulders before I've made it halfway across the room. I have never seen him so furious. "You will stay exactly where you are. And that man," he enunciates slowly, as though he's chewing, "will never step foot in this house again. Is that understood?"

I frown down at my shoes. "Yes, Father."

A moment later I hear Fritz's voice again. I half expect Jared to appear at the door covered in fur and bristling with bloody blue anger. Wisely, he doesn't. Their voices drift away, down the corridor to the front door. An engine turns over. Wheels screech as a car speeds away, and Jared with it.

The rest of the party ignores the scene like nothing at all has happened. Our mother prattles away about our impending Reveal while Resnikov reels off question after question. But Margot taps at her thigh to draw my attention. Her eyes are dark, hooded, filled with an unnamable dread I'd as soon say mirrors my own.

"Do you think they'll find her?" Margot asks me. It's late. The city has dulled to a quiet hum. A breeze ripples through the floating curtains of her bed where we snuggle together, two peas in a pod.

"Who? The witch? I don't know," I murmur. This particular witch could be anywhere. She could have been eaten by the Plague. Or like the goners, she could have just packed up and left.

Silence wraps around us, making us feel almost alone in the world. "Do you think we'll ever see them again?" I can tell how much it costs her to ask me.

I stroke her hair, her cheek. "Of course we will." She doesn't ask how I know. "Picture," I say, starting one of our oldest games.

Margot taps her bottom lip with a finger. "Mmm, hot sandy beach, waves that go on forever. Cotton candy clouds." I smile at her choice of perfect memories, pictures we would like to press ourselves into. She turns to me. "Picture."

But as I stare into my sister's eyes, I realize there is really only one picture worth playing for.

"Pile of corpses. Our enemies strewn in the streets. Jared and Torch and Mohawk beside us. Nolan Storm standing on top of the pile of bones wearing Dominion's crown."

Margot's quick intake of breath is horror-filled. "Why would you say that?"

"I'm tired of being hunted. Aren't you?"

"Yes, but Lucy," she pleads.

"Go to sleep, Margot," I say, quiet-quiet, brushing my fingers through her hair. "I'll watch over you tonight."

Tap, tap, tap. Not at Margot's garden door but mine. I lay still, listen carefully to its unfamiliar rhythm before gathering myself from Margot's bed and heading to my room. A dark silhouette fills the glass. My heart knocks in my chest like a fist, in time with the rapping. I think about pretending I don't hear him. But for all I know he can see me. He can probably smell me through the glass. From the darkness a pair of indigo eyes wink owlishly.

I cross the room to open the door. "What are you doing here?"

He listens at the threshold before stepping in and closing the door behind him. "What do you think I'm doing?" he growls.

Something brought him to my bedroom door, but now he seems unsure of himself. I can almost see him sifting through the scents in the room, shoulders relaxing by degrees as he casts furtive looks in all the shadowy areas.

"You look better," I say, hoping my relief isn't too obvious.

"You smell better." He grins and flips a lock of his hair. The casual, laid-back Jared is back.

"So," I say, "you made quite an impression on our father tonight." I move over to the bedside table and switch on the rose-colored lamp.

"Turn it off. It might bring attention." His voice is so quiet it's as though it floats through the air on a string.

I switch the lamp off again. "How did you get in here, anyway?"

"I'm going to have to talk to Shane about your father's security measures. They're paltry."

"Says the cat."

"Yeah"—his eyes rake over me—"says the cat." It's then I realize that the silence following his words isn't just awkward. Jared is *listening*.

"What are you listening for?"

"Is your father always such a peach?" He grabs my arms and maneuvers me over to the bed. I sit down while Jared stands over me.

"No, sometimes he's even peachier."

Jared snorts. "Funny."

"You didn't answer my question. What are you doing here at—three in the morning?" I wince at my bedside clock. Jared rubs his nose like it hurts. "Did you break in so you could tell me my parents have issues? Because—Feedflash—I already know."

"Lucy…" Jared sighs and crouches before me. His glittering green cat's eyes slowly travel up my pajama-clad body. They rest here and there, frustrated and slightly lost, on my thighs, my breasts, my shoulders. "Look, your father made it perfectly clear he expects me to stay away from you two. And he'll probably fire Storm before he'll listen to details of the attack. I—couldn't just leave and let you think I'd abandoned you."

It's not the confession I expect. As I stare down into the shadowy planes of his too handsome face I wonder if he is just as taken aback. "So…what's the plan? Storm has a plan, right? Because frankly, I'm flat out of leads to follow on my own."

The familiar Jared—jerky Jared—resurfaces. He pats a patronizing hand on my knee but forgets to remove it, where it burns a slow hole through me and heats my blood. "Sure." He snorts. "You won't see us, but we'll see you."

"Jared." I move my hand so it sits on top of his. "You didn't see the man in the living room, did you?"

A dozen expressions flit over his face. "No," he says cautiously.

I lean down slowly and curl a protective hand around his ear before whispering. "It's like he's Richardson's twin, Jared. Tell Storm his name is Leo Resnikov. He's up to something. Something weird is going on and…I'm scared." Jared doesn't move away, not at first. He clenches his fingers around my knee, his back stiff and straight. When his feral eyes meet mine, I'm taken by surprise at the heat burning through them. "Don't leave us," I plead, clawing at his hand.

Jared's clothes blend in with the darkness of the room so I almost don't see him move when he cups my cheeks. For a fiery second his lips meet mine, fierce, hungry. He rests his forehead against mine and draws long hauls of air into his lungs. I can't tell if he's trying to control his temper or to bathe in my scent.

I almost don't recognize him when he sits back on his heels. The lines of his face have become sharper, longer, the nose short and soft. His words are slightly muddled, as though he's drunk. "I got you," he pledges, sharp teeth punctuating each syllable. Jared tips his head back and snarls once, a grumpy kitten more than a terrifying panther, before sailing out the balcony door.

23

"Don't be a bore. Play something uplifting," our mother tells Margot in a tight voice. Then she turns her attention to me. "Lucy," she hisses. "Do that song you used to do with your sister."

As I join my sister at the piano, I feel her heaviness, like a rain cloud about to burst. Margot opens with a soft chord. I follow. At least singing gives me a chance to take in the elaborate scene being played out before us. The room is a giant stage, with the piano and us girls as its centerpiece. Candles flicker romantically from sconces, chandelier lit low, throwing prisms onto the faces of the guests: Senator and Mary Kain to the far side of the room. Betts Gallagher and her husband George seated behind them. Some of our father's other business associates. A diplomat from France. And the smirking, amused Leo Resnikov.

His eyes follow us everywhere, as though those eyes have bought and sold us a dozen times over. I can tell from the way

Mary Kain flirts with him that people think he's handsome. Maybe it's the long face with the dimples, the sandy, boyish hair. Still, underneath his tailored black tie, I'd as soon call him a wolf.

When the polite spattering of applause for our performance dies down, I overhear our mother speaking with Betts Gallagher. "Of course, due to the timing we'll keep it small—a hundred or so. But I think the intimacy will make it feel a little more exclusive."

Our Reveal party. It's all our mother has spoken about since she returned. The plans are "shaping up nicely," she tells everyone within range. "Everyone will just die with envy," she says. Beside me, Margot mouths, *or just die*.

Betts leans over, her signature red sequins falling away from her ample bosom as she tells our mother in a dramatic whisper, "It's all anyone can talk about. It will be the party of the year." I listen to them prattle on with half an ear, the other half watching the wolf work the guests across the room. I'm so caught up in the game, I almost miss what passes between the ladies. "He'll play escort to one of the girls, of course. But I'm leaving it up to him which," our mother drawls. "A month ago I would have been sure he'd pick Margot, but she's been so withdrawn lately." Betts *tsks*, the sequins across her bosom swaying back and forth like a pendulum as she shakes her head. "Lucy isn't as adventurous as her sister, but she has a certain edge about her these days that I think appeals to Russian aristocracy."

As Betts bobs her head in agreement and gulps down her drink, I finally comprehend something of the larger picture. Resnikov is to be the guest of honor at our Reveal party, not us. It's a showpiece for *him*. What I don't yet know is *why*. A month ago I would have been offended that my parents were giving Margot and my special day to a stranger. Now, though, I just want answers. Our parents have never let someone else choose who will be our escorts. Leo Resnikov has a kind of power over them I've never seen before.

A ripple in the room alerts me to a visitor. A woman in a long white trench coat stands at the threshold of the living room, flanked by an embarrassed Shane. Her frizzy nest of hair has been pulled into a tall bun. It makes her look even more severe, with a long neck and a gaze that fastens on you like she's just pulled a gun. Those eyes bead on my sister, then me. There's a message in them as she argues with our father, who has appeared out of nowhere to "deal" with our unwelcome guest. I meet Margot's eyes. My sister is near the fireplace—too far to be of any help. And of course, she is trapped in conversation with Resnikov.

Snippets of their conversation drift over to me as I draw near. "Sir." Dorian Raines pulls herself up and stares our father down, no easy task. "I will tell you one more time. I am here to see your daughters on medical authority. I am not at liberty to discuss it with you. By right of Section 3. 4.1 of the Health Code—"

"Surely you're not invoking the Code in my home. With all my guests here." Our father's voice cuts through, silk underlaid with steel. If she had any sense at all, Dorian Raines would turn and run.

"I'm merely here to seek out a moment with your daughters. Alone."

It's too late. The damage is done—not that I think he ever would have let her speak to us anyhow. The Health Code was something they dreamed up when the Plague came, like writing a eulogy for a funeral that has already taken place. It was supposed to create a Protocol for handling the illness. What it did was, it gave doctors, especially geneticists, unprecedented authority for dealing with the ins and outs of the disease.

It should have protected her. Had Dorian invoked the Code in any other household, in any other situation, people would have bent over backward to accommodate her.

But this is the Upper Circle. And here our father is king. The last thing the king will put up with is a threat to his authority. And I've done the unthinkable: gone outside his boundaries and seen a doctor not on his payroll. Worse, she's exposing us in front of our father's business associate.

"Dr. Raines." I sweep in and grab one of her hands. She's cold, shaking with rage. "I'm so glad you found the place."

She stares at me for a long second before I see the shift behind her eyes. "Lucy, how good of you to greet me. I think there's been some misunderstanding. Your father says I don't have an appointment."

And with that one little line, she overplays our hand. "Dr. Raines will simply have to make another appointment." Our father's smile tightens like a noose as my stomach sinks. "You'll call her office in the morning and set something up, won't you?" Meaning, of course, never. He waves a dismissive hand at the doctor, which signals a new man sporting a merc-style buzz cut and oversized muscles, to step behind her as Shane melts away.

"I'll just escort Dr. Raines to the door, shall I?" Murder is written in our father's eyes. The merc trails us, but for the next minute and a half, I have Dorian Raines to myself.

"Lucy," she starts.

I shake my head and cut her off. With a smile that might not look too frozen, I ask, "Storm sent you?"

But Dorian's blue eyes are startled. "Not exactly."

"Did they find the witch?" The door is too close. I slow down, pretending to show Dorian the lintels and the sconces. Buzz cut stops at an appropriate distance. Hopefully, out of hearing range.

"No, I don't know anything about a…" She stops, hands on hips. "I'm here because of the blood tests."

"What about them?"

"You need to hear. You both do."

"We have about twenty seconds before we're rudely separated," I bite out.

"The blood work showed slightly different properties between your and your sister's blood. I ran the test again and again, but without more samples the results remain uncertain."

I come to a dead stop. "What does that mean?"

This is not the Dorian Raines I have become accustomed to: the calm, no-nonsense, unflappable doctor. This Dorian has high color in her otherwise pale cheeks, a disturbed, excited gleam to her blue eyes.

This Dorian Raines has discovered something unthinkable.

"Tell me," I demand.

"We knew there's something peculiar to your blood. And there is. Listen, your blood type doesn't even register. I've never seen anything like it. And to make matters more complex… Don't you realize? You and Margot were conjoined. You should both have the same blood phenotype. As in, *exactly* the same."

A wave of dizziness. Heavy steps behind me. I look up to see buzz cut coming toward us, chiseled face intent.

I turn and grip Dorian's hands. "So good to see you." I smile. "Please tell Jared to drop in and see us sometime."

But confusion fills her face. "Jared? But I was under the impression—"

"Father will be expecting me to see to our very important guests now, Doctor. But I'll be sure to set up that appointment tomorrow. I'm sorry we've been so unforgivably rude." I bow my head, pretending to blush as buzz cut comes to stand at my back with the clink of his rifle against his belt buckle. Dorian looks the man over impassively.

"Yes, of course, do that," she murmurs.

"Please be sure to pass on my remembrances," I tell her, tightening my hands around hers. "And drive safe."

Buzz cut whisks her out the door before I can say anything else. Maybe it doesn't matter. Dorian Raines is a smart woman. The kind of woman who puzzles things to death until they make sense.

At least, I hope she is.

24

There must be a dozen girls waiting for us as we arrive that morning. Shane grumbles his good-byes and idles the car by the curb while we are engulfed in a gaggle of blue plaid-wrapped flamingoes.

"Spill it." Harmony Everett puts a hand to Margot's chest and holds her there. "It's only two weeks away already. Why so secretive?"

They would never believe the truth. So as I push Harmony's hand away, I tell them what they want to hear. "We were sworn not to reveal any details. It's for security," I say, and am amazed when I can fake a blush.

Margot must be amazed, too. "Lucy," she seethes at my lie. But this just confirms the story for the girls. We've been holding out.

"What is it—celebrities?"

I shake my head with a tragic air. "No, no one you'd know. Just some foreign *dignitaries*," I stress, hoping she gets the point.

Her blue eyes widen. She grabs for the hand of her long-haired friend in a near swoon. "You're kidding." She drools.

I pause dramatically, looking down at my shoes. "We've got to go, Margot," I say in a quiet voice. She darts past me as we run up the stairs and into our stone haven.

"Was that really necessary?" Margot's whisper is fierce. But a smile hovers on the corners of her lips.

"Yes," I say back. A grin overtakes me as Margot's life throbs within me, bright and shiny for one beautiful, brittle moment. "It absolutely was."

Robbie Deakins corners us in the hallway on our way to lunch. "You're serious?" he practically yells. I've never seen him so annoyed. No mocking smile sits on his usually pretty lips. He tosses back his glossy head of short curls and glares at us.

"What's wrong with you, Robbie?" Margot calls as we stop before him. But Robbie leans an arm against a post and manages to look even more annoyed.

"You got another date to your party, Margot?"

Oh. So that's it. "You know we don't get to choose, Robbie. Our parents aren't as liberal as yours."

"Am I even *invited*, now that you've got some prince attending?"

The gossip chain has been very, very busy. "We never said," Margot starts, raising an eyebrow at me.

I jump in with the sternest voice I can muster without laughing. "Nobody is supposed to know about that, Robbie."

Robbie waves his arms expansively. "The whole damned school is talking about it, Lucy. I feel like such a fool!"

He's pouting. I can't see what my sister ever saw in him. And maybe Margot can't, either. "You feel like a… Robbie.

You're being ridiculous."

"I thought we were going to be together."

"Robbie!" Margot snaps her fingers in his startled face. "Get with it. It was never up to me. It never will be." Her voice curls bitterly. "I'm quite sure your family is still on the guest list. I'll be lucky if our father allows us to have a dance. That's it. That's all it's ever been." She sighs.

And suddenly I feel the weight of Margot's exhaustion: the prison of our family, the heavy sadness of the past month, punctuated by the terror of not knowing what is brewing in our blood and bone.

How can we not have the same blood?

I reach for my sister's hand just as she reaches for mine. "Let's go outside to eat," Margot murmurs, tugging me from the hall.

"Sorry," I tell her as we head out into the bright gray of outside. "I went too far."

Margot tosses her hair. "You didn't go far enough," she tells me darkly.

One moment I'm daydreaming about him. The next? He's crossing the quad on catlike feet as I sit, bathing in a patch of pearly white light in the crisp, cool air outside the school. He'd stick out a mile even outside of my exclusive private school: he might have the arrogant manner of a Grayguard Academy grad, but Jared Price is messy. Tousled blond hair clashes against the bright red of his shirt stenciled with an enormous black question mark. On his feet he wears a pair of brown, twisted leather sandals, just peeking out from the frayed hem of his pants. Still, it's my heart I'm worried about as he saunters over.

"Who dresses you?" I ask as I take him in, piece by piece, pretending I've not been starving for a glimpse of him. The indigo eyes, the mocking twist to his full lips. A flip of his hair trails down his forehead. I am distracted by a long scratch poking out from the top of the slightly stretched neckline of his shirt.

Jared shrugs, eyes sweeping over the small octagonal courtyard—accessible only by two doors on either side—before landing back on me. I brace myself, waiting for the sting I am sure is coming. Instead, he flashes a coy grin. "Us poor folk have to dress ourselves, Princess." What's this? A joke…? From Jared? "What are you doing out here alone?"

This particular courtyard is safe enough: the only real way in, aside from the heavily armed school, is via the roof. But I'm not about to explain that to Jared. Nor will I tell him about the extra security running patrols up there. They have promised us, again and again, that there will never be another situation like the one from the other week. More importantly, they have promised our father. Still, I am happier in this space, confined on all sides by a prison of bricks and mortar, a dry, bleak jail yard, than I am just about anywhere else these days.

The bigger mystery is how Jared snuck in. "How did you get here?"

"Dammit, Princess, answer the—"

But I'm getting better at navigating the arrogant, bossy True Born. "What happened to your neck?" I reach out and trace the angry line of red with the lightest of fingertips. Jared sucks in a quick breath and rears back as though I've hit him. Lightning fast, he grabs my wrist, even angrier than he was a second ago. "Where is your security?" he grumbles. "Where's Margot?"

"Inside. The bathroom." I don't know how I manage to sound so calm and collected as pleasure washes through me. I like knowing I've thrown him off-balance, even if I have no idea how or for what purpose. "She'll be back in a moment."

He nods, shoulders relaxing a fraction, but he forgets to let go of my wrist. "You shouldn't be out here. Not alone," he lectures.

"I shouldn't be alive. That doesn't stop me from breathing. Besides, I'm not alone, am I?"

"I swear, you are the biggest pain in the neck I've ever met."

"Right back at you," I tell him, dry as toast.

For just a moment his eyes flare full green. He takes another step back, still grasping my arm, and pulls me into the shadow of the wall. But his eyes are serious rather than angry as they hook on every inch of me, heavy as caresses: my hair, my shoulders, the curve of my neck, my fingers, the fall of my skirt and my bare legs ending in short leather pumps. With a funny stare he reaches out and cups a bouncy curl that skims my shoulder. Currents ricochet through my body. "Did you cut your hair?"

I swallow, not trusting myself to answer.

"Lucy," he starts.

A helicopter sounds directly overhead. It's loud, jarring, close enough to be a concern—or so Jared clearly believes as he sweeps the sky and curses. The courtyard door creaks. Before I have time to see who it is, Jared has me flattened against the wall behind the door. It isn't Margot. Male voices— soldiers' voices—break the air. Jared's hand flies over my mouth, trapping whatever I was going to say, along with my breath. His other arm snags around my waist. Alternating between glaring at me and glaring at the door, he mouths at me to keep my trap shut. His nose twitches angrily, his eyes a luminous bright green. I reckon we've been here before.

But this feels...different. Jared's chest rises and falls against me like the sea. I can smell him, too: woodsy and familiar, a scent I can only call his. I wonder if he can feel the trip of my heart as it knocks against his chest.

The door slams shut, cutting off the voices. Jared's shoulders inch down but he still seems ready for a fight. I pluck at his hand, still plastered over my mouth. A weird expression creeps over his face. He watches my efforts but doesn't move. I wonder if he's being amused at me as he says, "I don't know if I should set you free," and continues to stare down at me, his hard length pressed against me. It's as if he's forgotten where we are, forgotten everything as he stares at me quizzically.

"I really don't get you, Princess," he tells me with sincerity. I glare at him from beneath my bangs. He smiles, more tender than I thought he had in him, which just makes me want to punch him all the more. Then, like he's forgotten his train of thought, his mouth perks up, popping out a dimple I haven't seen before. "Today you look like a cross between a kitten and an angry pixie." Slowly his hand comes away.

"Do that again and I'll show you an angry pixie," I shoot back. Jared's head tips back as he laughs. I want to kill him, but I haven't seen him look so relaxed since...well, not since we danced around Storm's living room, if I'm honest. "I really don't get you, either," I whisper, feeling something unknot in my chest.

Jared sobers. "Dorian passed on your message."

The way he says it, so matter-of-fact, makes me livid. "Forget it. Go back to Storm and leave us alone." I turn my back on him and head back for the table.

He grabs my arm. "I swear to God, Princess. You make me so crazy I could just—"

"What?" I twirl back to him, yelling. "Leave us alone as prisoners in that house? With that *man*? *Ignore* me? *Who cares!* Is that the worst you've got?"

"Stop it." He grits his teeth. "We're doing what we can."

"Are you? Did you know our father is pawning one of us off on Resnikov? Do you even know what that means? Something terrible is happening, and we have no idea what it is and no clue what to do. And we're *alone*." My breath heaves like I've run a mile. I put a hand to my stomach and breathe deeply, attempting to calm myself. In truth, even I don't know what Leo Resnikov means for our lives, but it surely can't be good. Jared considers me for a good long while, features softening.

"I reckon we need to do a better job communicating," he finally says.

"Come again?"

"We haven't forgotten about you, Lucy," he hushes. His hand slides down my arm, fingers scalding my skin, as though I'm a frightened colt. "There's a plan."

"Yes, well, our father has a plan, too."

"You need to trust us."

"Trust Nolan Storm's True Borns?" I scoff.

"Trust me then, Lucy. Just me."

Tears threaten, but I can't let them fall. I choke the words out over the lump in my throat. "Why would—why would I trust you?"

"Because. Because even though you make me so damned crazy I could tear up a room…" He hesitates, suddenly a lost little boy. "You know. You *know* I'd rip apart anyone who so much as looked at you funny." The words sound like a revelation even to himself. My breath catches in my throat. Does he protect all of his clients this fiercely? Or am I—I don't let the thought progress an inch further. Now isn't the time to contemplate Jared's role in my life—now is the time to save it.

I rub tears out of my eyes and look at him. Really look. Purple shadows sit beneath his eyes. His cheeks are pale and hollow underneath light blond stubble, like he hasn't bothered to shave in a while. He looks tired. Worn.

"She said our blood is different."

"Yes," Jared acknowledges. "But we don't really know what that means yet."

"What about the witch?"

Jared performs another visual sweep of the courtyard. "There've been some leads but we're still looking."

"Oh," I say, downcast.

"Lucy." He sounds exasperated as he pushes a strand of hair from my mouth. Then he rubs the back of his neck as though I really have given him pain. "Even if there is such a thing as this witch… She's probably dead. If Westfall had any sense at all, he would have killed her."

"How can you say that?"

He shrugs. "It's what a smart man would have done."

Sometimes I lose sight of what Jared really is. A soldier. A killer. *True Born.* I can't afford to forget. But is he *my* soldier? My killer? My protector? I don't have the time, or the means, to find out.

"So what now?"

Jared shrugs again and gives a bored flip of his blond locks. "We keep looking for her. And we have a plan."

"Have you seen Richardson again?"

"No. He's gone underground."

"And you aren't going to share your plan with us?"

"Better that you don't know."

Our Reveal is just two weeks away. Resnikov and our father are clearly up to something. And Richardson—who is he? Resnikov's evil twin? Doppelganger? Whoever he is, he's running around somewhere with a falcon man, looking for us, but we can't know the plan?

"It's for your safety as much as ours."

"Oh." I hadn't considered that. It makes sense. If Margot or I are captured, would we not tell our captors anything they wanted to hear? "Right. Well, I'll continue on with my own plan, then."

I stumble against Jared as he suddenly pulls me close. He catches me and rubs his mouth against the shell of my ear, working a shiver up and down my spine. "Trust me, Lucy Fox. I won't let anything happen to either of you."

I don't even have time to finish thinking, *You can't protect us from everything*, by the time he's pulled away and has darted across the courtyard. The door opens without a protest. And Jared Price disappears like he'd never been there at all.

I hear the sobbing before my eyes open. The room is dark, half lit by dawn. I am alone in my bed. It takes me another moment or two to realize the sobbing comes from me.

Margot bursts in the door and rushes for me. She checks me over with her eyes before sliding into bed beside me and throwing her arms around me.

"What's wrong?"

I shake my head. "Dream," I say, and that's as much as I want to tell her. I don't dare tell another soul about the images floating through my mind, over and over again. Of the Lasters crushing into the gate, their limbs running red. The blond lady with the white, unseeing eyes in the yard, holding out her hand to me as though she sees me. Only me.

The yard awash in blood. *Laster. True Born. Splicer.* Witch.

Because, as I shake off the remnants of sleep, I think I finally might know who my dream lady might be.

"Margot?" I croak through the lump in my throat.

"Shhh. It's going to be okay."

"I don't think so. I think—"

She scoots back into the headboard. "Don't say it. Okay?"

I hang my head, defeated. "Do you believe they've abandoned us?"

She knows who I mean. Margot's gray-green eyes spark with anger. "I don't care. I'm looking forward to our party and then...then maybe we'll take a trip," she says with false brightness.

"Do you really think our parents are just going to let us go off somewhere together?"

Margot bites her lip. "I heard them talking about a trip."

My eyes narrow with suspicion. This is the first I'm hearing of it. I can't imagine our parents benevolently sending us on a relaxing cruise. "What kind of trip?"

"I don't know." Margot shrugs. "Something with the whole family, I guess. I think even Resnikov is coming."

I'm nauseous at the thought. "You can't be serious."

"I reckon he's a really important business contact. It will be so good to get away from the preacher men and... everybody."

"Margot," I yell, shaking her slim shoulders. "Snap out of it! We're never going to get away from the preacher men. There will be preacher men wherever we go."

Margot twists viciously out of my grip. "You don't know that."

"And there will be True Borns, too. Only I doubt they'll be as nice as Storm. They'll be more like Richardson and that weird bird guy."

"Stop!" Margot covers her ears, like we are children in a fight.

But we're not children, not anymore, and the stakes are far too high. "Margot," I say, gentle now as I pry fingers from ears. "Margot, we've got to stick together. If you hear anything else, and I mean anything, you need to tell me."

Margot stares at me as the minutes tick by. "I'm broken, you know. And for a little while, when we were with them... when he... I felt I could at least pretend everything was going to be okay. But it's not going to be okay, Lucy. I'm never going to be okay."

"Yes, you are, *shh*," I soothe, pulling her head to mine and running my fingers through her silky tresses. "Margot, you're going to feel better. You're not broken."

"Oh, Lucy, yes, I am. Yes, I am," she repeats through fresh tears. She hasn't cried for days now, but as the gray light of morning rises we are back in that room, that terrible room, mourning the loss of our innocence.

25

"I suppose it can't be helped," our mother says sourly as she pens yet another hand-written invitation. We are at breakfast, one big happy family, although their new best friend, Resnikov, is oddly absent from the table. Usually he doesn't miss an opportunity to look good in front of our father by lavishing attention on us.

"Certainly it can," says our father. He puts down his NewsFeed and grabs at the leather gloves sitting beside his plate like shiny black beetles.

Our mother casts a shrewd glance. "Just the other day Betts told me that the families are beginning to take a real shine to him. He's been invited everywhere. Not to invite him will cause a stir."

"*We* decide who is invited everywhere."

"Yes, dear, but we already invited him in, haven't we?"

Margot and I watch the fine verbal volleying between our parents and we trade signals, placing bets on who will win.

Our usual vote would be our father. But in the case of social standing and etiquette, our mother is the cage match victor. Death or Society.

Our father glares. "We can just as easily rescind his standing."

"Yes, Lukas, but not without people talking. He's one of the wealthiest men in Dominion now, if not the State. Clearly a good businessman. And you put the security of your own daughters in his hands. If you back off now...I hesitate to say it but people might start to question our good judgment."

Our father tightens his grip on a glove as the rest of us hold our breath. Under the silence is the wooden ticking of the clock in the hall. Each ticking second sounds like a mini-explosion. "Fine," he says grudgingly, and we all remember to breathe.

Margot pinches her thigh under the table and rubs a circle there. Small victories. Storm will be invited to the Reveal. I flash her a quick grin. "Will Robbie Deakins and his parents be coming? We're particularly concerned that someone our own age comes, as well," she pipes up.

Our father curses under his breath. "That social-climbing monkey?"

"Father," Margot scolds as our mother's sharp voice rings out, "Lukas. Henry Deakins has been a true friend to us. Robbie and the girls have practically grown up together." She stares at our father pointedly. "They're on the list."

Our father grabs his gloves and whips them across his palm once, twice, as he gets up from the table. "Girls," he says. His smile is terrifying. "Your escort for the party will be Leo Resnikov. Everyone else will have to check with him before speaking to you or dancing with you."

Margot gasps as our mother shoots our father an annoyed look. "Such a kind way of breaking it to them."

"This has nothing to do with kindness. This is duty." Our father leans over the table. "*And they will do theirs*," he seethes and sails off for the day.

We wait until he's out of earshot. "Mother?" Margot asks, trying to mask the rising note of panic in her voice. "What is he talking about?"

Our mother spans a hand across her pearls, holding them as though they have severed her neck. She hesitates, not at all like her, and won't meet our eyes. "I didn't want you to have to find out like that. But, your duty to your family requires that you show Mr. Resnikov a great deal of respect and favor. You will both be considered under escort by him."

Margot gasps, her face turning an ugly shade of purple. Rage boils under her skin. "Our Reveal is going to be about some random business deal? We're not your whores, Mother."

A slap rings out. I reckon several seconds tick by before either Margot or I are lucid enough to comprehend what has happened. My flesh throbs, hot and stinging.

Patches of red dot our mother's high cheekbones, too, as though she's the one who's been slapped. "You'll keep your panties on until we advise you otherwise," she seethes before turning on her heel and leaving.

"You all right?" I ask Margot. She stares back at me in wordless horror.

I stand up on shaky legs and move over to the small, OldTime mirror adorning the wall leading to the hallway. One of my cheeks is deathly pale. The other carries the livid red imprint of our mother's hand.

I catch Margot's reflection entering the mirror. Our eyes

meet. Slowly, she puts a hand to her cheek, where I can feel the throbbing skin, where the mark should be.

But isn't.

Margot meets me at the great wooden doors of the academy, and we stroll outside to wait for our ride. Outside there isn't a single Laster, as though the streets have been swept clear. Shane steps forward as we come down the stairs of the school. He's wearing a new white shirt with a round of ammo clipped around him, like a beauty pageant sash, looking as ugly as it comes: the nose that has been smashed and rebuilt so it tilts slightly left. A scar the length of an orange rind kisses the skin beneath his ear, like a kid's drawing of a moon.

He glowers at us and nods before turning toward the street and completing his sweep. Other bodyguards flank the steps to perform the same task. He told us once that the Personals, as they're known, look out for one another's charges.

But they are staring out at nothing. The streets are empty and gray, charged with an eerie silence. "Where is everyone?" Margot asks, taking the words right out of my mouth.

Shane shakes his head. "Streets have got too quiet since the last attack." He opens the door of the OldTime car and we slide onto the hard leather seats. He shuts us in, glaring about uneasily, before climbing in front and starting the car, muttering something ungentlemanly under his breath.

"What do you mean?" I press. "You mean they're just all gone? All the Lasters have vanished?"

"Doubt it," he answers wryly. "Probably just gone away to a preacher jamboree." My skin shivers at the thought. "They're around here somewhere," he continues. *Just not here.* The words remain unspoken but it's clear as day. Downtown Dominion has been abandoned.

"Why do you say that?"

He nods in the direction we're driving. "That new tree that's sprung up in Emerson Square. Some folks a'been leavin' ribbons and such on it through the night. Putting up string cans. Scares the bejeezus out of the coons when they bang together."

Beside me, Margot's breath hitches, and I feel something like heat emanating from my sister. "Why would someone do that?"

"Not just a someone. Loads of someones, I reckon."

"Can we go by it, Shane? Please?" Margot begs.

Shane grumbles but turns on his signal light. "There might not be anything to see," he warns. "The Staters have been pulling stuff down as fast as it goes up," he says, using the slang the mercs use to indicate the local policing force. From the way the mercs talk, we've gathered that the "Staters" are about one step up from pet rocks.

"Why?" I ask.

"'Cause they're trying to figure out how to tear down the entire tree. But it all goes back up again the next night."

We hear it well before we see it: tinny, hollow clapping that sounds a bit like the bells they ring when two Splicers marry. The tree has grown since the magic bombs were lobbed. At first we can't see the top. The entire corner is dwarfed by the massive tree, rising at least five stories and eating up the entire width of the major intersection. But it's much as

Shane has described: the lowest branches are hung with tin cans dangling on strings, ropes of paper, colorful strings like a child's version of a Christmas tree. A breeze kicks up and the cans knock and bang together, a symphony of bones.

Margot points to the paper strips that hang in thick icicles. "What are those?"

Shane stops the car. There's nowhere to go under the shadow of the enormous tree. "Messages, I guess."

"What kind of messages?"

"Prayers to get well. Prayers not to get sick." He rubs a hand down a stubbled jaw.

"What's that?" I ask, pointing to a spot left of the tree. Shane doesn't answer, but it's just as well. I know what it is. I just don't want it to be true. We stare at one of the enormous blond stone office buildings, abandoned for years now. But on the side of the building someone has drawn two red circles, conjoined in the middle. The red paint sprawls twenty feet across, maybe ten feet high. A figure huddles underneath, knees drawn, hood pulled over his features.

As we stop, he looks up. The hood slips off, revealing the bony face of Father Wes's boy. His boyish face has grown harder still, if that's possible—or maybe it's the dirt that makes it seem that way. He stares at the car as though he can see through the tinted windows before slowly, deliberately, rising to his feet. He makes some sort of gesture with his hands, interweaving his fingers until they are two circles, joined in the middle.

"We need to get out of here, Shane. *Now*." I pluck at Shane's shirt.

Shane doesn't ask questions. He turns the ignition, and the car jumps to life. He guns the Mercedes backward, swerving into a lane before righting the car forward and hitting the gas. Still, the shadow from the massive tree swallows us for a good long time until we break free. The boy's eyes haunt me for a long spell to come.

It's hard to reconcile miraculous trees and True Borns with the mundane horror of dress fitting. I pose beside my sister in the sewing room of Madame Elise's, stuck with so many pins we're life-size voodoo dolls. It's our final fitting before the big Reveal, just three days away. Our mother has become progressively grim.

She's overseen every tiny detail of the event with the martial air of a true military mind. Cocktails at six, followed by a formal dinner at seven. At nine-thirty the ball will begin with our presentation. The Reveal will be at midnight, saving the best for last. Special, embossed invitations only. Of all Dominion's elite, only one hundred families received the cream linen invitation. We thought the pressure was bad at school—our mother has been fending off attacks from her so-called friends who would do just about anything to wrangle a golden ticket to our party.

Make that Resnikov's party.

"You're about to become women." She stares fondly at us in our party frocks, as though we are pieces of jewelry she can price at a glance. Our dresses are similar but not matching: Margot will wear a fitted emerald green sheath, sweeping to the floor. I will be in a sleeveless pale violet dress with a sweetheart neck, cinched at the waist and belling out to the floor in a grand sweep. I wonder what Jared would say if he could see me in this dress, then erase the thought as quickly as I can. I can't afford to think about him, I remind myself, though he's been popping into my head for days.

I wonder how anyone enjoys this primping, all just to hear whether you'll live or die. Even though we're luckier than most—at this point it seems unlikely to be a death sentence we'll hear—dressing for the occasion feels like wrapping yourself in a winding sheet for burial. Oblivious, our mother fiddles with the buttons running about two inches up my back. "A bit tighter here," she tells Elise. The woman nods a mouth full of pins at our mother. "You're lucky, you know," she continues, sounding almost wistful.

"Yes, Mother, we know," Margot replies. Our mother's eyes flash at the hint of rebellion in her tone.

"You are," she repeats. Her hands snag the back of Margot's hair, twisting it into a severe chignon. "Maybe something like this," she murmurs, more to herself than us.

After all, what does it matter what we want? We have not been consulted in anything: not the dresses, nor the guest list. Not even the menu. We have been, as always, relegated to the sidelines like two chess pieces that will adorn a game table.

"It's a big deal, the moment your future is Revealed."

"What was your Reveal like, Mother?" I ask, trying to deflect attention away from Margot.

Our mother's elegant, cold eyes meet her own reflection in the floor-to-ceiling mirror. Her full lips purse, making her cheekbones into hollows. "It was different in my day," she says coyly. She stares at her reflection a beat longer before staking her eyes on my exquisitely tailored gown.

"How so?"

"For one thing, I didn't have Russian counts courting me."

"Is that what he's doing? Courting us?"

"He's an old man," Margot raises her voice.

"He's not an old man," our mother fusses. "Should either of you have the opportunity to catch his eye, you'd be lucky. And what if you get the opportunity to go to Russia with him? Think of the opportunity," she repeats, her face tight.

"Mother," I say patiently, "we're not going to Russia."

"You might be," she snaps back. Margot recoils. My stomach drops.

And in that moment I have the proof that our father and mother have cooked something up with Resnikov. They are—there's no better word for it—selling us. One by one? Or have we been sold as a set?

I pour all the sugar I can into my next words. "Mother, people have been asking but I have no idea… What is Mr. Resnikov's business?"

"Oh"—she waves a vague hand—"he's a business man."

"What kind of business?"

"A dabbler, if I remember correctly. He has a lot of land, obviously, so he's into lumber. And pharmaceuticals, I think."

Pharmaceuticals? I arch an eyebrow at Margot. She slides two fingers across the inner skin of her wrist as I watch. *Us*, she means. This has something to do with us, specifically. The Protocols. Our blood. Our DNA.

I try to mask the horror I feel, also shared from Margot to me, as we stare back at our mother. We need Dorian Raines. We need Storm. We need that witch.

I need Jared, I think desperately.

26

Margot stares moodily out at the sky through her bedroom window. It's full light at half past eight in the morning, but not so you can tell. The air is heavy and thick, like curdling cream, as the sky turns the greenish black of a bruise. For the past two days the NewsFeed has been blaring warnings of a massive Flux storm headed our way. Looks like it will hit today of all days, the day of our party.

Extra mercs have been arriving for the past two days and have been busy setting up a secure perimeter. Through Shane we hear our father even broke down and solicited Storm's advice on new security measures. Now I can almost hear the boots thudding overhead as the bought soldiers pace back and forth on their rounds. Our front gate has become as difficult to cross as the border between here and Europe. Two hold shotguns at the ready while a third checks the credentials of the man driving the delivery van and runs his thumb print through the human signature machine.

Shane also told us, much as he no doubt wishes he hadn't, that there have been rumors. Rumor is, the Lasters are planning something against Dominion's government although details have been vague on exactly what. Protest? Attack? There hasn't been a full-scale attack on the government since the first wave of the Plague when our parents were children. The government retaliated by instituting martial law, which hasn't been lifted since.

But by far, the Flux storm is the biggest concern. They're predictable only in their unpredictability, these harsh-weather storms. They must have started before the Plague, but if they did, nobody cares. Now they are just another sign of our broken world, along with the omnipresent gray-white sky and the empty buildings, silent streets.

The last Flux storm ripped up the entire eastern tip of the city, demolished it with a mighty swipe of a funnel before dipping over the lake and drinking up the water, only to turn around and dump it on the still-smoking city. Lasters caught in the massive electrical fires drowned in seconds. The smell of charred and bloated flesh hung over the city for months afterward.

I rest my chin on Margot's shoulder and squeeze her round the waist. "I reckon it will be nasty."

"The storm? Yes, I bet," Margot replies, distracted.

She's been this way since the final fitting: lost in some dark train of thought I can't follow. "Are you all right?" I sigh against her neck and immediately feel the tickly shiver on my own.

Margot turns on me. "Stop asking me that, okay?"

"Mar, I just—"

"I know you're just looking out for me, Lu. But I'm fine,

okay? I just have a lot on my mind."

"Mar, wait," I call after her as she disappears into the bathroom. When she re-emerges, her hair is a shiny mass that floats over her shoulders. Her face is scrubbed clean and pink. And she's donned a fancy pink-and-white-striped frock for breakfast.

"Think of this as the Last Supper," she says, striking a glamour pose.

I giggle helplessly. "You look too good," I tell her. "Resnikov won't leave you alone."

Something dark creeps along my sister's face. "Yes, well. I always wanted to see Russia."

"Don't even." I snort.

"Do they have a two-wife policy in Russia? We could marry him together." She grins.

I burst out laughing. I laugh until my sides ache. "Please, stop." But Margot has already sobered. Her eyes trail out the window again, and she moves toward it as if magnetically drawn.

"Do you think they'll find her? The witch?"

"Maybe." I shrug. "Does it matter now? We have so much else to worry about."

"I don't know." Margot bites her lip as she turns back to me. "You know, it's nothing like I expected today to be."

The wrenching fear we'd been living with as we went through round after round of Protocols is gone. But along with that fear, our sense of certainty has also leaked away. If we're not Lasters, or even Splicers, what will we be? What will our parents announce tonight in front of their special guests?

"We need to think of the end game," I tell my sister. "They want us to go with Resnikov, so what will they tell us and the Circle?"

"That's so calculating." Margot frowns.

"So are they."

Margot nods, but I can feel her unhappiness stretching between us. Her beautiful eyes, mirrors of my soul, stare into me. "If I were them, I'd tell the world we're Lasters and send us away on one last trip. That way he gets both of us."

And no one will say a word when we never return. The knife in my stomach twists a little more.

Margot's eyes fill with tears. "Do you really think Storm has a plan?"

"If he doesn't," I whisper back, taking her pinkie in mine and shaking, "I do. My plan is we escape. Okay? We run."

My sister takes my measure for a long moment before slowly, reluctantly nodding. It's the sentence next to death, running away from our family. But maybe it's next to the only choice remaining to us.

Our mother's designer set afloat pale pink lanterns in small pools all through the ballroom. Beside the pools, the patterned wood of the floor gleams like sun on waves. Six-foot tropical plants group together in made islands, with discreet wooden benches tucked beneath them to give our guests' rest and privacy.

As we wander into this lush paradise, stretching before us with a thousand twinkling lights, Margot and I gaze at the throng of admiring guests. But I, for one, cannot be glad, I think as I squeeze my sister's hand. In the face of everything—Resnikov, Richardson, Father Wes, even the Lasters—this so-called perfect party is a fool's paradise.

Beneath the veneer is the plaster and tape that holds everything together. Pale-faced Lasters—come out of the woodwork for a paycheck but who, if the rumors are near truth won't be well-paid—circulate trays of tulip-stemmed champagne flutes. Some of the tropical islands have been taken over by mercs who mumble into their mouthpieces as they scan the crowds. A metal detector set into the doorframe whines once, twice, while a team of mercs frisk the unsuspecting man who's tripped it. Unless he's a senator, he'll undoubtedly be hauled into the guardroom for a proper pat down before being allowed to rejoin the festivities.

We wait for our cue at the doorway. Margot's face is untroubled, though that is just her careful mask. She looks so beautiful in her dress, so sophisticated and so much older than I could have imagined. I wonder if my own face holds the same expression: have I, too, become an ice queen? When all eyes fall on us and a hush descends, our hands unclasp and we fall into perfect, synchronized curtsies to the roar of applause. Resnikov appears before us in his black tailored tux and bows low, first to Margot and then to me. My stomach clenches with regret. What would it have been like, I daydream, to be greeted by someone we cared about? An image of a blond rebel prince with startling green eyes flashing over blue pops into my mind. No good can come of that, I tell myself sternly.

Anger sizzles through me as Resnikov offers us each an arm, as though we really are his two harem wives. He promenades us down the center of the ballroom, as has become the custom for girls, just as I catch sight of a gleaming set of antlers rising from the throng of delighted faces.

Storm.

Has Margot seen him? *And where's Jared?* an annoying inner voice whines. I try not to stare, but Storm is a good head taller than most of our guests even before the rack of antlers. Our eyes meet and he nods, a tight, pensive smile stamped on his handsome features. Just then the endless wind rattles the house, flickers the lantern light. The gale has been battering at everything all day, toppling the car hotels, which now block the streets, according to the NewsFeed. Our guests don't seem overly concerned.

We arrive at the back of the room and curtsy again, this time to Resnikov, who bows to each of us again in turn before sweeping Margot into a formal dance. I suppose he could be called handsome in his black tux and crisp white shirt, I critique as I stand back and watch my sister glide around the room. If only we could trust his motives. Resnikov smiles down into Margot's eyes. Yet I can't help think how cold he is, how calculating. Compared to Jared's fiery personality, though, everyone seems cold. When Jared smiles, his eyes crease into a patchwork of laugh lines that make him seem comfortable in his own skin. Where are Resnikov's laugh lines? No, for Resnikov we are a business deal. But just what does he think he's purchasing?

And then there's the question of Richardson.

Our father touches my shoulder with one soft leathery fingertip, pulling me from my reverie. He's wearing his gloves, which, paired with his pristine tuxedo, make him look like a terrifying version of royalty. "May I have this dance?" he asks and pulls me onto the dance floor. I have always felt as if he could read our minds, if not our faces. It makes me want to hide from him now—especially now, as the storm lashes outside, and I know he's up to something terrible.

"You and your sister look very beautiful tonight," he says quietly.

We both glance over at Margot, who could be a queen as she whirls around the ballroom with Resnikov. "Thank you, Father."

"Tell me, Lucinda, do you think your sister likes Resnikov?"

"I couldn't say, Father."

"Come now." He scoffs. "I thought there was nothing you and your sister did not share."

I shrug delicately. "What is there to think about, Father? Mr. Resnikov is your guest. We have done everything we can to make him feel welcome. We hope we have not displeased you."

Not happy with my answer, the leather of his gloves creaks slightly as his fingers tighten against my waist, my hand. "No. With notable exceptions, you have been the ideal hostesses," he admits before a thoughtful expression crosses his severe, handsome features. "I suppose it does not matter, anyway."

"I'm sorry, Father, what does not matter?"

"It's time you heard. Your sister has decided to accompany Mr. Resnikov back to Russia."

I gape in shock at our father's words, sure he must be joking. "Th-that's not —" I stammer.

"I assure you it is possible. I spoke with Margot earlier today."

I flash back to earlier that day: Margot, looking dully at the window, mute and even more withdrawn. "What did you do?" I choke out.

"Why do you suspect I have done something?" Red patches creep over his cheeks. "Who are you to question me? Your sister is a grown woman. She makes her own choices.

As do you," he says meaningfully.

"What do you mean?"

"Your sister has chosen to visit Russia for a good length of time. The question is, will you accompany your sister or will you remain here?"

"That's not a fair choice, now, is it?"

"Why not? Russia is beautiful. Why wouldn't you want to be treated like a queen at Resnikov's estate? He is a very rich man."

"And what will you have us do for him there, Father?"

We stop dancing as he glares down at me. "Nothing. But the doctors tell me...you and Margot will have to continue with the Protocols. You are freaks of nature, both of you, and no one is certain of your fate."

Breath hisses out of me as I force my hands out of his. "What is this Reveal for, then, Father? What will you be announcing to our guests?"

He doesn't even pause. "Naturally, we will tell them you are both Splicers."

In a blinding flash, I finally understand: Lukas Fox has always seen this as a con, nothing but a game of announcing your victory over life and death. Rich and powerful families can't afford to be seen as Lasters or True Borns. It makes me wonder: how many other families have lied about their children's results?

And then I'm struck with the very real thought that maybe they never had any intention of telling us what we really are. We are just "good girls" to do their bidding. We don't ask questions. And they don't have to give us answers. Even if we were Lasters, fated to die no matter how many trips to the Splicer Clinic—and our father's cynical words prove beyond a doubt that we're not—they'd let us die without ever telling us the truth. Or, they would dangle lies over our heads to force us into compliance.

Disgusted, I turn away, but he grabs my arm and twists. "Just where do you think you're going?" His voice is cold steel, eyes glittering murder.

I look him straight in the eye with a saccharine smile as I pluck at his bruising fingers. "It's my turn to dance with our escort, Father," I chirp.

Our mother catches up to me before I can flee the ballroom. She's a wraith in a sequined black tube dress, her hair piled artlessly on top of her head. Around her neck is a heavy onyx and diamond-crusted necklace, a piece I've never seen before. It looks as though it's holding her head on a platter. A fitting tribute in the Fox family, I think as a hysterical bubble of laughter threatens to burst.

"Where do you think you're going?" She has several guards behind her. I suppose they are there to make sure I stay in the room.

"Nowhere," I say, refusing to meet her eyes.

"Did your father tell you?"

"That he's sold Margot? Yes, he told me." I expect her to slap me, as she did Margot the other day. When nothing happens, I open my eyes and stare back at our mother. She's not angry as I expect but…resigned.

"It's not what you think. It's not the money, although there will be some."

"What is it, then?"

"A debt."

"You're in trouble?"

Her head tips back. She grabs at her throat. Her long,

beautiful neck arches as she laughs. "You don't have a clue, do you? How do you expect that your father has become such a powerful man? This has been in the works for years."

"Father and Resnikov?"

"It was a long-standing promise. From before you were born. It's *why* you were born."

"I don't understand." I shake my head in confusion. "You're not making sense."

Our mother puts a hand to my cheek. I can almost still feel the sting from the slap she gave Margot. Two for the price of one. *Lock and key*. She looks at me with almost maternal pride, turning the hard blue of her eyes into something soft and faraway.

"He was right, you know. You both excelled every expectation," she tells me quietly. "I'm sorry this party wasn't more in your taste. You both deserve a nice party."

"Mother, please." I grab at her hand. "You're not making sense."

"May I have this dance?" Resnikov's smooth, low tones startle me. I jump, as does our mother, who drops her hand as though it's on fire. "Am I interrupting a mother-daughter moment?" He throws a charming smile at us, white teeth flashing, but it doesn't reach his eyes. An air of menace wafts from him despite the tuxedo and carefully slicked back hair threatening to tumble down over his eyes.

He extends a hand. Our mother pushes me forward. I get the message. My hand is small in his, which is thick and calloused, as though he's used to hard labor. I swallow and look up at him. Resnikov gazes down at me dispassionately as he wheels me into the fray.

"You look lovely tonight," he opens. I nod my head and

murmur my thanks. He smells of cigars, but underneath that I can smell *him*, dark and strange. I try to listen to the music. The orchestra is playing something light and impersonal. Resnikov tightens his grip on my hand. "You're also very quiet tonight."

"Not much to say, I guess."

"Tell me, Lucinda." His accent always thickens around my name. *Lyoo-cinda.* "Do you think we can be friends?"

It's not a move I expect. I glance up. His frank appraisal unbalances me.

"I-I'm not sure. Why do you ask?"

Resnikov whirls me around before answering. "Because we can do this the easy way or the hard way. Either way, you have just been informed your sister is coming back to Russia with me. Correct?"

So much for subterfuge. I swallow hard before asking, "And what would be the easy way?"

His whole chest vibrates as he chuckles. "I like you," he tells me. "You are a smart young woman. The easy way would be if you come, as well. Of your own free will, of course."

I surprise myself by asking, "And what happens to me if I don't want to come?"

Resnikov shrugs, his dark eyes boring into mine. "You come anyway. Only you're not so comfortable."

We dance a moment longer before I decide to take a wild stab in the dark. "Do our parents know that?"

His smile is genuinely amused as he answers. "You are far brighter than your father gives you credit for, I think." He whirls me to the side of the room and bows low over my hand. "I'll let you consider my offer. You can give me your answer in the morning." He melts into the crowd.

And how can he think I'll just sit here and wait for him to

kidnap my sister and me? Because they can make sure no one takes me in. Because they know there's nowhere for me to go but the streets. *Because the room is filled with mercs strapped with guns. And who do they answer to?* Not me.

A second later I'm swept into a waltz with Storm. He towers over me even without the antlers, but he's so gentle and light on his feet I feel like I'm dancing on a cloud.

"You're not supposed to dance with us without asking Resnikov." I frown. But then, because the tears threaten to spill I add, "We're going to Russia."

Storm nods tersely. "Get a few things together in a bag. Essentials for just a day or two. Nothing else. Be at the foot of the staircase in ten minutes."

"I don't know what to do," I murmur. But Storm either doesn't hear me or doesn't want to. The song ends and he slips into the crowd and I quickly lose sight of him.

I wheel around, hoping to find my sister. But the ballroom is a giant crush. I reckon I couldn't find my way to the door unless I'd lived here all my life. I rush into the room dedicated as the ladies' withdrawing room. Margot is not there. Running out onto the balcony I catch our father standing with a few of his cronies. Thick blue smoke curls from their hands, which hold gleaming glasses of dark golden liquor and fat, lit cigars. I retreat, hoping to run upstairs before our mother notices me. And back up with a thump into a hard body.

I turn, an apology on my lips. Only to be met with the dark, menacing face of Richardson.

27

"**Y**ou're a hard lady to catch." Richardson's lips twist with sarcasm as he grabs my arm and pulls.

"Ow," I say as loudly as I dare. Sadly, he won't be taken for a bad guy, I think, noting the tuxedo, the black silk eye patch and more importantly, the fact that no one is around to help me. "I don't recall seeing your name on the guest list."

"I don't recall giving my name at the door." He smirks and marches me down the dimly lit demi-corridor that separates the ballroom from the balconies.

I dig in my heels and give an outraged screech. "Where do you think you're taking me?"

"Time's up," he snarls. "Consider your decision made. I'm taking you to your room to pack. You're too much of a flight risk."

My brain trips over his words. *Flight risk.* "What decision?" I ask. But inwardly I'm wondering how he knows—*unless he really is Resnikov?* But his accent, his face—he's not even in the same tux as Resnikov, I realize, noting the cheaper cut to Richardson's suit. But how does he know? And what happened to giving me time to consider?

I dig my heels in hard enough that he's forced to stop. "Who are you—his brother?"

Richardson's smile finally reaches his remaining eye and crinkles the corner, just as it does on Resnikov. "Good guess," he says, studying me. "No."

"What, then? Cousins?"

"Think of us as cousins if it makes it easier. Let's go. I do not want to have to damage you."

Damage me? "Why would you bother with me? You have Margot. You only need one of us, right?" It's only a guess but it seems I've hit the mark.

His mouth curls up into an oddly disarming smile. "Insurance."

I may have no choice in the matter, but I sure as hell won't give him the honor of going quietly. Not in the middle of my own Reveal. Not wanting to miss a chance, I slam my hand against his nose with a sharp, upward jab. He winces, and when he lets me go, I grab at his face, pulling his black eye patch down and revealing pitted sunken scar tissue. He's distracted only for seconds, long enough for me to bring my knee to his crotch. Shockwaves run through his body as I pluck up the bell of my skirt and run like hell.

As I run for the main staircase of the house, I realize what a dilemma I'm in. Storm is nowhere to be seen, but there are guards with guns everywhere. Guards Resnikov had a hand in hiring. *Is he even Russian?* I wonder hysterically as I force myself into a fast walk. I glance over my shoulder, expecting to see an enraged Richardson appear with a gun, but he's not there. Not yet.

Neither is Storm—or my parents—and I'm desperate. I toss a smile at the guards at the staircase. Would they prevent me from going upstairs? Trap me? They don't so much as raise a finger as I reach for the door handle and rush outside into the night air.

The exterior of the house is flooded with light. The same designer that helped our mother with the lanterns and pools convinced her to continue the theme on the exterior. Our house looks like a gigantic block of light. I blink at the ostentatious waste of electricity, and reckon that if they didn't before, every last one of the rabble in town now knows where we live. But that hardly matters, I think to myself as I look past the gate.

Because they've found us. All of them.

There must be three hundred—maybe four. Guards line the fence, guns pointing at the massive sea of bodies. The street is deadly quiet—the kind of quiet that makes you think someone has died. The Lasters stand still as stone, blinking, calm faces lit by the garish glow of the building.

"Lucy?" A voice laced with a hint of fear breaks through the panic racing through my blood. "Lucy, for once in your life do what I say and don't move."

I almost sag with relief and a strange, bubbling joy. I'd know that voice anywhere. But why does he sound scared? I turn. Framed against the shiny black and gray cars lining the grass along the driveway is Jared, who holds the arm of a breathtakingly beautiful woman. She's not dressed for the party, but then again, she wouldn't have to be. She's the kind of woman who would be stunning in a sack. Tall, slim as a pencil but still curved, she shakes a mane of white-blond hair that ripples down her back from two decorative side combs. It's her eyes that catch me: beautiful, almond-shaped eyes, and I'm stabbed through with jealousy. But then I see why Jared holds her arm that way. Those eyes of hers are covered in the bluish-white sheen of cataracts.

My stomach sinks with recognition. *Her.*

I glance over my shoulder at our bedroom windows, Margot's and mine. And yes, there is my sister, framed in the window. Her lovely hair curls around her face in wisps as she puts her hands on the glass. As though we can reach each other through the glass and a two-story drop.

No. No. No. No nonono. "Margot," I whisper, whipping my head around. "Jared?" is all the warning I get to mutter before all hell breaks loose.

The wind howls through the streets like a hungry animal even as a weird chanting fills in the air behind them. The Lasters move forward like a well-trained army. The gates buckle as they press into the thin metal bars.

Behind a raft of people a figure pulls up to the gates on something like a makeshift stage. It's an awkward wooden thing—salvaged wood from the look of it—on two large wheels, like a wheelbarrow. As the awkward contraption sidles forward I see Father Wes astride the cart like the demented preacher man he is. With one hand he holds on to a post driven up the center of the cart, and with the other, he shouts into a megaphone. "Salvation is at hand," he hisses, "salvation is ours for the taking."

Jared and the blond woman step around a shiny black car. "Get back, Lucy. Get the hell out of here," he growls.

I ignore him. "You're the witch."

Shaking her head, the woman regards me sadly with her sightless eyes. "No."

"But you have to be." I reckon I'm whining because she looks at me piteously.

"I think you mean my mother. She's missing…has been for years now."

"But your eyes." I trail off. I know I'm being rude, but I can't seem to help myself, and we're running out of time. Hands reach through the bars of the gate and are battered down by the butt of a gun. Blood arches in a delicate spray across the pavement. Some of it lands on the woman's hair and face. She doesn't blink, her unseeing eyes trained on me like she's seeing under my skin. She traces a finger around my body in the air, following the tracks of my veins.

"Get back, Serena!" Jared yells as he tries to pull the mysterious woman back.

But she ignores him, too. "Your blood," she says, clearly fascinated by something. "I've never seen it before… Like his, only different." Already pale, her eyes turn the dead white of winter.

"His?" I say, but I don't need to ask. I know who. Nolan Storm. "It's my blood, isn't it? And my sister's."

"Yes" — she nods quickly, and the words are a whisper as she points at me — "special blood."

In a flash of recognition, I blurt out, "You're a Salvager, aren't you? I thought those were just stories."

Salvagers. The kids at school snicker over the comic book versions of them, the Allan Quartermains of our new world order. Salvagers aren't respectable types of True Borns. No fins or tails or gills. A Salvager has only one gift: the ability to sniff out True Borns like a tracker dog. Lowest of the low.

"This storm isn't normal," she breaks the train of my thoughts. "It's been hatched. We need to find shelter before it does." I blink in confusion. Clouds, thick as blankets, roil around in shades of dark bilious green and black. Lightning cracks through, singeing the tip of a distant building as the clouds begin to knit themselves into a funnel the length of several city blocks. "It's coming," she warns again.

A ferocious crack sounds as the wind picks up into a gale. Dust and debris whip us in the face, blinding us. The Lasters don't seem to mind as they press the gate, dirty, desperate faces reaching for us as though their lives depend on it.

I need to know for sure. I've got to hear what these men and women and children would die for.

I need to know what we are.

I grab the woman's forearm. "What's our blood for? What kind of True Born are we?"

Her head tilts back as she gazes at me, sad and troubled. Her thin hand comes over my hand but she doesn't move. "What binds the people?"

What desire binds together the people of Dominion? Not money. Not love. Nor family or power. Not anymore. Not since the Plague came riding through town and ate through everything, everyone. No—the one thing people want is something they have no control over. Their bodies. Their lives. The ticking time bombs built into their genetic design.

Life and death.

"The Plague," I breathe.

I used to dream of someone who'd swoop in like the heroes of the OldenTime books and halt the Plague in its ravenous feeding frenzy. Never in a million years could I imagine that an answer lay hidden in our blood, the blueprint stamped in our nearly identical genes. I think back to what happened to Margot at the Clinic. Those men who lured Margot, trapped Margot. Stole from her.

And if they knew, how many others?

The woman says nothing more, but glides her unseeing eyes over the crowd. "Wrong people are behind that door." She nods toward the house.

Wrong people?

I don't have a chance to ask. Guards I don't recognize stand sentinel on the upper balcony of the house. They point their guns at the crowd at the gate, and the air fills with the sound of gunshot, screaming, instant death.

I scream, too, and cover my ears. "What are you doing?"

Someone tugs at my arms and all but drags me toward the house. My eyes are shut tight against the horror so it takes me a moment to realize that it's Jared.

He grabs my face between his hands. "Lucy." He's not yelling so I know it's serious. "Get into the house. Grab your stuff, and we'll get out of here, just like Storm said."

I shake my head and try to pull away. "I can't just leave, Jared. I can't leave Margot. My family." My hands twist against Jared's chest.

Jared's eyes narrow. He swallows hard and blinks at the sky. A long, ragged sigh drags from his lungs. I am nothing if not a pain in the ass for Jared True Born Price.

But when he finally sweeps his eyes over me again his face is a mask of anguish. Splotches of red run up the skin of his neck, the bones of his nose pinched, as though he's about to change. "You can't stay here, Lucy." The words are low, soft. "You can't stay here with them."

My heart rips. I know what it means if I let them take us:

the end of our world as we know it. And a very uncertain life of duty. But this is what we were born to. This life of privilege and wealth—it was always just on loan to us. This was the price we were always meant to pay for being Lukas and Antonia Fox's daughters.

I curl my fingers around Jared's hands, which still gently cup my cheeks. "Jared," my voice cracks as I plead for him to understand. Out of everyone, I need him to understand. "Jared, they're our parents. I don't know what he has on them but I can help." I may not have had a messy childhood, or a silly one, or even a particularly fun one, but I was safe, I had always been safe. In their own way, my parents did all they could to protect me. I can't now turn my back on helping them, can I? I may be angry, but in the end, there is only family.

"Listen to yourself." Jared's words become urgent as he brings my face in close to his, inhaling me. "Lu, they want to take you and Margot away, and you'll never come back. Never have a life of your own." Resting his forehead against mine, Jared breathes me in. His lips are so close to mine. So close. "You deserve a life of your own," he murmurs. And then, so silently it is almost lost in the storm, he adds, "With me."

Closing my eyes, I tremble against his hands. It hurts to want something so badly yet know I can't allow myself to have it. Reminding myself of everyone that I'm protecting, I pull myself from his arms. "I—I have to go now."

Jared curses, loudly and with color. I open my eyes just in time to see Richardson stride out from the wide double doors of our home. With a snarl, Richardson bounds down the front stairs and kicks Jared in the face, sending Jared sprawling back. I fall to my knees as someone grabs my arms from behind. I can't see my attacker but I can tell they are strong. The wind howls and pulls at my dress and hair as my arms are stretched back. I'm forced to my feet and dragged up the front stairs backward.

From this position I can see the carnage at the gate. Horror twists through my guts, leaving me sick and empty. Lasters are mowed down by gunmen. More take their place, the dead and injured bodies pulled back behind the crowd. *How will our father paper over this?* I'm shoved roughly once again and almost tumble off the steps. I stumble down two or three, hands splayed out to catch me, and turn back to see Storm grappling with one of the unknown merc guards at the door. It's not a fair contest. The guard swings the butt of his semi at Storm, who ducks and punches, just one blow, to the gut. The guard heaves, reaching for the ground with one hand. With his other, he reaches for the trigger of his weapon. Storm gets there first. A vicious kick to the hand and the gun flies over the guard's shoulder, his body crumpling around broken, flayed fingers.

Storm snarls and the earth trembles. His antlers burn bright blue-white, eyes misty pools. He paws the ground with one foot, tossing his antlers angrily. The howling wind breaks into lightning. It flashes down, connecting with the branches of Storm's antlers. His eyes blaze as he stomps and holds the storm within him.

This is what a True Born god looks like, I muse. Distracted, I'm caught up and swung over a thick shoulder. I kick and scream until a pushed-past-annoyance Jared grunts and yells, "Cut it out, Princess. I'm not above spanking you."

"Jared, no," I shout at his back as he marches me toward the guard's entrance. "Put me down. I need to get to Margot."

"Too risky," he yells.

"Jared, *please*. I will never forgive you!"

He pauses, and for a moment I think he might put me down. But he bounces me a little higher on his shoulder, grabbing my legs tightly, and starts moving quickly toward the gate. "I can live with that risk," he yells up at me through the chaos. I am about to unleash holy hell when something arcs across the sky, doing it for me.

I don't see the bomb lobbed over the gate at the house, but I hear it. It makes a deafening sound as it impacts, a shrill scream just before the air bursts into violet pink hues. Jared and I are knocked down. My wrist crumples beneath me as we hit the ground.

He scrambles on top of me, stretching himself flat around my body and curling my head under his arms and torso. I am surrounded by him, but I don't feel him. For once, I am not aware of Jared Price. I can't see, can't breathe. I'm not even sure I'd want to as the air transforms into a pink and white dragon.

It doesn't smell like any fire I've ever been close to. I struggle beneath Jared, who curses but eventually lets me poke my head up. A streak of dirt mars his beautiful face. A deep cut next to his eye bleeds freely. I reach up as if to touch it, but he grabs my hand and tries to stand us both up.

"No," I scream, looking at the house. There is a hole in the front of the house. It slashes across the second floor. From here I can see the mess of matchsticks my bed has been made into, debris littering the room. Where is my sister? Someone from outside the gate is shouting about retreat, something about screwing up. It doesn't sink in until I see the guests streaming out from the double doors leading out from the ballroom on the other side of the house. Women with shocked faces, grim men in their evening wear.

Jared pulls me back up in his firemen's pose before I can protest but quickly comes to a dead stop. From under Jared's arm, I spy an upside-down Richardson. His hair is mussed, his face battered and swollen and filled with murder.

"Put her down," Richardson snarls. Feathery hands grab me from the side and haul me off Jared's shoulder none too gently.

Jared's face elongates, the bones in his cheeks becoming more pronounced. His eyes transform, indigo to emerald, his nails lengthen, as he turns into the stuff of nightmares. His hair-singeing battle cry rises up over the sound of the wind before he pounces. They tussle across the grass of the front lawn, rolling end over end until Jared is on top and beating the ever-loving tar out of Richardson. Talons break through the skin of my upper arm. I stare into the inhumanly round, yellow eyes of the falcon man and realize I've had enough. I bow my head, going slack, until he's forced to relax his grip. Then I knee him in the groin, hard enough to make him double over. He doesn't let go but his grip isn't as strong as it was. I slap my palm as hard as I can with the awkward angle against the bridge of his nose. A sickening crunch sounds and the wide eyes blink closed, giving me an opportunity to break free and run for shelter.

Lasters rattle the gate until it sways like a sapling. I run for the row of shiny OldenTimes cars lining the driveway, out of sight from the guards at the house—who are busy with the chaos set off from whatever the Lasters threw at our house—and hopefully out of sight of the falcon man, the Lasters, and the Preacher man.

A blur of dark feathers blends in among the panicking

guests. Not sure I'm safe, I crouch behind a car and search for
signs of Jared and Richardson. A body flies through the air,
and Jared pounces after it like a cat chasing a chew toy. I stand
up to get a better look, but the car I'm leaning on suddenly
ignites, burning me with its exhaust pipe. The car backs up as
I glide out from behind, just in time to hear the *smack*! as it
slams into the car behind, then floors it into a U-turn toward
the still-locked gate.

Tires squeal. More cars pull out from the parked line.
The first car speeds up as it hits the gate, crunching against
steel and bodies. Screaming. So much screaming. The car is
dented as it backs up about fifty feet and rams the gate again,
this time shattering the locking mechanism and leaving a
trail of bodies on either side as it forces the gate open, inch
by squealing inch.

The Preacher's rabble pour through the gate, shouting
bloody blue murder. I stand there, a deer in the headlights,
unsure where to turn. Behind me, the house is ruined. The
smoke has died to a curl. But where is Margot? And then I
feel it, that tenuous bond, bright and thin between us, growing
thicker.

Margot appears at the front door, her upper arm held by
Resnikov. Falcon man stands behind them, feathers ruffled
and a thick trail of blood coating the down around his face.
And a second later, my parents appear, harried and mussed
but safe. I want to sag in relief.

My attention fastens on Margot. She's pale. A tiny streak
of blood smears her temple and there are tiny red spatters
on her dress, but otherwise she seems fine. I would have felt
it if she wasn't. She scans the chaos with a blank expression
of horror. *Margot*, I tug at her, but of course she can't hear

me. I start toward her when I'm knocked off my feet again.

A dirty hand covers my mouth. I gaze into the crazed eyes of a skin-and-bones man. His shirt is torn and bloody, his dark pants a soiled mess. He shouts at me, his shaggy hair falling into a blotchy red face, but I can't understand what he's saying. A hand snakes out. I don't realize what's happening until the punch lands in my face and the world shuts off like a light.

28

It's the Flux storm that rouses me. Water falls in trickles down my neck. Pain overwhelms me as I open my eyes at the ground swaying beneath me. The Laster has me hooked around his neck where I dangle like a carcass.

I hear a boom, so loud it's as though the heavens have opened. Another. Then another. The Laster holding me pauses, shouts something unintelligible to his comrades. He turns just long enough toward the gate that I catch a glimpse of the house. Margot and my parents are still on the steps, held there by a few dozen Lasters and the chaos all around them. It's not too late, then. And suddenly the earth stops.

Storm pounds down the steps of the house. Lightning dances across his antlers like he's connected to the heavens by strings. On his face is a look of pure rage, which he proves as he grabs an unsuspecting Laster stupid enough to rush him. A neat twist of his hands and he breaks the man's neck. The Laster falls to the side. Storm walks on like he's riding the rain. Bombs of rain now fall, soaking the grass, the cars, bodies awash with blood and dirt running into the ground.

Storm turns. I catch my breath as he takes in the scene of chaos and charges the Lasters. The smart ones stop in their tracks and back up as the rain begins to fall harder, obscuring the green-gray sky.

Another jolt and I'm on the ground again, covered in mud. I roll a few feet away and watch as Jared bites the cheek off the Laster who was holding me seconds before. The panicked man tries to dig his fingers into Jared's face. I hear a terrible crunch as Jared bites first one, then the other hand. Bones crack and break as Jared shakes and tosses his head, splitting the man's skin. Casually he spits pieces of bone into the grass. His chin drips blood on the screaming man as I try to right myself. I don't want the man to die, even if he has hit me. Crawling over to Jared I put my hand on his arm. Feral eyes, filled with bloodlust, greet mine. I've miscalculated. He takes in my swelling cheek and eye and those eyes tighten a little more. He looks down coldly at the captive trapped between his thighs. He straightens his fingers so they are stiff knives before he drives them through the Laster's temples. A final death cry sounds from the head, which explodes like a ripe melon. Jared rubs his hands clean on the Laster's filthy shirt and stands up. I look away, not sure how to be gracious with this violent love poem.

I glance over at the door. Margot and Resnikov look like a bizarre parody of the newly married, surrounded by the uninvited. I have just seconds to get to them if I'm to go. They'll not wait for me in this chaos.

"You have a bad habit of attracting the wrong men, Princess." Jared stares at me a long minute in the rain before putting out a hand, as though we're about to waltz around the ballroom. A strange, charged silence stretches between us. "I'll help you," he tells me. His eyelashes flutter. But he makes no further move to touch me. "I'll help you, I swear. I can help you get her back. But for God's sake, do it from a safe distance. Do it smart. Do it with me."

It's not that simple, I want to scream at him. I'd be giving up my life. My family. My friends. The entire Upper Circle. Yet, as my pulse jumps and I stare at the gore-covered True Born before me, I suddenly understand that old life was already gone. Whatever deal our father has made with Resnikov, it doesn't include us continuing our cozy life in Dominion City.

More than that: as the rain and smoke flatten my pretty dress and wash over the hot bruises on my face, for the first time in my life it occurs to me that I no longer want to be dictated by duty. I want to forge my own life. *And if I had a choice?* a quiet voice inside me asks. *What life would I choose? Who and what would I choose to be?*

And then I don't hesitate. I place my fingers, slim and slight, in Jared's large, rain-washed hand. I expect him to lead me away, but instead he pulls me up into his arms. I feel his chest vibrate with the long, deep breath he takes, as though he's been starved of oxygen. He holds me tighter, arms drawing me close, mouth hovering over my skin, before murmuring in my ear, "Hang on."

We follow Storm out the gate. Jared snarls with long canines every few seconds. The Lasters pull back, forming a corridor, suddenly quiet. I wait for a bomb or whatever it is they'll pull next, but nothing happens. Nothing happens. Even if I wasn't tipped off by the hopeful glances they throw my way, I can feel it, an air of satisfaction swirling through their ragged ranks. Guests are still flying into their cars. I take a last look back at the window that was my bedroom. A tendril of green pokes its way through the gap, aiming for the sky.

My parents and sister have vanished, along with the mysterious Resnikov. At least Margot is alive. Wherever she is she has access to her hands—she pinches her thigh, hard enough to draw blood then rubs it, a silent goodbye. I can't reach my leg to pat the stinging flesh. Wouldn't want to. The cord between us stretches, golden and fragile, until it becomes a thin, silent string.

My eyes glaze over until I spy the witch—no, the witch's daughter, I remind myself—pull herself out from behind a line of cars reflecting red light in the gloom. She sets out at a stroll, a smile tugging at her lips. A commotion to my left catches my eye, and I watch as a massive man covered head to toe in marmalade fur tosses Lasters aside like they're garbage bags. He's a spitting angry, man-sized cat, ears flattened against his head under a black bolo hat. Cat man has paired his hat with a white undershirt, black leather pants, and rounds of ammo lacing his shoulders and torso. His feet, marmalade paws ending in four-inch claws, are bare.

"There you are," he says in a whisky voice to the witch's daughter. Cat man pulls out a cigar and sticks it between two sharpened cat teeth. His fingers rummage through pockets.

"Don't smoke those here, Carl," the blond woman returns in a tired voice. "They've gone and set off bombs."

Cat man grumbles but shoves the cigar back behind his ear as he follows her thin figure through the parted crowds. Father Wes is nowhere to be seen, although I suspect he's too smart to have been shot.

Storm must be thinking the same thing. He stops in the

middle of the crowd, which has formed a healthy gap around him. Dirty, dark-streaked, and hungry faces stretch as far as the eye can see. How many are here now? Hundreds, maybe thousands. Storm stamps one foot. The ground shimmies and booms. His antlers angle sideways as he glares at the crowd.

"Where is he?" his voice shakes the air. Pin quiet settles through the rabble until, far in the distance, the wail of a siren rises over the city. Our father has gone and called in the fire department. It will cost him a fortune. "*Where is he?*" Storm booms again. The Lasters shift uneasily but no one says a word. "Fine," he spits. "Tell him Nolan Storm has just taken Dominion for his own. Tell him," he says with a feral grin, "I'm coming for the man who would steal little girls."

The Lasters shrink back even more, happy looks wiped from their faces, and we walk off into the deepening gloom of twilight. No one looks particularly bothered about Father Wes's morality. The Lasters stretch all the way to Mercy, two streets away. There hasn't been a congregation so large since the Plague first started eating through our ranks. Whatever else can be said about the man who'd steal little girls, Father Wes inspires devotion in his followers.

We keep walking, though, a tribe of dark angels amidst the ruined people. No one bothers us. And we don't bother them as they shuffle closer to my parents' wrecked house.

29

The air steams with rain as we head toward the rendezvous point. "What happened to Richardson?" I croak in Jared's ear.

"I killed him."

I punch Jared's shoulder, but it's a weak and pathetic attempt, even for me. "You shouldn't have done that. We needed him for information." It should concern me, how quickly I have become immune to Jared's violence. How quickly I have become a plotter in this giant game. I wonder what a lifetime of exposure would do to a person, what they turn into.

"I know." He looks down at me, a trace of regret in his eyes. But behind the nugget of remorse lies something else: he's happy he got to be the one to do it. "I'm glad I got to kill the other guy, too," he says as though he's read my mind. His smile doesn't last long as he takes in the rapid swelling of my eye. Soon I reckon I won't be able to open it. Soon, I reckon, I won't care.

"They still took my sister," I whisper.

Jared's arms tighten around me as we near the big black car. "I know," he tells me with real sadness.

Those few words are all it takes to make it real. I hold in a sob as Jared places me carefully in the back seat and slides in beside me. *Just like old times*, I hear myself think. Except it isn't. There's no rescued Margot beside me when Jared pulls me close to his body. His hand riffles through my hair, and I hear his indrawn breath as he methodically recounts the events of the night.

Did I make the right choice?

The front door opens, and Mohawk slides into the driver's seat.

"Where the hell have you been?" Jared growls.

Mohawk snorts. "You're welcome, Grumpy. I love driving your snippy ass around."

"Where's Storm?" I don't ask about the witch's daughter or the cat man. I simply don't have the energy.

Mohawk turns to give me a saucy smile. "Antlers and cars don't mix."

For the rest of the drive back to Storm's, we're silent. The rest of Dominion is empty, as though someone had opened some doors and every citizen fled. A body slumps against a tired building, but that's it: no mercs or bodyguards, no fancy Oldworld cars riding around, not a single living Laster. But on the walls are the markings they have left behind: two circles, joined in the center. And the bloody red letters accompanying their hieroglyphics.

Evolve or die.

...

Jared carries me into the bedroom I'm beginning to think of as mine. He gently strips off my high-heeled shoes and pulls one of his oversized shirts over my head before unbuttoning me from my ruined dress. He pulls the pins from my hair, raking his fingers through it, and warms up a washcloth for me to wipe my face. By then he's slung me into the bed and has changed into a pair of sweats and a faded blue shirt. I'm too tired to fight it when he slides in next to me and curls me in close.

We sleep through the night and half the day before Jared's whiskers scratch my skin where he rubs against my cheek. His breath tickles strands of hair framing my cheek.

"We need to get some ice for that eye of yours." His voice is gravelly and deep. I try to look at him but one of my eyes isn't quite cooperating. I push back an inch.

"I reckon I look like hell warmed over." His answering chuckle confirms my suspicions, but I still don't move. Even as he gently brushes strands of hair away from my face. "What do I do?" I whisper. I'm not certain what it is I'm even asking about. Am I asking about Storm, or Margot? Or am I asking about something deeper, more mysterious—like the thing scratching between myself and the wild man beside me?

Jared's fingers freeze on my face as though I've uttered magic words. I think he's about to roll out of bed and tell me we'll speak with Storm. But he surprises me. He takes my chin in his hand and stares deeply into my eyes.

"I don't know," he confesses. His fingers trail over my ears, down the back of my neck where he tangles with my hair. "I'm like an addict," he says without humor. "All it took was one look, one scent, and you were hardwired into me."

"You don't even know me," I say. At least half the time I am convinced he hates my guts. And the other half? I suspect I hate his.

His smile is rueful. "I guess not in the traditional sense. But"—his fingers trail down my shoulder, rousing my skin as he brushes my back—"scents don't lie. Not like people do. Not that it matters." He sighs. His heat curls up inside me.

"Why?"

"It's my job to protect you." His face is bathed in shadows and stubble as he cracks a serious blue eye at me.

Against the sinking pool of disappointment in my belly I return, "I don't know what that means."

He shrugs, but I can see shadows creep into his eyes. "You come first. You'll always be first," he tells me fervently.

I want to unravel every thread he's just laid bare, but everything beats urgently inside me. And I need answers. I need a plan.

"Jared." My hand splays across his chest. I can feel his heart beating wildly under my hand, pulsing under the muscles of his chest. "Jared," I say again, wetting my cracked lips. "The woman with the white eyes said my blood is different. She didn't say it exactly, but she made it seem like it can do something to the Plague. But Dorian told me my blood was different from Margot's—our blood is different." My mind leaps in horror from one realization to the next. "They were going to kidnap me, too. I think whatever they wanted us for, they needed me, too. I need to get her back."

His warm, calloused hand closes over mine. "I told you I'd help you."

And in that moment I know everything I need to know.

...

"Good, you're up." Storm breezes into the kitchen where I'm busy sucking up a bowl of cereal while watching the NewsFeed. I look up. He looks rested, younger than before, if possible.

"Senator and Mary Kain are still missing," I tell him. The headlines all scream about the missing Senator and his wife. The strangeness surrounding their unexpected departure. Were they killed during the bombing or were they ripped apart by the Lasters?

My own family does not appear in the NewsFeed. Nor do the thousands of Lasters who stormed the gate, the dozens that were killed. They have simply vanished like the genetic sequences that burn their lives away. And my own parents? Have they gone away with Margot and Resnikov? Will they watch over her? Whatever their plans are, I reckon they've just begun to hatch.

My spoon clatters in the bowl as Jared glides into the kitchen, looking cool and relaxed and showing too much skin in his boxer shorts and shirt.

"Yes, I know."

"You know?" My attention diverts back to Storm. "What happened to them?"

"I suspect Resnikov happened."

My brain short-circuits. "What does that mean? Were they in on everything—the protocols? Did they—"

Storm's hands smack down on the counter like hammers. "Let's not get ahead of ourselves. Why don't you come and speak to me in my office when you're through here?"

"I'm coming, too." Jared gives Storm and me his biggest killer cat grin.

"I see," Storm says thoughtfully as he starts out the opposite door toward his office.

"Storm, wait," I say, getting clumsily to my feet. He turns and waits for me, patience stamped into every feature. "Did you—do you know about us? About Margot and me?"

His head tilts to the side, studying me. There's no apology in his gray eyes, no sense of remorse as he tells me, "I've had suspicions."

"Suspicions."

"There are a lot of players on the board, a lot of people who seem to want to get their hands on your blood. As you know, big money runs the Splicer Clinics. I've suspected for a while that there's something different about you girls. But do I know exactly what you are? What your blood is capable of?" Storm shakes a fiery head. "Not in the least."

"Did you know our father was going to sell us?"

"No." The words are just that: flat, emotionless.

"Is she—I mean, the witch's daughter. Is she coming back? I'd like to talk to her."

He nods, a spark lighting his eyes. "As a matter of fact, she and Carl will be here in about"—he consults his wristwatch—"half an hour."

I nod back, glad there will be some lead, however fragile, to help me repair the stretched cord between my sister and me. There are too many things to repair, I realize as Jared tugs me back to the breakfast bar. My father and mother, wherever they might be. But first, Margot.

When I had finally crawled out of bed that morning, it had been from a dream where the witch's daughter watched with her sightless eyes while I sobbed and sobbed from above the city. As I cried, my tears became rain, watering the dark brown patches of urban darkness. Everywhere my tears fell tiny lights blossomed.

When I opened my eyes, I was sure I felt Margot, tugging at me like a fish on a line. Not scared, exactly. Not angry. But some gray zone in between. Someone was stroking Margot's arm. Softly enough, but she felt menace. In the next moment it was gone—like someone had shut off a tap.

Like a lock and key that didn't fit together anymore.

I turn a hard, dazzling smile on a stunned-looking Jared. Despite everything that has happened, everything I've lost, I've good reason to smile. I have an ally, someone I can trust. Maybe more than one. And I've got a plan: come hell or Plague fire, I'm going to get to Russia. And once I'm there, I'm going to find out what Resnikov knows, what my parents obviously want to keep secret. And I'm going to get my sister back.

A wash of bright green floats across Jared's eyes as he tugs me over the threshold of the kitchen and into the hall. I have one more reason to smile, I muse as I pause.

Today is my eighteenth birthday. And my own future has yet to be Revealed.

Acknowledgments

Books are universes that coalesce into beautiful worlds. I have many stars orbiting through mine. Thanks to Monica Curtis for being my perpetual first reader, Erin Churchill and Taras Grescoe for the writer's retreat, Irwin Adam for sharing nuggets of Russian with me. I also want to thank everyone at Entangled: I owe a huge thanks to Liz Pelletier, editor extraordinaire, from whom I have learned so much. Thanks also to Melissa Montovani and Heather Riccio, the Art Department for the stunning cover, and finally, Madison Pelletier and Stacy Abrams for being such great readers. Thanks also to Raincoast Books and Fernanda Viveiros for all the support in Canada. I owe a special debt to my agent, Robert Lecker for making all this stuff happen and being a true champion. I also want to send a shout out to Melanie Windle of Glamazon Productions, whose enthusiasm and insights into these characters has helped me grow.

But here's where I also need to thank the legion universe of Wattpad readers for their encouragement and unflagging enthusiasm for True Born. There is absolutely nothing better for a writer than an army of avid readers who tell you they love your characters, your world and they want more. I adore you, people. From the bottom of my heart, thank you—your passion for this story inspired me to turn what was supposed to be a novella into a trilogy and has kept me going over the bumpy parts.

READ ON FOR A SNEAK PEAK OF

TRUE NORTH

L.E. STERLING

1

Sometimes flesh and bone are as inexplicable as magic. I was but seven years old when I first realized that the song of blood-to-blood could hold sway over death. Margot was out with our driver that day. I don't recall the why now, except to say we were always uneasy to be separated, and more so that morning. Jenks was our old-timey driver with the bushy eyebrows. He wore a black cap tilted on an angle over his thinning hair. His suits were always a touch too large. I'd noticed, in a child's offhand way, that those suits were getting larger. When the Plague bit into him that morning, his foot stuck on the accelerator. He drove wildly through the town, drowning in wave after wave of agony, while Margot clung to the backseat like a burr.

At home, they tell us, and miles apart, I was hysterical. No one would listen to me. Not the staff, nor our mother and father. Desperate, I ran out of the house and started one of our father's many cars. I'd go after my twin on my own.

I thank all the gods in Dominion that it was Shane riding the gate that day, our father's man who knew us well—knew we were different. By the time Shane had a dragnet stop the car, poor old Jenks had cut a swath of destruction through the town. He died before they delivered a tear-stained Margot home. Bruised and shaken but miraculously not hurt, my twin looked at me as though she'd seen through the veil.

They were halted thirty feet from the lake. Just thirty more feet and they'd be underwater, and my sister's flesh tangled with the deep.

That was the day I came to know the power of our bond: if we listened closely to our bones, fought hard enough, showed the world we'd not back down, my sister and I could pull each other from the jaws of fate. I learned my lesson that day as my raging grief clawed back the tides of death—that, and that the only thing worse than feeling my twin's suffering was the fear of not feeling her at all.

It was a hard and terrible and wonderful lesson, and I learned it well.

I squat at the roots of the giant tree, sliding into the bark a long, thin pipette to gather a sample. The slim tube fills and I add it to the sample case, counting off vials along with how many months it's been. *One, two.* I imagine this is a new game Margot and I have devised: the game of the missing sister. *Three. Four.* The air buzzes with the sound of machinery. Startled, I look up and try to sight the choppers whirling overhead. The sky stays white and blank, though the sound rises and falls. Rain slicks my face and runs down my neck to pool at my collar.

"It will be dark soon." Beside me, Doctor Dorian Raines packs away her tools. "We'd better finish up or Storm won't let us come back here for a month." One of her springy curls defies the rain and gravity to stand on end. A spade hurls through the air and lands at my knee. "Make sure you get a proper sample from under the root this time," she teases me.

She has reason to, I reckon. Over the past months Doc Raines has had to teach me a great deal. The first time we'd come to take samples of the massive, unnatural thing known across Dominion as the "Prayer Tree," I'd pulled vials of broken asphalt rather than the loamy soil from which the tree sprang.

I'd been tired and distracted and suffering from "too much glitter," as Margot would say. But all that glitter—the parties, the meetings, the endless social events—was robbing me of sleep. And what dreams I did have were shadowed with what the glitter hid. My life now isn't so much about digging for soil samples as digging for answers.

I'm on a hunt for my sister.

Four short months ago my world—and Dominion City— had been very different. The glitter had been my every day, though of a different variety. Coming from one of the most prominent families of Dominion's Upper Circle, it was expected of my sister and me to attend social events, to play hostess for the rich and powerful. That had all come to a crashing halt the night of our Reveal. That night, our world had exploded. The Lasters, led by the crazy preacher man,

Father Wes, led a revolt on our house.

So many had died that night, so uselessly. And I had been left alone. I reckon I could have gone with my parents and Margot and the dark Russian aristocrat, Leo Resnikov, who held sway over them. I opted to remain behind in Dominion—I'd wanted to stay with the wild, emerald-and-indigo-eyed Jared Price and the rest of his tribe. I wanted to get as far away from the corruption of my father and his ilk as I could, trusting that the True Borns and their enigmatic leader, Nolan Storm, would help me get Margot back.

I gave myself a choice: I could curl up in a ball and let the Plague take me. Or I could have faith in the magic buried deep in our blood and bones.

I chose to believe.

Four months on, things haven't worked out quite as I'd expected. I reckon I feel as I did all those years ago when I first thought my twin would be taken from me. Helpless. Lost, as though my body and my world had been ripped in two, and the better part of me vanished. The True Borns are helping, or so says Nolan Storm, though there has been no progress to speak of. And I'd trust Jared Price with my life, though he doesn't make it easy. Ever since that night, Jared has been the perfect merc: cold, professional, distant.

Yet I'll not soon forget the moment I decided, when he looked at me and the masks between us fell.

Stay with me, Lu.

I shiver at the memory and idly tune in to a rising tide of chatter from around the tree. Childish voices scratch at the air. Something like the song of a bird grabs my attention. It's unnatural, out of place here. I glance up. From this short distance you can see the bits of silver and red and white flashing from the tree's lush canopy. Grown in mere hours from the seeds of a so-called "magic bomb," the deciduous now dwarves the intersection it's eaten—a place the Lasters have renamed Heaven Square. It crows over the red-graffitied buildings of Dominion City's wasteland. And this is where Doc Raines, Nolan Storm's semi-official clinician scientist, and I, her assistant, dig for answers. Literally.

The birdcall sounds again, this time from another direction.

"Oh, bother," Doc Raines mutters under her breath. She swiped a lock of hair from her eyes with the back of a gloved hand. "Not again."

"You think?" I say, trying not to sound too excited.

Doc Raines picks up the pace of her packing. "What else could it be?"

The swarmings happen fast. Before you can blink, the kid gangs will arrive en masse and strip you of money, your clothes, the gold from your teeth. We've protection here, courtesy of Nolan Storm, but that's of little comfort. A team of thirty or forty could overwhelm us. There's no shortage of little thieves in Dominion.

"Hurry, Lucy," Doc Raines calls impatiently.

"Just one more sample," I tell her, crawling deeper under a bough.

The sounds rise, more like a warning than harmless birdsong. I can sense, rather than see, small bodies maneuvering around the buildings plastered in a mess of graffiti. Everywhere you look, the red tags appear: the same two circles, conjoined in the middle like a pair of crossed eyes. *Evolve or die* is scribbled beneath the best of them, sometimes even spelled right. The dying part is easy enough to understand in a city like Dominion. Thanks to the Plague, people here are dying by the bucketful.

A shout. It's Derek, one of our guards for today. Then I hear it: a shrill battle cry that raises the hair on the back of my neck. It comes at us from every angle. I push my way closer to the trunk. It would be hard to attack me under the tree, I reason. But the shelter also fulfills another need of mine.

"Lucy!" Derek yells. "Stay where you are!"

The sounds grow louder, more ominous, chilling the blood in my veins.

Derek shouts over to Penny, our other guard. If the gangs think they've hit an easy mark here, Penny—whom I think of with affection as Mohawk—will have them thinking twice. I imagine her grinning sharp teeth at the children, scaring them silly just before she laughs and tears one of them limb from limb.

Doc Raines whispers something urgently at me but I'm too far out of range to hear. I creep farther into the deep, reaching out my fingers until I touch bark. The kids' shrill sounds fill the air like a screaming murder of crows. I can't think, can hardly breathe.

And suddenly I'm not alone.

GRAB THE ENTANGLED TEEN RELEASES READERS ARE TALKING ABOUT!

PROOF OF LIES
BY DIANA RODRIGUEZ WALLACH

Some secrets are best kept hidden…

Anastasia Phoenix has always been the odd girl out, whether moving from city to international city with her scientist parents or being the black belt who speaks four languages.

And most definitely as the orphan whose sister is missing, presumed dead.

She's the only one who believes Keira is still alive, and when new evidence surfaces, Anastasia sets out to follow the trail—and lands in the middle of a massive conspiracy. Now she isn't sure who she can trust. At her side is Marcus, the bad boy with a sexy accent who's as secretive as she is. He may have followed her to Rome to help, but something about him seems too good to be true.

Nothing is as it appears, and when everything she's ever known is revealed to be a lie, Anastasia has to believe in one impossibility.

She *will* find her sister.

ISLAND OF EXILES
BY ERICA CAMERON

On the isolated desert island of Shiara, every breath is a battle.

The clan comes before self, and protecting her home means Khya is a warrior above all else. But when obeying the clan leaders could cost her brother his life, Khya's home becomes a deadly trap. The council she hoped to join has betrayed her, and their secrets, hundreds of years deep, reach around a world she's never seen.

To save her brother's life and her island home, her only choice is to turn against her clan and go on the run—a betrayal and a death sentence.

REDUX
BY A.L DAVROE

Their domed city is in ruins. With nowhere to go, prodigy hacker Ellani "Ella" Drexel and a small band of survivors escape the wasteland *she* unknowingly created.

But malfunctioning androids and angry rebels make sanctuary hard to find. Worse, the boy she loves is acting distant, and not at all like the person she first met in *Nexis*.

Ella needs to turn back and make a stand to reclaim her home. She's determined to bring a new—and better—life to all who've suffered.

Or die trying.

INFINITY
by Jus Accardo

There are three things Kori knows for sure about her life:

One: Her army general dad is insanely overprotective.
Two: The guy he sent to watch her, Cade, is way too good-looking.
Three: Everything she knew was a lie.

Now there are three things Kori never knew about her life:

One: There's a device that allows her to jump dimensions.
Two: Cade's got a lethal secret.
Three: Someone wants her dead.

GUARDIAN OF SECRETS
by Brenda Drake

Sure, jumping through books into the world's most beautiful libraries to protect humans from mystical creatures is awesome. No one knows that better than Gia Kearns, but she could do without the part where people are always trying to kill her. Oh, and the fact that she and Pop had to move away from her friends and life as she knew it. But someone has to save the world from the upcoming apocalypse, and it looks like that's going to be Gia. Maybe. If she survives.

ANOMALY

BY TONYA KUPER

Reality is only an illusion.
Except for those who can control it…

Worst. Birthday. Ever.

My first boyfriend dumped me—happy birthday, Josie!—my dad is who knows where, I have some weird virus that makes me want to hurl, and now my ex is licking another girl's tonsils. Oh, and I'm officially the same age as my brother was when he died. Yeah, today is about as fun-filled as the swamps of Dagobah. But then weird things start happening…

Like I make something materialize just by *thinking* about it.

When hottily-hot badass Reid Wentworth shows up on a motorcycle, everything changes. Like, *everything*. Who I am. My family. What really happened to my brother. *Existence.* I am Oculi, and I have the ability to change reality with my thoughts. Now Reid, in all his hotness, is charged with guiding and protecting me as I begin learning how to bend reality. And he's the only thing standing between me and the secret organization that wants me dead…